DON PENDLETON's

MACK BOLAN.

VENGEANCE

A GOLD EAGLE BOOK FROM

WORLDWIDE.

TORONTO • NEW YORK • LONDON
AMSTERDAM • PARIS • SYDNEY • HAMBURG
STOCKHOLM • ATHENS • TOKYO • MILAN
MADRID • WARSAW • BUDAPEST • AUCKLAND

First edition December 1999

ISBN 0-373-61469-1

Special thanks and acknowledgment to
Mike Newton for his contribution to this work.

VENGEANCE

3-

"I need everything you have on Malik al-Salaam."

"He is American."

"You'd think so from his passport," Bolan replied, "but you couldn't prove it by the company he keeps."

"Malik regards himself as an ambassador of unity to Muslim people everywhere," Filali stated. "His arrogance is such that he believes he might somehow unite the several factions that have fought each other bitterly for centuries, and forge from them a strong united front against the unbelievers of the world."

"So how's he doing?"

"So far he cannot get around their hatred and mistrust."

"But if he does…?"

"If he does, then the West might face an enemy unrivaled since the time of the Crusades."

*Other titles available in
this series:*

Too long a sacrifice
Can make a stone of the heart.

—William Butler Yeats,
"Easter 1916"

Some would say that my heart turned to stone
years ago. Right or wrong, it's time to teach
those who would needlessly sacrifice innocents
what a hard heart is really all about.

—Mack Bolan

For the victims and survivors of the
August 7, 1998, embassy bombings
in Nairobi, Kenya, and Dar es Salaam,
Tanzania. God keep.

PROLOGUE

Algeria

Come with me to the Casbah.

The salacious, half whispered come-on was so ancient, so clichéd, that Joseph Pangborn couldn't for the life of him remember who had said it first. Some character in a forgotten movie, playing on the Late, Late Show.

Pangborn didn't really care who said it first. The point at issue was who said it last—in this case, Ralph Wakefield, a fellow paper-pusher at the U.S. Embassy. Wakefield looked so hokey, when he came right out and said it, that Pangborn had to chuckle.

Still, here they were.

It wasn't just the two of them. Wakefield had made the rounds of those who weren't assigned to work on Friday night—those who possessed a personality, at least—and rounded up a group of five, himself included. There was Eddie Bittaker, John DeSalvo and Barry Gunness. Bittaker was one of the Marines assigned to guard the embassy, off duty now just like the rest of them, and out of uniform.

A boys' night out.

Six months on station in Algiers, and this would be the first time Pangborn had set foot inside the seedy Casbah district. He knew all the stories, including tales of sex and drugs for sale; of European females snatched and sold to harems in the hard-core Arab states; of tourists who had disappeared without a trace, and some who had allegedly been found butchered and stripped of everything a wily thief could use or sell in some dank alleyway. Pangborn didn't know which to believe, or which were simply urban myths, but all of them came flooding back at once as he approached the Casbah with his friends.

They walked, because borrowing a set of diplomatic wheels required specific paperwork in triplicate, and none of them wanted to spin a fairy tale to fill the box headed Reason for Use. It was the little fibs that boomeranged and smacked you in the rear end when you were least expecting it—a flat or fender bender on their way to have some raunchy fun, for instance—that made a kind of blot, though trivial, which could sometimes shift a promising career into neutral for years on end.

They could have ridden in a taxi, but DeSalvo had suggested saving every dinar they possessed to spend on "wine, women and song—without the song, of course." Pangborn, twenty-eight and counting, with no sex to speak of since he left the States, had seen the reason in DeSalvo's plan, and helped convince the other two. Besides, it wasn't all that far to walk. The streets had cooled a bit since sundown, and the stroll allowed him to anticipate coming events, while simultaneously bolstering his nerve.

Besides, thought Pangborn, they could always catch a taxi going back if it was too damned late—or they were too damned drunk—to walk.

Going in, you smell the Casbah before you realize that you have crossed the border separating one world from the other. Breathing deeply, Pangborn tried to sort out the aromas that assailed him. There were cooking smells, some more inviting than others, but he was more interested in the other scents that told him he had crossed the line. Some were familiar to seasoned travelers, from every slum in the world: human waste, unwashed bodies, a general reek of decay. The climate helped a bit in that respect: it was a dry heat, as they say, and baked a goodly portion of the stench from filthy paving stones. As for the other smells, he picked out incense, perfume, rich tobacco smoke and something else, compelling yet so subtle that Pangborn suspected it was conjured by his own imagination.

Sex.

Show me the honey, Pangborn thought, and chuckled.

"What's funny?" Barry Gunness, walking to his left, peered owlishly at Pangborn from behind his wire-rimmed spectacles.

"Nothing," Pangborn replied. "I just feel good."

He had been looking forward to the outing for the past six days. It was a chance to let his hair down, figuratively speaking, and to sample some of what he had been missing since he left the States. Eternal optimist that Pangborn was, he had two condoms in his pocket, just in case. It didn't trouble him particularly that he would be buying any sex he got this night.

When in Algiers, he thought, and this time caught himself before another chuckle could escape. Around them, market stalls were mostly shuttered for the night, although a few still offered jewelry, ornate daggers and the like. The wicked knives made Pangborn wonder just how safe they really were, but he immediately shrugged it off. He had been taught from childhood that negative thinking invited a worst-case scenario, and he deftly sidetracked his thoughts toward a more pleasant terminus.

Sunni Muslims might run the country, their faith installed as the official state religion, but they weren't fundamentalist fanatics, and visitors to the Casbah could still find a surfeit of sin with which to amuse themselves.

"I'm ready."

"Ready for what?" asked John DeSalvo, on his right.

"Sorry?"

"You said, 'I'm ready,' and I asked you—"

Pangborn felt the color rising in his cheeks, realizing he'd spoken out loud, but he was saved, after a fashion, by a gibe from Eddie Bittaker. "I'll tell you what he's ready for," the young Marine declared. "Same thing I am. He wants some poon."

"Well," Pangborn said, deciding there was nothing to be gained from playing innocent, "I wouldn't turn it down."

DeSalvo ginned and said, "You know something? I'm ready, too."

The five of them were laughing as they left the modern city's neon blaze behind and moved through narrow, darkened streets in search of something they would long remember.

ADNAN AL-QADIR FOLLOWED the five Americans at a reasonable distance, careful to present the image of one who moved in the same direction, without necessarily having the same destination. Tracking them was easy, since he knew the city better than they ever would, each winding street and narrow alley of the Casbah rabbit warren etched indelibly into his memory. The Americans were strangers here, out of place in every sense. He could have tracked them just as easily on a parallel street, following their loud, abrasive laughter as a hunter followed birdcalls in the wild.

There had been ample time to plan the interception. Four whole days, in fact, since Adnan al-Qadir had learned of the Friday-night foray planned by these five. His man inside the U.S. Embassy was invisible to those around him, a native sweeper of floors and swabber of toilets who kept his mouth shut, his eyes and ears open. Granted, he wasn't much of a spy— the Americans would never discuss pressing matters of state with a broom-pusher in the room—but his attentiveness had paid off well enough, this time.

Al-Qadir couldn't have named the five Americans or stated their positions on the diplomatic staff to save his life. In fact, he didn't care exactly who or what they were. It was enough for him that they were representatives of the Great Satan, demons once removed, who walked the streets of al-Qadir's homeland as if they owned the place. He despised them, hated them in fact, as he despised and hated Europeans, Russians—anyone at all who came into his country and attempted to dictate how things should be.

Al-Qadir's grandparents had been murdered by French Legionnaires in 1959, at a time when Algeria was deemed "an integral part" of France. The French were finally expelled, his father taking part in the revolt against the colonists, but peace was still elusive for the faithful who believed that God meant exactly what He said in the Koran, and that a day of reckoning was due for those who flaunted His divine precepts. For eight long years, the civil war had raged, since free elections scheduled for the early days of 1992 were canceled by the ruling government, from fear that Muslim fundamentalists would win the vote hands down. There had been nonstop mayhem ever since, atrocities committed on both sides, and there was still no end in sight.

This night, in the Casbah, al-Qadir would strike a telling blow against the foreign enemies who, tacitly or otherwise, supported the oppression of his brothers in the faith. It mattered not to him that his selected targets were oblivious to the events that sealed their fate. He frankly didn't care if they were agents of the CIA or simple office lackeys at the U.S. Embassy. This night, they were examples to the world at large, and they would serve him well.

The Browning automatic pistol tucked into the waistband of his trousers, underneath his baggy linen shirt, was warm and heavy, pressed against his flesh. The muzzle prodded at his groin with every step he took. It was the older, single-action model that he carried cocked and locked—a live round in the chamber, hammer back, the safety on. If he was forced to use it, if the others failed somehow, each microsecond would be precious to him when he drew and fired.

He hoped it wouldn't come to that. Al-Qadir had killed before, perhaps a dozen times in all. He wasn't frightened by the thought of spilling blood, although he didn't relish it. If he was forced to use the Browning automatic, it would mean his planning for the ambush had been flawed in some respect, that those he picked to do the killing weren't equal to the task. And while the failure might be someone else's fault, blame always settled, ultimately, on the man in charge.

This was his second operation in the field, in a command capacity. The first, a car bombing in Skikda, had gone off like clockwork, though the final body count was smaller than he might have wished. Still, there had been no comebacks, no arrests, and the reprisals launched in answer to the blast had only served to generate more hatred of the ruling government. His maiden outing as a team commander, thus, had been a clear success.

But he couldn't afford a failure. Most particularly with Americans involved. There would be repercussions from his strike this night; they were anticipated and desired. If he should bungle the attack, though...

Angrily, al-Qadir reached up and flicked his fingertips against one ear, as if to frighten off a buzzing gnat. It stung, the sudden pain clearing his head, allowing him to focus on his adversaries and the task at hand.

He wouldn't fail.

Three men with automatic weapons waited for the five Americans a few blocks farther on. One of their number had a plastic dime-store walkie-talkie in his pocket tuned to the same frequency as the one al-Qadir carried. They had spoken only twice, and briefly: once, when the Americans emerged from the embassy, moving on foot toward the Casbah; and again, several moments ago, as the targets reached their destination. Al-Qadir would not use the radio again unless his targets deviated from their present course, veering off into one of the narrow side streets.

The Casbah was a maze to strangers, but the main drag ran fairly straight and true, through the heart of the district. It featured taverns, most of them with dancing girls and prostitutes, plus tattoo parlors, small "clinics" where the healers specialized in curing impotence, and dingy shops where the most sought-after merchandise was never placed on public display. You could buy guns and sex toys here, children and drugs.

A surefire passport to the Casbah underworld was cash.

Only the heartiest of tourists strayed far from the Casbah's central artery of commerce. Those who did were sometimes lost forever in the labyrinth, while others came out penniless, with dazed expressions on their faces, frequently unwilling to divulge what they had seen—or done—while they were out of touch

with civilized society. Police who ventured past the
fringes of the Casbah came in numbers, flying squads
of four to six the standard rule, and even then they
trespassed on the devil's ground reluctantly. Tourist
advisories had thinned the flock of foreign sheep in
recent years, but there would always be enough to
keep the Casbah's underground economy well in the
black.

This night, al-Qadir intended to supply a splash of
crimson, for variety.

Trailing the five Americans, watching their every
move, he was grateful for the chill that settled in his
chest. These men meant nothing to him. He felt no
compassion for them, for their friends and loved ones
at the embassy, or back in the United States. It wasn't
that he hated them specifically, as individuals, but
rather that he held their nation in contempt, willing
to use them any way he could in service of the holy
cause. If they could understand his reasoning, these
five might see that he was justified in what he was
about to do.

He spied one of his shooters, lounging in the doorway of a tavern up ahead and on his left. Al-Qadir
was startled when the five Americans approached the
tavern, and he flashed a rapid hand sign to his soldier,
warning him to wait and hold his fire. Frustration
gnawed at al-Qadir, as the Americans lined up and
disappeared inside the tavern.

Never mind.

This way, he had them trapped. They had to come
out sometime, and al-Qadir would be there waiting
for them, with his soldiers, even if it took all night.

"LE'S FINE ANOTHER PLACE," Ralph Wakefield said, slurring his words enough that Pangborn knew the wine was kicking in. He had the makings of a buzz, himself, and that was cool. It was the whole point of their outing, after all.

Well, one point, anyway.

Pangborn wasn't about to let himself get sloppy drunk. No way. For one thing, he had sworn off public vomiting and passing out when he was still a Stanford undergrad; and for another, he had no intention of abandoning his self-control on unfamiliar ground, where he could wind up getting robbed—if not worse.

It was agreed that they should move along and find another place to spend their money, while it lasted. Not that any of them found the dancers disagreeable, by any means; it simply struck them as a waste of time and energy to spend the whole night in the first establishment they spotted. There was still so much the Casbah had to show them, and the night was young.

Pangborn was steady on his feet when he stood and trailed his comrades toward the exit. No one tried to stop them, pleading with them to remain and spend more money. They had left a decent tip, and the employees of the tavern seemed to know that others would be stopping by to take their place before the night was through.

Emerging from the smoky tavern, Pangborn was surprised by how much the night air had cooled off in the past hour. Still comfortable in shirtsleeves, he nonetheless experienced a taste of what it had to be like for nomads in the desert, seared by day and crouched around a fire by night, as Mother Nature dragged them back and forth between extremes.

"I need a woman."

"Me, too," Eddie Bittaker said.

Pangborn blushed again, and cursed his tendency to think out loud. He was about to make some quip about the liquor talking, when the most amazing thing occurred, freezing his vocal cords and drying up the words before they reached his lips.

As Pangborn turned to face him, Bittaker began to do a jerky little dance, arms flapping like ungainly wings, his face distorted in what might have been a grimace or a scowl. His sport shirt rippled, as if there were hornets trapped inside and trying to get out. A heartbeat later, something *did* burst free, but it was warm and wet, spattering Pangborn's face.

He heard and recognized the muffled sound of automatic gunfire, even as he understood that Bittaker was dying, stumbling back against the tavern's stucco wall and leaving dark smears on the beige paint as he fell. A quick glance to his right showed Barry Gunness hit and staggering, still on his feet, but obviously wounded, clutching at his side.

Instinctively, Pangborn dropped into a crouch and swung back toward the tavern's doorway, seeking cover there. Before he took three scuttling steps, he saw a dark-skinned figure framed there, blocking his retreat, bright muzzle-flashes winking at him from a weapon held against the shooter's hip. The sound was muffled once again, more like an air gun than the automatic weapon it so obviously was.

They had silencers, he thought, but it was useless

information at the moment. Before he even had the chance to reason out his choice of "they" as a descriptive pronoun, Pangborn knew there were at least two shooters, maybe more. He saw another muzzle-flash, across the street, and then Ralph Wakefield seemed to stumble on some unseen obstacle, arms outflung to catch himself as he fell. He hit the pavement with an ugly crunching sound and did not move again.

Pangborn turned back in the direction they had come from, toward the embassy so hopelessly beyond his reach. He didn't know where Gunness was, and didn't care. Unarmed, outnumbered, there was nothing he could do for anyone except himself. And even then—

When he was hit, it didn't feel the way he had imagined being shot would feel. Instead of piercing, burning pain, it felt more like a solid punch or kick delivered to his side, forcing the air out of his lungs. He couldn't keep his balance, feeling lucky that he landed on his knees, instead of sprawling on his face.

He had to get up.

He had one foot braced under him and was pushing off, when he was hit again. This time it pierced and burned, as if someone had run up behind him with a red-hot blade and stabbed him in the back. The impact punched him forward, and the pavement rushed to meet his face. He felt his nose crack, but it hardly mattered, like a bee sting to a man on fire.

Pangborn was still alive, still conscious, when one of the shooters reached him, bent down, rolled him roughly over on his back. He might have screamed, but there was something in his throat, and it was all that he could do to catch his breath. The shooter studied him up close and personal for several seconds, finally straightening. His gun came into view, nose-heavy with a foot-long sound suppressor attached. Pangborn could see a thread of gray smoke wafting from the muzzle.

A moment later the world exploded in his face.

CHAPTER ONE

Libya

The key to getting in and out of Libya alive was two-fold: running overland while beating the watchful eyes of radar operators, and dodging erratic border patrols. The first part came down to logistics; the second relied on dumb luck. Khaddafi's roving desert squads were liberated from specific schedules. Each team had a sector to patrol, but how they did that job was generally up to them.

As long as no one entering or leaving Libya slipped through the net.

Mack Bolan recognized that luck existed—bad, as well as good—but he rebelled at trusting his life or the lives of others to a whim of Fate. If he was meant to die this night, if some omniscient power at the dark heart of the universe decided it was time to tap him on the shoulder, there was nothing he could do about it. Since he couldn't read Fate's mind, however, Bolan had a perfect right—a duty—to protect himself and those he cared about with every means at his disposal. If the gods, in fact, helped those who helped themselves, the Executioner was a prime candidate for some celestial aid.

While he was waiting, though, he would continue doing what he could with what he had.

The border crossing into Libya, for instance, was a calculated risk. The four men riding with him in a dusty U.S. Army-surplus jeep were volunteers, each one a seasoned warrior, amply blooded in the crucible their homeland had become since 1992. The driver, Gholomreza Kordiyeh, was Bolan's ranking contact in Algiers, the other three his handpicked choices for the best men he could find to watch a comrade's back in killing situations. Bolan knew their names—Kemal, Ari, Faisal—but little else about them.

That was where the trust kicked in.

Their target was a desert campsite, six kilometers across the border into Libya, and twice that far below the border city of Ghalamis. It was occupied and operated by the Armed Islamic Group—or GIA, for short—one of the largest and most deadly factions active in Algeria's domestic war. The GIA trained killers there, with arms and ammunition from Khaddafi's arsenal, then sent them home again to raise whatever hell they could.

So far, the terrorists had done a bang-up job.

Since January 1992, Algeria had averaged some ten thousand political murders per year. Many of those killed were women, children and the elderly, slaughtered in brutal raids that reduced whole townships to smoking ruins. Spokesmen for the state denounced the violence on both sides, but when state agents acted, some alleged, they did so on behalf of covert death squads armed and funded by the reigning government. Troops were dispatched reluctantly to deal with new "disturbances," and by the time they reached the scene—even when it was within sight of their barracks—nothing typically remained except the dead and wounded.

Bolan knew the GIA wasn't responsible for all the violence raging through Algeria, but soldiers of the Armed Islamic Group had done their part.

Besides, he had to start somewhere.

The border was behind them by moonrise. The jeep was running dark, but Kordiyeh still managed to avoid most of the potholes, circumnavigating clumps of spiny growth and detouring around gullies as if he knew the way by heart. Their final sit-down had included the study of a map, which Bolan carried in a pocket of his desert camouflage fatigues, but Gholom-reza Kordiyeh didn't appear to need it, even driving in the dark.

"We are almost there," the driver said, in English more precise than most of what the Executioner was used to hearing in the States. "One more kilometer, I think."

"Okay."

Like his companions, Bolan packed an AKSU assault rifle, the short-barreled, folding-stock version of the venerable AK-74. Chambered for the Soviet 5.45 mm cartridge, the AKSU boasted a cyclic rate of 800 rounds per minute in full-auto mode, although the stubby barrel made it hard to control in sustained full-auto fire.

Rugged dependability aside, the "baby" Kalashnikovs, if lost or captured on the field of battle, would also help to mask the identity of their owners. Manufactured by the millions in Russia, Eastern Europe and China, the AK rifles turned up everywhere. No paramilitary group on earth, from Manila and Myanmar to the badlands of Montana, felt its arsenal complete without at least a few Kalashnikovs.

The team's backup weapons were equally anonymous: 9 mm CZ-75 semiauto pistols, manufactured in Czechoslovakia before the collapse of the Soviet Bloc; Russian-made RGD-5 antipersonnel grenades and a motley collection of razor-edged fighting knives. None of the fighters carried any personal ID, and any labels within their well-worn clothes had long since been removed.

The jeep was coasting to a halt. Kordiyeh pointed through the windshield toward a subtle glow of lights on the horizon. "There," he said. "Five hundred meters, more or less."

Bolan could feel the old excitement taking over, energizing him. Without the engine noise, he thought that he could pick out the faintest sound of human occupancy, carried to them from the campsite on the cool night breeze.

Five hundred meters. It was nothing but a warm-up, if you took your time and no one saw you coming. Coming back, if they were under fire and fleeing hot pursuit, it would feel like five hundred miles.

He thought about a final run-through of the plan, deciding it would be an insult to his four companions and a waste of precious time. Instead of going through the script again, he simply said, "All right. Let's take a walk."

Bolan stepped out of the open jeep. A tug adjusted his combat webbing and the bandolier of extra magazines for the Kalashnikov. The desert hardpan crunched beneath his boots as he set off to find his enemies.

ASIM TABARI HATED standing watch at night. He didn't fear the darkness as a child might—not while he was carrying his AKM assault rifle, at any rate— but watching out for enemies in this place simply struck him as a waste of time and energy. The very point of setting up a training camp in Libya, protected by Khaddafi's sympathetic government, was to insure security against their enemies. If they were safe, why should a guard be necessary, day or night?

It would be quite a different thing, Tabari thought, if they were fighting the Israelis. Tel Aviv was unpredictable. The Jews might send their Phantoms anywhere to bomb and strafe suspected terrorists, but there was no such danger from the fat, complacent slugs who ruled Algeria. Tabari's hated government would no would more risk a border incident with Libya than it would launch a rocket to the moon. Assassinating individuals and raiding unarmed villages was one thing; waging war against a neighboring state that could—and would—respond in force was something else entirely.

Still, Tabari spent one night a week on sentry duty, roaming the perimeter incessantly, with nothing but the desert rats and scorpions for company. Sometimes, he almost wished the enemy would come, a raid to break the tedium of watching out for nonexistent adversaries. The notion lingered for only a fleeting moment, though, before he settled back into the dull routine.

Because he didn't really want the enemy to come. Not here. Not on his watch. Tabari wasn't sure exactly how he would react if suddenly confronted with a foe who sought to kill him. Would he panic? Freeze? Run for his life?

He had been trained, of course—was being trained, with six weeks left to go before he graduated as a full-fledged soldier of the Armed Islamic Group—but there was still a residue of doubt. He had no shortage of contempt for those who were his enemies, and he had even killed before, but under circumstances that he didn't care to talk about.

The riot in Tilimsen had been one of those affairs that seemed to blow up out of nowhere, sparked by rumors of a confrontation that might well have been imaginary. By the time the story reached him, it had grown from ugly words and rumored shoving to a tale of rape and murder, several of his nameless coreligionists cast as victims. The mob formed swiftly, armed with makeshift bludgeons, knives and axes, moving toward the nearest Sunni neighborhood, from which police had suddenly, mysteriously disappeared.

The Sunnis fought back in defense of homes and families. The battle lasted for an hour, maybe longer, with Tabari mostly ducking bricks and stones that flew in his direction. It was nearly over, with the main force of the mob retreating, when he spied the boy, no more than nine or ten years old to Tabari's manly seventeen. The boy had flung a stone that grazed the teenager's hairline, drawing blood. He turned to flee, but stumbled, dropping to his hands and knees. Before he had a chance to rise, Tabari overtook him, swung the length of jagged metal rebar that he carried, smashing it across the youngster's skull.

One blow was all it took. He knew the boy was dead before he turned and ran away. It was the way his body crumpled, with the crimson halo spilled around his broken head, that told Tabari he had killed. Days later, when he shared war stories with his friends, the boy became a stout, black-bearded man, a full head taller than Tabari, armed with a wicked kukri knife. The others bought it, or appeared to, and his status with the men who mattered had increased. A place was found for him within the GIA, and he was sent for special training like the rest, in Libya.

Now, here he was again, on sentry duty in the middle of another boring night.

A low-pitched scraping sound, somewhere in front of him, halted Tabari in midstride, his weapon snapping up in search of targets. Startled, he could hear the solid thumping of his heart against his rib cage, and his finger tightened on the AKM's trigger, taking up the slack. Another quarter pound or so of pressure, and he would release a stream of automatic fire into the brooding darkness.

Something scuttled into view, moving from left to right across his path, in the direction of the camp. He squinted, making out the sleek form of a large, gray desert rat. It was most likely headed for the mess tent, where it would find scraps aplenty, even when the cooks had finished cleaning up.

Tabari let his pent-up breath escape between clenched teeth, relaxing his grip on the rifle, slowly lowering its muzzle toward the earth. It would have been humiliating to arouse the sleeping camp with gunfire, frightened by a rodent scratching in the sand. He stood and watched the rat until it vanished into the shadows near the mess tent. Even with the conscious effort to relax, Tabari still was nearly deafened by the throbbing of his own accelerated pulse. He felt the angry color in his face and cursed his hands for trembling as they gripped the AKM.

He asked himself—not for the first time—whether he was truly suited to a soldier's life. A killer he might be where unarmed children were concerned, but could a few weeks' basic training in the desert make a fighting man of him? And if, upon returning home, he found himself unable to perform his duties as commanded by the GIA, where could he go to hide?

Another scuffling sound, and while he tensed at first, Asim Tabari didn't turn to watch the second rat emerge from hiding, racing toward the camp once he had passed.

A strong arm snaked around his neck and tightened, cutting off his wind, a boot sole catching him behind one knee. Tabari felt his leg go and tried to squeeze the trigger on his AK-47, but the knife thrust beat him to it, cold steel driving home behind the angle of his jaw and probing for the spinal cord. Pinwheels of light exploded on the inside of his drooping eyelids, swallowed instantly by darkness as his soul took flight and left its shell behind.

TRUSTING THE TALL American enough to follow him had been a stretch for Gholomreza Kordiyeh. In modern-day Algeria, it took an idiot to *not* be paranoid, with neighbor killing neighbor in the dead of night. Survival hinged on trusting no one until he had proved himself beyond the ghost of any doubt, and even then it was a gamble. Kordiyeh had known the grim-faced stranger less than thirty hours, and already they were in the field together, facing odds that should have put him off the expedition altogether.

Still, there was something about the American— Mike Belasko, he called himself; undoubtedly a pseudonym—that inspired confidence, demanded trust. He had been recommended unequivocally by Kordiyeh's contact in the CIA, but that didn't explain the feeling he inspired. No, it was something from within the man himself, transmitted by the war-weary eyes that seemed to penetrate Kordiyeh's very soul.

If he was killed tonight, Kordiyeh reckoned that it wouldn't be Belasko's fault.

The training camp in Libya had been an open secret for the past two years, but Kordiyeh and his associates had never found the wherewithal to strike before tonight. This stranger had empowered them, somehow, to move against their enemies, and now the first of those was dead, cut down before he had a chance to warn the camp.

Kordiyeh wiped his dagger on the dead man's shirt and sheathed it, slipped the compact AKSU rifle off his shoulder and released the safety. Even as he found his place on the perimeter, he knew the others would be fanning out and taking their positions. Faisal, Ari and Kemal he knew as tough, determined fighters. As for Belasko, Kordiyeh had seen death in his eyes and had no doubts about the stranger's martial skill. It was the odds that troubled him as he crouched in the darkness, waiting for the bloodshed to begin.

It was believed that at least fifty fledgling soldiers of the GIA were housed within the desert camp at any given time. They all had automatic weapons and were trained to use them, more or less, which placed the odds, including their instructors and the normal staff, at something over ten to one against survival for the members of Belasko's team. One sentry dead would make no difference in the scheme of things, but they still had the marginal advantage of surprise. If they could use it well—

The sound of automatic fire, away to his left, made Kordiyeh flinch. He checked his watch and saw that it was forty seconds early. One of his compatriots had either failed to synchronize his watch correctly or had encountered opposition that couldn't be silenced with a blade.

No matter.

It was too late to correct the problem, and he had no time to waste in speculating on what might have gone awry. If one of his commandos had been seen and shot, that raised the odds appreciably, and he could only hope to balance the books by striking swiftly, lethally, before his enemies were fully roused from sleep.

His primary target was a wooden barracks building, dark and silent for the moment, forty yards in front of him. Erupting from his crouch, Kordiyeh closed the gap in seconds, palming one of the Russian hand grenades as he ran. Sliding into the west wall of the barracks with jarring force, he yanked the grenade's safety pin and lobbed the bomb through an open window, set into the wall a foot or so above his head.

Breathless, dizzy with the first rush of adrenaline, he charged around the corner, slowing as he neared the open compound proper, crouching in the darkness as he waited for the blast.

The shock of the grenade's explosion stung him, even through the barracks wall. Before the echo died away, he heard men screaming, gasping, cursing. On the far side of the compound, there was yet another blast: another barracks hit, a flash of lightning as the darkened windows vomited their shattered glass, smoke pouring out behind it. Someone in the dark was shouting orders, but no one was responding to him, yet.

The first visible survivors of Kordiyeh's grenade blast were staggering out of the barracks, some of them carrying weapons, others clutching bloody wounds or cupping hands to ears. He counted seven bunched outside the door before he made his move, the AKSU's folding stock extended, braced against his ribs.

Kordiyeh came out firing from the hip, no milking short bursts for precision as he had been taught to do. He sprayed the sleepy, frightened soldiers with his bullet hose and watched them crumple, jerking, twitching as they fell. He couldn't swear that all of them were dead, but they were down, and that was all that mattered at the moment.

Two more youths armed with rifles lurched out through the doorway, stumbling on the bodies scattered in their path, and Kordiyeh dispatched them with another searing burst before they had a chance to find their balance. Every corpse that hit the ground was like a counter in his mind, shaving the odds. Even if none was dead or injured in the barracks, he had dropped nine of the enemy—ten, with the sentry—and that meant the odds were down, at worst, to something in the neighborhood of twelve to one.

Gunfire suddenly erupted from the barracks that was Kordiyeh's secondary target, and he ducked as bullets rippled through the air a foot or so above his head. It was impossible to say if they were strays, or if he had been sighted by the enemy. In any case, he had to neutralize the danger for his own sake, and the safety of his comrades.

Running in an awkward crouch, Kordiyeh slid into cover at the corner of the barracks designated as his secondary target. Fumbling with another hand grenade, he almost dropped it in his haste, then willed himself to take it slowly, making no mistakes.

Extract the pin, wind up the pitch, duck backward as the crash of glass assured him that his aim was good. Another moment, and the blast reverberated through his flesh, screams trailing in its wake.

He edged back to the corner, waiting for survivors to emerge.

A BURST FROM BOLAN'S AKSU rifle cut the legs from underneath two soldiers who were rushing toward the nearest burning barracks. Even in the mottled firelight he could see how young they were—late teens, perhaps early twenties—but he put it out of his mind. If they were old enough to take up arms and plan to massacre their neighbors, they were old enough to face the consequences.

Bolan saw a fourth barracks go up in flames, but this one had already emptied, its occupants spilling into the firelit compound with weapons in hand, looking awkward in various states of dress. He moved in their direction, briefly counting heads before he came into effective firing range. The AKSU's 5.45 mm rounds could reach a target farther out, but with its stubby barrel, Bolan opted not to take the chance.

How many of the would-be soldiers in the compound were already dead or wounded? The Executioner didn't know, and he wasn't particularly interested. The goal of this preliminary strike was not so much to score a body count—although he would seize any opportunity available to whittle down the hostile odds—but rather to unsettle his opponents, let them know beyond a shadow of a doubt that there were no more sanctuaries, no safe havens where they could retreat to plan their next atrocity.

In that regard, he reckoned that the strike was already a success, regardless of what happened next. Of course, it would be meaningless if he and Kordiyeh were killed, and their first strike turned out to be the last.

Bolan had urged his contact to remain at home,

choose English-speaking fighters whom he trusted, but the tough Algerian refused to wait behind the lines while others did his dirty work. At first, for something like five seconds, Bolan had considered that he might be on a would-be hero trip, a macho fantasy, but then he realized that Kordiyeh already was a hero, battle tested, wearing scars on both his body and his soul. He wouldn't stay behind and wait for sitreps from the killing ground. He wouldn't pass the burden of his cause to others while he had the strength to carry it himself.

Bolan was close enough to cut loose on his targets when one of them spotted him. The terrorist was short and skinny, standing in his faded boxer shorts and sleeveless undershirt. He aimed an index finger at the Executioner and started speaking in Arabic, a warning to his friends, cut off abruptly when a 3-round burst from Bolan's rifle opened up his chest.

The others got the message then, a couple of them swinging weapons in the general direction of the threat, the rest—he counted half a dozen runners— scattering in search of cover.

He took the stationary shooters first, chopping them down with eight or nine rounds that left his rifle's magazine half empty. Even as they crumpled to the hardpan, going slack in death, he had forgotten them, tracking the others in their flight. Because the troops had scattered, Bolan recognized that one or two of them would almost certainly escape. And that was fine. He needed someone to convey the story of this night's events, and while the leader of a burial detail could do the job, it would have greater impact coming

from a terrified survivor, still unsettled by his brush
with death.

He swiveled to his left and caught the nearest runner with a short burst between the shoulder blades,
slamming him facedown in the dust. A "good guy"
never back-shoots anybody in the movies—well, at
least he never used to—but the rules of combat lose
a great deal in transmission from the firing line to
Hollywood. In battle, where a person's life is riding
on the line, the easy shot is taken when it presents
itself.

Still tracking, Bolan framed another target in his
sights and dropped the runner in a boneless sprawl.
He left the lithe body tumbling in midair and found
another target, farther out. This one had dropped his
weapon and was running with his shoulders hunched,
head tucked in like a turtle's. Bolan made a judgment
on the spot and let him go.

Not so the next. This guy had almost reached the
nearest barracks. It was already in flames, but it was
still an obstacle to place between himself and sudden
death, its drifting smoke potentially a further shield.
The first dark tendrils were already reaching out to
welcome him when Bolan's bullets took him down.
One moment, he was high-stepping across the camp;
the next, his legs appeared to tangle, somehow, and
he went down on his left side with a solid thud, to
rise no more.

One left, and that one had already stretched his lead
to fifty yards or so, while Bolan dropped his comrades. It was still a fairly decent shot—not guaranteed, of course, considering his weapon; simply do-

able—but Bolan let it pass and watched the runner disappear.

He palmed the compact walkie-talkie from his belt and thumbed down the transmission switch. "All Foxfire units," he said, using the code name Kordiyeh had chosen for their strike force, "disengage ASAP and fall back as agreed. Repeating, disengage and fall back to point B."

He hoped they were alive to hear him, but he didn't wait for a response. Clipping the small device back on his web belt, Bolan obeyed his own order, breaking off contact with the dazed enemy, retreating westward toward the strip of darkened desert where his team last stood united.

How many would make it back?

He shrugged off the useless question and let the drifting smoke envelop him. The Executioner became a midnight shadow, one of many drifting through the firelit compound, homing on the rendezvous.

CHAPTER TWO

Mukhtar Haddad still didn't know how many soldiers he had lost, but instinct told him the attack was over. Automatic weapons' fire still sputtered on the northern fringe of the camp, but there were no more blasts from hand grenades, no hostile fire incoming from the vast, dark mystery that was the desert. Over by the motor pool, a handful of survivors were engaging shadows, venting fear and anger through their weapons, but Haddad had sent off a sergeant with orders to restrain them.

It was over, but it wasn't finished, yet.

Haddad had scanned the wreckage, flashlight beams directed by his order toward the shadows where the firelight didn't reach. He hadn't counted corpses, though he had a fair idea that roughly half his men were either dead or wounded. More important at the moment was the fact that he had found no unfamiliar faces staring at the midnight desert sky with lifeless eyes.

Which told him all of the attackers had escaped, if not unscathed, at least still fit for travel, able to elude his untested guerrillas as they fled.

And that was unacceptable.

He started shouting orders, rallying the troops. Haddad cared nothing that a number of the men responding to his call were walking wounded. They were warriors, first and foremost. This would be their chance to prove that training them to fight for God's mighty cause wasn't a waste of time.

The compound's motor pool had somehow weathered the assault with relatively minor damage. One jeep sat nose-down on flattened tires, reminding Haddad of a camel kneeling to accept its rider. Yet another had a punctured fuel tank, aromatic gas fumes cutting the dust in his nostrils. Two more were bullet-scarred, one having lost most of its windshield, but he thought both would run. The other three, together with the half-ton military truck, were all undamaged, six working vehicles in all.

More than enough.

He gave another round of orders, splitting his strike force into four-man teams, one piling into each of the five jeeps. They left the half-ton where it was, with seven of the wounded and a disappointed sergeant to protect the camp.

Haddad wouldn't divide his force, which meant that they could only chase the fleeing enemy in one direction. If his choice was incorrect, their effort would be wasted, and the raiders would most certainly escape.

Which way to go?

Haddad imagined how he would have staged the raid, if he had been the hunter, rather than the prey. It helped to know his enemies, and who his friends

were. Some in Libya no doubt resented the establishment of training camps for foreign nationals, but few
of them—if any—would be rash enough to risk Khaddafi's wrath by mounting an attack against their
leader's personally invited guests. That knowledge
told him that the raiders came from outside Libya.
With the border so near and the GIA's most ardent
adversaries fellow natives of Algeria, where else
would he seek his enemies, but to the west?

Haddad was in the lead jeep as the caravan rolled
out of camp, its high-beam headlights boring through
the night like feral, luminescent eyes. He could redeem the situation, to some extent, if he could only
overtake the raiders, capture them and find out who
they were. Before he executed them, of course. Unfortunately, it was probable that none of them would
view surrender as an option. He guessed that he
would have to kill them all, in lieu of letting them
escape, but even corpses sometimes told a story, if
you paid attention.

He could photograph the dead, for one thing, cir-
culate the Polaroid photos back home to see if any of
the faces sparked a memory. Haddad would only need
one name, one link to any of the several groups that
stood in opposition to the Armed Islamic Group, and
it would justify reprisals on a massive scale. If all
else failed, he would assume connections to one or
another of the private armies that opposed the GIA.

Why not? When you had God on your side, all
enemies were equal and deserving of the same swift
punishment.

But first, he had to insure that none of those who

had besmirched his honor managed to escape. Whatever happened in the next few hours, he could not—
would not—abide the prospect of another failure.

"Faster!" he demanded of his driver.

Each passing moment brought him closer to his
enemies, and brought *them* closer to the border. If
they crossed back into Algeria, he would have lost
the race.

Haddad sat rigid in his seat and clutched the
AK-47 in his lap.

He would not permit his adversaries to escape.

It was unthinkable.

"THEY'RE COMING," Kordiyeh remarked, as if com-
menting on the possibility of rain.

Bolan turned to face the east and saw the headlights. They were running single file across the waste-
land, thus preventing any comprehensive count of vehicles, but he guesstimated three, then doubled it for
safety's sake. Six jeeps could carry thirty gunners, if
they packed them in, but Bolan doubted there were
thirty able-bodied soldiers in the camp, and some of
those would almost certainly be left behind to douse
the fires and salvage gear.

Say twenty, then, and hope that he was guessing
high. If Bolan had a choice, he would prefer to over-
estimate an adversary's strength and be prepared to
face the absolute rock-bottom worst. In mortal combat, wishful thinking was a one-way ticket to the
grave.

They had another hundred yards to go before they
reached their own jeep, standing in the shadow of its

rocky hideaway. He made the calculation automatically and knew that running for the border now would be a waste of time.

"Let's go," he said, and started double-timing toward the jutting slab of stone. It was imperfect as a fortress, more a backstop than a true defensive sanctuary, but it offered cover of a sort and altitude for plunging fire into the hostile vehicles.

All five of them were decent runners, but the caravan pursuing them had horsepower behind it, gaining rapidly. Even a cautious driver, with the high beams to direct him, could make thirty-five or forty miles per hour on the desert flats, swerving around the minor obstacles, which meant that Bolan's team would reach their vehicle and rocky bastion with no more than seconds left to spare.

Robbed of the chance to organize a true defense, Bolan gave orders as he ran. "Go high, above the headlight beams, and take them out the best you can." It barely qualified as planning, but he couldn't tell his companions where to go and what to do. He hadn't scouted out the rocky jumble when they parked beside it, and he had no time to do so now.

"Grenades," he told them, almost as an afterthought. "Grenades first. Shake them up before you give them any muzzle-flash to zero in on."

There was no answer from the four Algerians, but he hadn't expected one. They came from desert-dwelling stock, and probably knew more about what they should do in this extremity than Bolan did. Still, he had felt compelled to offer something, minimal as it might be. The four men were there because of him, and if they died, their blood would stay with him.

Assuming he survived to bear the weight.

The outcropping might once have been a monolith, but it had weathered over the millennia since it was thrust up from the earth, split by an earthquake sometime in the century or so before white men arrived to "save" the Arab peoples from themselves. Its highest point was twenty feet or so above the desert floor, sloping to east and north, the south face nearly vertical, a mound of tumbled shards and loose shale facing to the west.

Small favors, Bolan thought. They didn't have to climb hand-over-hand, like mountaineers, to reach the modest pinnacle. The outcropping was large enough to let five snipers pick their fields of fire, but only four were climbing now. Bolan detoured around the southern face and ducked behind the waiting jeep.

It was a risky choice—perhaps the worst position in a set already marginal at best—and so he had reserved it for himself. The four Algerians could strafe their enemies with plunging fire, but they still needed someone on the ground for mopping up, to keep the hunters from surrounding them immediately, storming up the rocky slopes and overwhelming them by force of numbers. On the flat, he had at least some combat stretch and flexibility, which would have been denied him higher up.

As for his cover, well, the jeep would stop a fair amount of the incoming fire. Its plural downsides were the jerrican of gasoline mounted in back beside the spare tire, and the fact that Bolan couldn't use the flats to best advantage while he hid behind the vehicle.

Upside: if he could draw enough fire from their adversaries in the early moments of the fight, it might allow his backup gunners to respond effectively with their Kalashnikovs.

Downside: baiting the enemy alone could get him killed.

And so, what else was new?

He ducked as headlights splashed across the stone behind him, picking out the jeep. Above the racing engine noise, he heard a shout in Arabic that came from somewhere in the motorcade, not from above him and behind. Kordiyeh and the others kept their mouths shut and their heads down, waiting for the enemy to close within effective killing range.

Bolan unclipped an antipersonnel grenade and pulled the pin, white-knuckled as he held the high-explosive egg. He counted off the numbers, watching as the gray stone face behind him lit up like a drive-in movie screen. A few more seconds, now...

He made the pitch without rising from cover, retrieving his AKSU while the hand grenade was still airborne. He had a fresh mag in the weapon, thirty rounds, full-metal jacket. In a crunch, he could unload the whole clip in two-and-one-quarter seconds, but that would be a last-ditch desperation play. Pinpoint precision might elude him in the present circumstances, but the Executioner would do his best with what he had.

The shock of the grenade explosion was immediately followed by a second and a third, Kordiyeh's troopers pitching in. One of the jeeps took a direct hit with the second blast, erupting into flames and swerving sharply, so that it tipped over on its side and spilled its load of burning, screaming mannequins. The other pitches were inferior, but still sprayed shrapnel at the open vehicles, eliciting more cries of pain and anger.

Bolan came up firing at the nearest jeep, eyes narrowed into slits against the muzzle-flashes blazing back at him.

IT HAD BEEN Kordiyeh's grenade that turned one of the charging jeeps into a rolling funeral pyre. He had been lucky on the pitch and had no reason to believe he could repeat that pinpoint accuracy with a second grenade, but he tried anyway, palming his second-to-last bomb and lobbing it at the final vehicle in line.

It missed, but exploded close enough to sting a couple of the gunners with shrapnel. Neither of them seemed badly wounded, and their vehicle was swerving out of sight around the corner of the rock pile by the time Kordiyeh grabbed his AKSU rifle and prepared to bring them under fire.

No matter. There were still plenty of targets, some of the GIA commandos firing from their circling jeeps, while others leaped clear to charge the outcropping on foot.

Kordiyeh had the AKSU braced against his shoulder, sighting down the stubby barrel, when a jeep rolled into view below him, trailing dust behind it like a smoke screen. Squeezing off a short burst to confirm the range, he saw his bullets stitch a ragged line of holes across the right-front fender and corrected slightly, leading his target. The next burst was better, half a dozen 5.45 mm bullets ripping through the driver and the seat he occupied, slamming him hard to his left, so that the man was dragged for several yards before he tumbled clear.

The vehicle kept going, the solitary gunman in the rear seat noticing too late that he had lost his driver. Reaching out across the empty driver's seat, he was about to grab the steering wheel, then saw that he was rolling toward collision with the capsized, burning jeep. Instead of trying for a course correction, he bailed out, a painful-looking swan dive, seconds before impact jarred the flaming barrier and set the second vehicle on fire.

Kordiyeh tracked the gunner who had bailed out of the jeep, was just about to drop him on the run, when bullets suddenly began to strike the rock around him. Some deflected into space as whining ricochets, while others shattered, spraying jagged bits of stone and copper. Several of the tiny missiles burned his cheek, and when he swiped at them, his fingers came back bloody.

Furious, aware that it meant death for him to be pinned down while other troops outflanked him, Kordiyeh risked a glance over the brink in search of the snipers. He glimpsed two muzzle-flashes, six or seven feet apart, before he ducked under cover, reaching for the last grenade clipped to his belt.

There could be no precision this time, but he needed cover, something that would keep the shooters' heads down while he tried to pick them off. He jerked the pin and flicked it back across his shoulder into darkness. When he made the pitch, Kordiyeh lobbed the grenade, hoping that it would fall to earth between his enemies.

In fact, he scored an airburst, peppering both men with shrapnel, but he never knew it. Waiting for the blast, Kordiyeh lunged from cover with the AKSU's stock braced tight against his shoulder, firing even as he cleared the rocky lip. One of his enemies was standing, while the other knelt, an arm raised to protect his blood-streaked face. Kordiyeh couldn't see the blood or make out the expressions on those hostile faces, nor did he attempt to pick out details in the dark. It was enough for him to catch them more or less off guard, their automatic weapons lowered for a crucial moment that might never come again.

He shot the standing gunner first, because he made a slightly better target, bullets punching through his chest and slamming him to earth with such explosive force that his shoulders hit before his buttocks touched the ground. Tracking a few short inches to his right, Kordiyeh fired a second burst just as the kneeling gunner dropped his arm and tried to raise his weapon. His adversary's skull disintegrated into crimson mist, the lifeless body toppling over sideways, spilling blood into the dust.

So far, so good.

He thought of the tall American, Belasko, and it occurred to Kordiyeh that the man was nowhere to be seen. Had he been picked off by a sniper's bullet, cast among the scattered stones below? Or had he ever scaled the rocky pinnacle at all?

Where was he? Kordiyeh couldn't help wondering. And was he still alive?

MUKHTAR HADDAD HAD never thought himself invincible, but neither had he ever felt so close to death as in the past few moments, since the first grenades had burst among the five jeeps of his motorcade. His vehicle had stalled out when the driver stopped a bullet with his face and let his foot slip off the clutch. The man was still alive, his lower jaw askew and streaming blood, and while he tried to start the jeep again, his fumbling efforts were a waste of time. Haddad bailed out and hunkered down behind the jeep with the two young soldiers who had ridden in the back.

It was a time for orders shouted in commanding tones, a rallying of forces, but Haddad couldn't think of anything to say. Not that his troops would hear him anyway, with all the gunfire and explosions. Even if he tried to rally them, they were as likely to ignore him and retreat as to advance in unison and storm the heights.

His own driver muttered something unintelligible, drooling blood, and gave the jeep another try. The engine caught, growling back to life, and the driver pivoted to flash a ruined smile at his commander. He was reaching toward Haddad when another bullet struck, his body jerking with the impact, slumping back into his seat. His dying spasm floored the gas pedal, and the tires spewed dusty gravel as the vehicle lurched forward, traveling another ten or fifteen yards before the engine stalled again.

Haddad and his companions were suddenly exposed, with nothing to protect them from the snipers ranged above. Retreat was hopeless, and he somehow found the nerve to rush the nearest boulder, feeling bullets in the air around him more than hearing them. He reached the cover that he sought, glanced back and saw that one of the men who had been crouched beside him lay facedown, his arms outflung as if embracing death. The other young guerrilla was up and running, deserting his commander as he sprinted toward some unknown objective, away to the west.

Haddad couldn't have said what made him rise and follow the young man. One moment he was relatively safe, crouched behind a massive glob of stone; the next, without a conscious thought to guide him, he was up and running in the soldier's wake, as if afraid of being left alone.

In fact, on some level, Haddad knew that it would mean death to simply find a hiding place and try to wait out the battle. His enemies had been outnumbered when the shooting started, based upon the fact that only one jeep waited for them, and he guessed that they were still outnumbered, even though the odds had been dramatically revised. Haddad still had a chance to crush them, if he kept his wits about him and didn't lose his nerve.

He had come out with nineteen men, and while that force was nearly cut by half, his enemies were still outnumbered roughly two to one. If he could organize suppressing fire from three or four of his best marksmen, lead the others in a bold assault to overrun the stony pinnacle, they could still win the day.

Sudden gunfire erupted up ahead, not from the

rocks, but at ground level. Slowing as he came around the corner, following the muzzle of his AK-47, he nearly stumbled on the body of the young man he was following. The trooper lay stretched out on his back, blood welling from the open ruin of his chest, eyes glazed and out of focus as they seemed to look for answers in the sky above.

Haddad had time to glimpse the jeep in front of him, a shadow-figure rising from behind it, then he hastily recoiled. His feet betrayed him, sliding on loose shale, but when he fell it was a blessing in disguise. His adversary, crouched behind the jeep, let fly a burst of automatic fire that would have killed him where he stood, except that Haddad was no longer standing. Pushing off with heels and elbows, he found cover as the faceless enemy unleashed another burst, chewing up the earth and spraying gravel into the Arab's face.

It seemed to be a standoff, but Haddad wasn't content to let it go at that. He had already given up on capturing a raider for interrogation purposes, but he still meant to kill them if he could. This one behind the jeep, for instance, seemingly hadn't been quick enough to scale the heights and join his comrades. Now he was about to learn that he had made a critical mistake.

Haddad detached one of the hand grenades that weighted his belt. He switched the AK-47 to his left hand, used that thumb to hook the safety pin and tug it free of the grenade, still holding down the spoon with his right hand. He edged up to the corner of the rock that separated him from his opponent, trying to recall how far away the jeep stood, how close it was parked against the rocky face. The images were dark and jumbled in his mind, but Haddad thought they were close enough for what he had in mind.

The hand grenade might kill his enemy—if so, so much the better—but he wasn't counting on it. What it would most certainly achieve was to distract and stun him, buying several precious seconds, wherein Haddad could approach and finish off the job with rifle fire.

He offered up a prayer to God, held his breath and made the pitch. Six seconds, give or take, and he would make his move, reduce the raiding force by twenty percent or more, with one well-placed bullet.

Mukhtar Haddad would be a hero yet. He felt it in his bones.

BOLAN DIDN'T SEE the grenade, per se, but there was no mistaking the familiar clang of metal striking metal when it landed in the jeep. It didn't sound the least bit like a bullet strike, and there had been no muzzle-flash behind it. His mind couldn't conceive of any other metal object that was likely to come flying from the darkness in the middle of a firefight—certainly, his enemies weren't reduced to throwing knives—and he moved almost before the conscious thought took shape.

Nowhere to go for extra cover, he stepped back from the jeep and launched himself into a headlong dive, hugging the earth, the AKSU rifle pressed against his side. When the grenade went off, most of the blast and shrapnel was directed skyward, the vehicle's passenger compartment serving as a kind of bomb-disposal bucket. Any hope of driving the jeep home went up in smoke, but it saved Bolan's life and shielded him from all but half a dozen ragged splinters, flesh wounds stinging him like wasps.

Before the echo of the blast had ceased reverberating in his skull, Bolan was moving, rolling toward the open desert, rising to a combat crouch. The smoking wreckage of the jeep obscured him from the view of an advancing gunner who was stroking short bursts out of his full-sized Kalashnikov, giving the vehicle a noisy coup de grâce.

The soldier saw Bolan a few seconds too late. He swung his rifle around, but the Executioner beat him to it, triggering a burst that took him through the heart and lungs. Haddad folded at the knees and toppled forward onto his face.

A storm of automatic fire cut loose behind Bolan, and he spun in that direction, closing on the action. Twenty yards, then ten. He edged around the corner, just in time to see the hunters mount their final, desperate assault.

There were six of them, attacking in a ragged skirmish line, all firing from the hip as they advanced. Two of the gunners fell before the Executioner could frame a target in the AKSU's sights, and in another raucous moment it was finished, everybody down, their bodies twitching as one of the snipers on the high ground emptied his magazine.

The sudden silence had a grim, unearthly quality about it. Bolan stepped into the open, let the others see him and relax, before they scrambled down to double-check the dead. He counted three, then saw that Kordiyeh was stooped beneath the deadweight of another.

Faisal.

"I shall take him home," Kordiyeh said. "His family deserves that much, at least."

"We'll need a jeep for that," Bolan said. "Ours is shot."

He moved to check the others, found one with a corpse behind the wheel and dragged the dead man clear. The engine grudgingly responded to a twist of the ignition key, and once he got it running, Bolan thought it sounded hale enough to get them back across the border.

There was silence as the others loaded Faisal's body in the back. They spent a few more moments stripping weapons from the dead, each man with half a dozen rifles in his arms as they returned, their trousers sagging from the weight of several pistols each, tucked in their belts.

"We always need more weapons," Kordiyeh told Bolan. "Shall I drive?"

"I've got it," Bolan answered. "We can talk about our next move on the way."

This night had been a start, but nothing more. The worst of it still lay ahead.

CHAPTER THREE

Virginia
Two Days Earlier

From the air, if anyone was watching, Stony Man Farm would seem to be a normal working farm, for all intents and purposes. A pilot who expressed unhealthy interest could expect to have his aircraft photographed, identified and traced, followed by an intimidating summons from the FBI, perhaps a shakedown visit by a pair of agents. If any uninvited visitors should try to land without permission, there were Stinger missiles and a battery of rapid-firing miniguns to make sure the intruders were stone dead before they hit the ground. The same applied to vehicular traffic.

The "Farm" had been created by a chief executive now vanished from the Oval Office as the nerve center of a covert war on terrorism and "untouchable" crime, and its mission remained unchanged despite shifting administrations and political ideologies. Conservative or liberal—whatever those terms even really meant, these days—each president-elect in turn had recognized the grim necessity of a concealed backup weapon, cocked and locked for use in unforeseen emergencies. The operation superseded standard judicial procedure—some might have said, correctly, that it circumvented laws and the Constitution altogether—but it had become an indispensable tool in a world where rules and regulations sometimes failed to do the necessary job.

Bolan's trip along Skyline Drive had been uneventful, but now he could feel the watchers tracking him as he approached the farmhouse, and he saw the helicopter that would have carried Hal Brognola down from Washington. The man from Justice was already waiting for him on the broad front porch as Bolan parked his rental car and switched off the engine.

"You made good time," Brognola said, while he was shaking Bolan's hand.

"It sounded urgent," the Executioner told his friend of many years.

"Urgent's the word, all right. You need to freshen up or anything, after the drive?"

"I'm fine."

"Okay. They're waiting for us in the War Room," Brognola replied. "We might as well get to it."

"THEY" WERE Barbara Price and Aaron "The Bear" Kurtzman. Price was the thirtysomething, honey-blond mission controller at Stony Man Farm, Kurtzman the bearded and bespectacled computer wizard charged with handling all communications at the Farm. Together, they were the primary brains and heart of the Stony Man team.

There was no need for introductions as Brognola

and the Executioner arrived to join the comrades whom he literally trusted with his life. When they were settled in and had disposed of the amenities, Brognola got the briefing under way.

"You're up to speed on the dissension in Algeria," he said, not asking Bolan quite so much as stating an accepted fact.

"Dissension hardly covers it," the Executioner replied. "They're on the brink of civil war, if not beyond the point of no return. Ten thousand deaths a year, on average, dating back to '92. It's like a lunatic asylum with the inmates in control."

"You're closer to the truth than you imagine on that score," Brognola said. "The UN launched a formal probe of the conditions over there in 1998, and issued a report that August calling for the powers-that-be to find out whether any of the several dozen massacres each year were being carried out by military forces or government-sponsored militias. It wasn't really a question, mind you. The investigative team went on record with a statement that Algerian troops and their paramilitary pals *were* responsible for mass murder of captured guerrillas and 'hostile' civilians. At the same time, the report linked Islamic dissident groups to similar crimes, including multiple kidnappings, gang rapes and murders of women. Needless to say, the first part of the UN report was denounced in Algiers as a slanderous fraud."

"No great surprise," Bolan said.

"None at all. It looks like the two sides could go on killing until they depopulate the country and Khaddafi claims it for a parking lot. Some big shots in Congress couldn't care less. They're old enough to remember when Algeria gave shelter to Weathermen and Panthers on the run from Hoover's FBI. They like to see the shoe on the other foot, especially when it's kicking ass. State has a travel advisory out on the country. Beyond that, as far as some of the old guard is concerned, the place can go to hell."

"Except..."

"Except," the big Fed continued, "that it got out of hand last weekend. Four staffers from the U.S. Embassy took a hike to the Casbah district, looking for God knows what."

"You want suggestions?" Price asked him, with a teasing smile.

"Not even," Brognola replied. "Leave an old man his illusions, if it's not too much to ask."

"I was about to say shopping for curios," she said.

"As if. It doesn't matter what the four of them were after anyway, because they never found it. As investigators reconstruct it, they stopped off at one place for some drinks, and there were shooters waiting for them when they left. All four were killed outright by automatic fire, and someone cut their ears off for the hell of it. Some kind of souvenir, I wouldn't be surprised."

"Suspects?" Bolan asked.

"Pick your poison. It's gotten so bad in the past five years or so that shooters from Hamas are taking flak as 'moderates,' because they're willing to negotiate with the Algerine regime on certain points instead of simply killing anything that moves. The really hard-core rebels have four or five private armies to choose from. The largest and most active are the Armed Islamic Group, or GIA, sponsored by Libya, and Islamic Salvation Front, or FIS, funded from Tehran. You want to talk extreme, the FIS has issued an open death warrant on all 'unbelievers,' including Algerian soldiers, policemen, journalists, artists, poets and—get this—singers. Of course, the GIA considers the FIS 'too soft' on so-called enemies of Islam. Take your pick, they're all as crazy as hell.''

''No possibility of government involvement as a provocation?'' Bolan asked.

''We thought about that, but it doesn't track,'' Brognola said. ''For all the UN complaints about human rights violations, we support the Algerian government financially, and they've been fairly civil since diplomatic relations were restored in 1989. Truth is, they need all the Western friends they can get, with Iran and Libya both supporting insurgent militias.''

''I was thinking more along the lines of a diversionary tactic,'' Bolan said. ''A little something to increase U.S. support against the rebels, for instance.''

''Anything's possible, I suppose,'' Brognola allowed, ''but the Company doesn't think there's any state involvement, and we've got a joker in the deck that makes me lean a different way.''

''Which joker's that?'' Bolan asked.

The big Fed nodded to Kurtzman. ''Does the name Malik al-Salaam ring any bells?''

''A faint one,'' Bolan said. ''He's an American, I think. Some kind of Muslim activist?''

"One and the same," Kurtzman replied. "Born Rodney Allen Tuggle, in Detroit, on February 15, 1965. The same day Malcolm X was shot and killed in Harlem, that would be. If you believe the hype, Tuggle had an epiphany on his eighteenth birthday, wherein he 'discovered' that he was, in fact, the host of Malcolm's reborn spirit. He changed his name legally about six months later, but he waited another year and a half to start pushing the story, recruiting dissidents and rejects from the Nation of Islam for a new Islamic Brotherhood, with him calling the shots. His basic rap is a mishmash of black pride, anti-Semitism and solidarity with Muslim states 'oppressed' by the United States."

"He's got a thing or two to say about Algeria, I take it," Bolan said.

"Worse yet," Brognola stated. "He's *in* Algeria. Has been the past three months, with side trips into Libya, Iran and Syria. The Company can't prove he's taking money from Khaddafi or the others, but I haven't met a soul in Washington who doubts it."

"What's his take on the assassinations?" Bolan asked.

"First thing he did was publicly congratulate the killer—while, of course, denying that he knew who pulled the trigger or had any link to the event himself."

"You think he's lying?"

"Either way, he's given us one hell of a black eye. More to the point, there are concerns about what he might try to pull when he comes home, about a month from now. The rumble is that Malik al-Salaam has found himself a Daddy Warbucks—maybe more than one—to help him put a big-time arsenal together, maybe start an active 'liberation front' here in the States.''

"You think that's credible?" Bolan asked.

The big Fed responded with a shrug. "He's talked about the 'coming revolution' ever since he organized the Brotherhood. In April 1998, customs and ATF intercepted a shipment of Kalashnikovs and plastic explosives headed for a warehouse in New Jersey, via the Bahamas. There was nothing they could hang indictments on, as far as Malik was concerned, but one of his lieutenants signed the warehouse lease agreement. The guy sucked it up and took the whole weight himself, six years and change. Malik offered sympathy and then dumped his ass 'for the good of the movement.' Everyone else skated clean on the deal.''

"Any link between Malik and the Casbah killings?" Bolan asked.

"Nothing beyond his comments and the company he keeps. He's been seen talking to the leaders of the GIA at different times, along with spokesmen from the Islamic Salvation Army and the Movement of the Islamic State. Some think he might have what it takes to mend the bridges over there and help create a tighter dissident coalition.''

"I'm surprised the government doesn't show him the door," Bolan said.

"State already suggested that," Brognola replied. "Algiers is sensitive to the appearance of religious persecution, even in the middle of the shit storm they've got going on. Essentially, they are a Muslim state, no matter that the rebels trying to dismantle the regime are Muslims, too. The honchos over there have Malik figured as some kind of spokesman for all Muslims west of Gibraltar or something. One thing you can't fault is his propaganda machine.''

"Something needs to be done," Bolan said.

"We're agreed, all the way to the top. Of course, it can't be done officially."

"I'll need a contact and interpreter," the Executioner remarked. The official language of Algeria was Arabic, with French and various Berber dialects also well represented. English wasn't unknown, but it was rare enough—outside diplomatic circles, at least— that Bolan would be a nonfunctional sitting duck if he tried to pull off the mission alone.

"I've got somebody lined up in Algiers," Brognola said. "A contract agent with the Company, Hassan Filali. Langley was encouraged to cooperate without too many questions. Rumor has it that they got a call from Pennsylvania Avenue."

"It isn't what you know—" Kurtzman began.

"—it's *who* you know," Brognola finished for him. "And you're absolutely right."

"Is he connected?" Bolan asked. "The agent in Algiers, I mean."

"Affirmative. According to the Company, he's tight with the commander of a group that's fed up with the dissidents and state terrorism alike. I wasn't trusted with a name, but you'll be put in touch once you get over there. Between Filali and his friends, you should have all the local color that you need."

"This group's agenda would be…what, again?"

"Democracy," Brognola said, "or something close enough, at any rate, to get the jackboot off their necks. They also shun fanaticism and are pledged to keep a group of crackpot fundamentalists from taking over, if and when the present state caves in."

"Okay," Bolan said, keeping any reservations to himself. "I guess we're good to go. First thing tomorrow suit everyone?"

BOLAN'S OVERNIGHT lodging for the visit to Stony Man Farm was a room at the northeast corner of the second floor, complete with private bath. Directly underneath him, the garage and workshop might be occupied, but heavy insulation kept the noise and fumes from traveling upstairs. Above him on the third floor, there was storage space, communications gear and ample hardware for a last-ditch stand, in case the whole place went to hell.

He didn't dwell upon the latter notion, not because it was impossible, but rather because it had happened some years ago, with a combination of enemies outside and a traitor within. The raid had put Kurtzman in his wheelchair, and it had also cost lives, with Bolan's former mission controller and longtime ladylove numbered among the dead.

He didn't go there often, in his mind. The memories were clear enough, but there was nothing he could do to change the past, and Bolan had no taste for pointless masochism. At the moment, what he needed was an evening to relax and kill some time with friends before he traveled halfway around the world to kill more enemies.

Or, maybe, this time they would do the killing.

Bolan shed the morbid train of thought with his clothing, padding naked to the bathroom, reaching in to turn on the shower, adjusting the temperature to a pleasant heat before he stepped beneath the spray. He stood for several moments, palms braced flat against the tile below the showerhead, letting the water pelt his face, shoulders and chest.

He wasn't sure how much time had elapsed before he reached out for the soap—and froze.

Something was wrong. He couldn't peg it as a sound, but he stood immobile for another moment, listening, then turned his face slowly toward the shower door.

A human silhouette stood there, separated from Bolan by three feet of steamy space and a thin pane of frosted glass. Another moment, and the shadow reached forward. The shower's door snicked open, and Barbara Price stepped in to join him.

Naked as the day she was born.

"We're really into water conservation here, these days," she told him, as her hair acquired a deeper hue and plastered to her skull.

"Suits me," the Executioner replied, and slipped an arm around her supple waist, pulling her into his arms. She fit against him perfectly, her nipples almost sharp against his chest.

The first kiss seemed to last forever, broken only with reluctance when Bolan had to stop and catch his breath. He was tremendously aroused, his manhood trapped between them, rigid, pressed against the downy softness of her lower abdomen.

"The soap," she said, and reached around him, clinging with her free hand, so that the delicious friction was maintained and amplified. She found the soap and quickly worked a lather between her palms, then started soaping Bolan's broad chest with the bar, her free hand gliding down to capture him.

"That's risky," Bolan said between clenched teeth.

"You're telling me?" There was a taunt behind her smile.

"I meant—"

"I know," she said, the slow glide of her lathered palm accelerating, while she soaped his nipples with the foamy bar. "We've still got hours before we have to meet the others in the dining room."

"That's not the way to make it last," Bolan said, finding her with soapy fingers of his own and taking up the rhythm.

"I know what I'm doing," Price told him, as she closed her eyes and moved against his hand. "Taking—oh, God!—taking the edge off."

"I can feel the edge," he said. "It isn't going anywhere."

"You wanna bet?"

She started stroking almost frantically, his own hand keeping time, until she arched her back and stood on tiptoe, almost eye to eye with Bolan.

"Last one there can be on top next time," she told him, with a tremor in her voice.

They raced each other to the finish line, all steaming heat, two minds and bodies with a single desperate goal. The moment was too intense to last, and Price cried out first, head thrown back. He followed her a moment later, gasping, clutching her fiercely underneath the streaming spray.

"Hmm. You could use a little more soap here and there," she said at last, smiling.

"I can—"

"Let me," she ordered, and immediately went to work.

Her touch was magic. Bolan felt the need again, as if he hadn't just been satisfied.

"Oh, my," she said, "this still needs looking after."

"Look away."

She finished washing him and turned off the shower, reaching out to fetch a terry bath towel from the rack. "For best results, you really should get off your feet."

"I lost," Bolan reminded her, stroking one perfect breast. "I get to be on top."

"Your loss," she told him, leading Bolan from the shower, toward the bedroom, "is my gain."

CHAPTER FOUR

Algeria

His latest war against the savages had started in Algiers, and it was coming home. Not to the Casbah district, yet, though Bolan still might get around to it in time. Some of the terrorists he sought were quartered there, he had been told, but they were mostly shooters, grunts in the ongoing conflict that had reduced Algeria to the status of a huge free-fire zone. For his part, Bolan preferred to start at the top, trusting that the pawns would find him, when he threatened their kings.

Algeria's several dissident militias were homegrown, for the most part—reinforced, some said, with gunners from Afghanistan, seasoned veterans of war against the Soviets—but they were funded from outside, the GIA drawing its support from Libya, while soldiers of the FIS were armed and paid from Iran. That disparate backing would have made them adversaries, even if their views on religion and politics had been identical, and Bolan hoped to profit from the rivalry between the leading groups of militants.

As for the government itself, he was content for now to pass on tangling with the soldiers, if they stayed out of his way. Of course, if he should meet an "unofficial" death squad in the meantime, then all bets were off.

His first target that morning was the downtown office building where a certain Wasim Ruholla conducted business on behalf of interests based in Tehran. Ostensibly, he was concerned with everything from oil exports to cultural events, but if the CIA wasn't mistaken, his primary function was insuring prompt delivery of cash and weapons to the Islamic Salvation Front. The ayatollahs in Iran especially appreciated FIS zeal in cracking down on "decadent" artists, authors and musicians in Algeria.

Bolan approached the twelve-story office building on foot, Kordiyeh at his side. Both men were dressed in business suits despite the heat; both carried imitation-leather briefcases—one black, the other brown—in their left hands, leaving the right free to reach for armpit-holstered hardware if they were accosted on the street. Each briefcase contained a Spanish-made Z-84 submachine gun, strongly resembling the venerable Uzi, except that its metal stock folded over the top of the weapon's receiver, instead of collapsing accordion-style. The Z-84 has a cyclic rate identical to the Uzi, at 600 rounds per minute, feeding on a 36-round box magazine inserted through the pistol grip.

There had been sketchy news of the Libyan raid on the morning news, short on detail and devoid of any reference to the GIA training facility. Bolan had expected more, but it made no great difference to his plans. His enemies inside the GIA knew they were hurting, and now it was time for the FIS paymaster to share their discomfort.

There were no guards on the street outside the office building, and a lone surveillance camera in the lobby didn't track them as they moved beneath it toward the elevator. Ruholla's office was located on the seventh floor. They rode the elevator up in silence, passing six floors before they opened their cases to remove the compact stutterguns. It took another moment to attach suppressors, though it would be a wasted effort if the office was defended by lookouts with unsilenced guns.

Both men were ready when the door scraped open to reveal a slice of plain but spotless corridor. No one was waiting for the car, their progress unobstructed as they left the elevator, turning right along the hallway.

Ruholla's office suite lay directly ahead at the end of the corridor, some legend Bolan couldn't read inscribed in Arabic, gold paint on jet-black plastic, bolted onto polished wood. They stepped into a spacious waiting room, a male receptionist-cum-secretary glancing up from his keyboard as they entered. He was about to ask their business when he saw the weapons, his mouth snapping shut with an audible click.

Kordiyeh leveled his Z-84 at the young man's face, holding it steady as he bent to set his briefcase on the floor. A terse demand in Arabic, and the receptionist hesitated only for a moment, then rose from his desk, hands well out from his sides. Exactly how he touched off the alarm eluded Bolan afterward. Perhaps there was a panic button on the floor, but there could just as easily have been a small perpetual-surveillance camera hidden somewhere in the waiting room, feeding its images to monitors offstage.

Whatever, Bolan had no sooner set his briefcase on the floor than half a dozen guards exploded through a door behind the young receptionist and through another off to Bolan's right. They came out waving guns, but didn't open fire immediately, and their fleeting hesitation proved to be a fatal error.

Bolan spun to face the three men on his right, squeezing the trigger on his SMG. The weapon made a sound like heavy sailcloth ripping, a storm of 9 mm rounds ripping into his targets, flinging them backward like rag dolls. One of the three men got off a shot from his pistol, but he was already tumbling backward as he fired, his bullet wasted on the ceiling's beige acoustic tiles.

Kordiyeh, meanwhile, had dealt with his own team of gunners. All three were on the floor, one of them moving sluggishly until another 3-round burst collapsed his skull. Only the young receptionist was standing, and the simple act of staying upright almost seemed to take more will than he possessed. His face was streaked with crimson from the splashback of a head shot, and his hands were trembling as he held them, stiff-armed, overhead. He didn't hesitate, this time, when Kordiyeh repeated his original command. Stepping across the bodies of three men who had been friends, perhaps, he led them through the door propped open by one fallen corpse, along a narrow hallway to Wasim Ruholla's private office.

One drawback of an end suite on the seventh floor was that the place had no back door. Assuming that Ruholla's office wasn't completely soundproof, the Iranian certainly had to have heard the gunshot from his waiting room. Most likely, there was also an alarm—albeit silent—that alerted him when his protectors rushed to deal with armed intruders in the outer office. Bolan knew the odds were good that Ruholla would be crouched behind his desk right now, perhaps aiming a weapon at the office door.

"You first," he said to the receptionist, with Kordiyeh translating into Arabic.

The young man swallowed hard, edged forward and knocked. There was no answer, and he pounded on the door a second time more urgently, before a cautious voice responded from within. It had to have been a question, for their pointman seemed to answer, then apparently received the go-ahead. He used both hands to turn the knob, as if one would be insufficient for the job, and eased the door back on its hinges, cautiously encroaching on the inner sanctum.

Ruholla's first shot struck his young employee in the chest and rocked him backward on his heels. The second plowed a furrow underneath the left side of his jawline, deep enough to sever the carotid artery and thus unleash a crimson geyser, spouting almost to the ceiling tiles. As the receptionist fell backward, dead or dying, Bolan stuck his SMG around the doorjamb, squeezing off a burst to keep the target's head down while they rushed him.

Kordiyeh went through the doorway first and ducked off to his right, Bolan behind him, going left. If not for the two bullets that had cut down their escort, they might have thought the room was vacant, waiting for its occupant to put in an appearance. Furtive scuffling sounds behind the teakwood desk told Bolan where their man was hiding, and they opened fire in unison, the Parabellum slugs inscribing zigzag patterns on the polished wood.

Both submachine guns still had rounds left in their magazines when Ruholla gave a squeal of panic, tossed his shiny pistol clear and started spouting what Bolan knew could only be a plea for mercy. Kordiyeh responded with a brusque command, and the pudgy Iranian emerged by inches, soft hands held in front of him as if the palms could stop a bullet.

"Tell him he's finished here," Bolan instructed. "Tell him that the FIS is finished in Algeria. The ayatollahs need to find another charity closer to home."

Kordiyeh translated the message, apparently adding some threat of his own, punctuated by a jerky motion with his SMG. Ruholla flinched, staring wide-eyed, and replied with a stammer.

"He says that he will leave tonight," Kordiyeh said. "He thanks us for his life."

"He owes me one," Bolan replied. "The next time I see him, I'll collect."

Another rapid-fire translation from Kordiyeh, and

the Iranian didn't respond this time, merely ducking his head in a nod, eyes downcast.

They left the office abattoir and walked back to the elevator, stowing their SMGs while they waited for the slow car to return. Kordiyeh seemed pleased with himself, unconcerned at the possibility of police waiting for them downstairs.

"He will not summon the authorities," Kordiyeh said, when Bolan asked. "What would he say? He has been funding rebels who attempt to overthrow the government in power. If he wants to die, he could save time and spare himself much pain by simply jumping out the window."

"Fair enough."

"And our next stop?" his companion asked, a beat before the elevator car arrived.

"We can't play favorites," Bolan told him with a smile. "We need to have a little visit with the Libyan paymaster for the GIA."

THE LIBYAN WAS Asem Kabir, a stocky man whose olive complexion was pocked by lighter, crinkled scars. The marks had been made by shrapnel, inflicted when, from his point of view, the madman Ronald Reagan tried to murder Colonel Moammar Khaddafi in April 1986. Kabir had been present with his leader when the so-called smart bombs fell on Tripoli, and he had lost the vision in his left eye when a white-hot piece of steel sheared through the optic nerve. At that, he had been lucky to survive the blast, afterward taking pride in the fact that his body had absorbed the shrapnel that might have injured—even killed—the Libyan chief of state.

It was a service Kabir was pleased to render, never mind the pain or how the women who had once found him attractive now pretended not to notice his off-kilter smile, the unpredictable tic that sometimes made him wink involuntarily.

Kabir served his country still. He was attached to foreign service now, in covert operations, and it pleased him greatly to disburse the arms and money that permitted other peoples to resist the tyranny of the United States. He hated Israel, too, of course—indeed, he had been raised from childhood to despise the Jewish state—but it was the Americans who scarred him, left him with a rheumy, winking eye and mangled taste buds that sometimes confused the flavors of his food. He was delighted with the chaos he had helped to spread throughout Algeria, no better in Kabir's one good eye than a client state, controlled from Washington.

Of course, the venal "statesmen" in Algiers still posed as Muslims, still made noise about recovering a homeland for the Palestinians, but they were feeble in their efforts, more intent on managing affairs at home, stockpiling luxuries and money for themselves. If that were not the case, they would have stolidly rejected foreign aid from Washington, perhaps even turned back the calendar to happy days when fugitives were welcomed to Algeria from the United States, protected, armed and trained against the day when they might journey home again and take their battle to the streets.

Those days *would* come again, if Kabir had anything to say about it. At the moment, though, he had a major problem on his hands.

The previous night, persons unknown had struck the Armed Islamic Group's chief training camp in Libya. A predawn message from Khaddafi's chief of foreign intelligence had demanded that Kabir find out the names and group affiliation of the soldiers who had staged the raid. Ten hours later, after grilling everybody he could think of who might know the answer to that question, Kabir still had no answer for his boss.

And that was bad.

Houari Boudiaf, commander of the GIA, was known for his explosive temper when frustrated or enraged, but his outbursts were nothing compared to Khaddafi's. To the world at large, it seemed as if the colonel who commanded Libya had mellowed, somehow, but nothing could be further from the truth. His close brush with death in 1986 had taught the man to be a bit more circumspect in covering his tracks, a trifle more obscure—and slightly less inflammatory—in his speeches on the subject of The Enemy, but he was still a battle-tested Saladin at heart, pledged to the annihilation of the Jewish state in Israel and exemplary attacks on her supporters in the West.

There was another factor working here, as well, Kabir realized. Khaddafi longed to build an empire for himself, expand from Libya to rule a larger territory. That ambition had prompted the colonel to invade neighboring Chad in 1977, touching off a conflict that lasted nearly two decades, until a negotiated settlement with the United Nations saw occupation troops withdrawn in May 1994. There had also been border clashes with Egypt, to the east, and now he gazed westward, imagining the territory he would gain if a Libyan-backed puppet regime was installed in Algiers.

Libyan support for the Armed Islamic Group was no secret. Indeed, the GIA's commander—Houari Boudiaf—had often boasted of his ties to Tripoli. With that in mind, Kabir attempted to succeed where all his spies had thus far failed, determining who stood to profit from disruption of the training camp in Libya.

His problem: there were too many suspects.

One of the most obvious, and first to cross his mind, was the competing Islamic Salvation Front. The FIS and GIA had been at odds for years, despite their mutual devotion to the creation of a fundamentalist Islamic state, and they had burned more ammunition fighting each other than harassing government forces. The FIS commander, Nabi Ulmalhama, might not hesitate to strike across the border—though, admittedly, he had refrained from making any moves in that direction for the past two years, since the training camp was established.

Kabir directed his thoughts beyond Ulmalhama and the FIS, to their sponsors in Iran. Granted, Iran shared no border with Algeria—as Libya did—but there were still benefits aplenty to be gained from the installation of a pro-Tehran government in Algiers. Chief among them was a yawning loophole that would finally permit Iran to evade American trade sanctions, in place since 1996. While sundry U.S. firms were penalized for dealing with Iran, there was no ban on trading with Algeria. A few cosmetic touch-ups on the paperwork, and it would be business as usual for Iranian oil men, agricultural exporters and the like.

But would the ayatollahs risk a foray into Libya, thus leaving themselves vulnerable to charges of making war on another Islamic state? There were several ways around that problem, Kabir knew from personal experience. A strike force from the FIS could be employed, for instance, or Tehran could simply field a team of mercenaries—Germans, Cubans, Japanese, whatever—to perform the dirty work. In fact, since the attackers were adept at covering their tracks and left no dead or wounded on the battlefield, there was nothing to identify the raiders, anyway.

But Kabir still had a job to do, whether his adversaries made it difficult or not. He couldn't go back to Khaddafi with the explanation that his orders were "too difficult" to carry out. The colonel would expect results at any cost in order to retaliate effectively against his enemies.

That was the problem. As for its solution, Kabir thus far had no idea how he would complete his task. Informants on the street and in the countryside—and he had many of them, purchased cheaply in a nation where the average annual income fell below four thousand U.S. dollars—had no information on who had staged the border raid or why.

If he did not come up with something soon—

The fire alarm went off, startling Kabir with its

clamor, making him jump in his chair like a frightened child. There was no one to see him, but he felt embarrassed all the same, more curious about the source of the alarm than worried that his life might be at risk. There was a fire escape outside his third-floor suite of offices, and he had no fear of being trapped inside the building, even if there was a fire. More likely, though, the cheap equipment had malfunctioned once again, and he would have to suffer another confrontation with his landlord.

As he reached the office door and wrapped his hand around the knob, a new sound reached his ears. It was the pop-pop-pop of gunfire, unmistakable despite the muffling effect of walls and doors.

And for the first time since he woke that morning, he knew fear.

As with the first strike in Algiers, Gholomreza Kordiyeh had mapped the layout of their target with a floor plan drawn from memory. The Libyan paymaster's office was a third-floor suite, located in a building two miles from the point where they had dealt with the Iranians, some thirty minutes earlier. If word of the attack had spread this far, it seemed to have no visible impact: no sentries were visible outside the building, although Bolan knew they could be watching from the windows of a dozen different structures or from any nearby vehicle. The street was busy, though, and he hoped that two more men in suits with briefcases in hand wouldn't stand out, despite the fact that one of them clearly wasn't a native.

It was a long block's walk from the public parking

lot to reach their target. If the probe went badly, they could easily be cut off from their wheels and cast adrift, afoot in old Algiers—assuming they weren't gunned down before they reached the street. The Executioner was well accustomed to such risks, but that didn't mean that he took them lightly or ignored the possibility of failure.

In addition to the submachine gun in his briefcase and the CZ-75 pistol slung beneath his arm, Bolan carried two smoke grenades under his jacket, clipped to his belt, well around toward the back. The jacket had some room to spare, and while the outline of the two grenades might still be visible to a discerning eye, he counted on the fact that few Algerians would be inclined to watch a stranger's buttocks as he passed them on the street.

Bolan had braced himself for soldiers in the lobby, ready to proceed if they were forced to blast their way upstairs, but no one moved to intercept them as they entered; no one seemed to give them so much as a second glance.

Again, they rode the elevator to preserve appearances, though Bolan might have opted for the stairs had he been working on his own. An elevator could become a death trap in so many ways: if they were spotted coming in, and there were gunners waiting for them up on three, prepared to hose them with automatic fire; if someone threw the switch that would trap them between floors; if their enemies went all out and used a small explosive charge to snap the cables, dropping Bolan and Kordiyeh into the basement with bone-crushing force. Retreating from the strike, unless they made it a clean sweep, they also ran the risk of meeting reinforcements in the lobby, either uniforms or private shooters summoned by their mark.

Bolan was hoping he could leave the Libyan alive, as he had done with Wasim Ruholla in their first urban strike. He would prefer to have a living messenger, unless it came down to the crunch and he was forced to kill the paymaster, along with any guards on hand. It would be Kabir's choice, finally, if he should live or die. In case the Libyan was feeling bold or trigger-happy, Bolan had a letter in his pocket, written in Arabic, that would explain the raid to anyone who came along and found the bodies after they were gone.

The elevator was an older model than the one in Wasim Ruholla's building, equipped with one of those brass accordion grates that had to be pulled across the open door before the car could shudder on its way. The outer door was frosted glass, and would provide no cover for the passengers if Kabir had gunmen waiting for them on the floor above. Nor, for that matter, were they hidden from the view of passersby on two, as they removed the automatic weapons from their briefcases and double-checked each submachine gun's load. Full magazines, with the suppressors snug in place.

There were no shooters visible as they arrived on three, but they could only see six feet of corridor from where they stood, well back inside the elevator car. There could be half a dozen gunmen lined up, ready to unload from left and right as they emerged, but

there was only one way to find out. Kordiyeh led the
way, by virtue of his language skills, although the
SMG he held against his leg would do most of his
talking in the next few minutes. Bolan watched him
glance both ways, nod toward the left, then followed
him immediately, holding the Z-84 well back, at least
partly concealed by his thigh.

There was a straight-backed wooden chair planted
outside the entrance to Kabir's office, occupied by a
swarthy, heavyset man in a rumpled gray suit. Beside
him, to his left, a canvas shopping bag was propped
against the wall, containing what could only be some
kind of weapon, from its size and shape.

The lookout had been dozing, but he heard the elevator's grate squeal open, and he watched the new
arrivals moving toward him, his expression stuck
somewhere between concern and apathy. His left
hand made a jerky movement, spatulate fingers groping for the bag and gun inside, but Bolan beat him to
it, raising his Z-84 and triggering a muffled burst before the sentry could reach his own weapon.

The Parabellum shockers hit him in the face and
splayed his cheeks, as if he had been riding on a
rocket sled. His skull rebounded from the wall, leaving a dent behind, and then he toppled forward, spilling from the chair to lie facedown, a heap of lifeless
flesh.

Bolan and Kordiyeh picked up their pace, brushed
through the outer door to find another male receptionist—apparently the norm for Muslim businessmen—already on his feet and moving toward a door
behind him. Whether he was responding to the noise

outside or had some other errand, they would never know. Twin muzzles locked on to his face and froze the young man in his tracks. Kordiyeh rattled off a sharp command, already moving forward in anticipation that the youth would do as he was told.

Instead, he gave a high-pitched squeal and bolted for the nearby door. Kordiyeh could have overtaken him on foot, most likely, but the warning cry had finished any hope of a surprise attack, and they weren't prepared to deal with prisoners of war. A short burst from his SMG was dead on target, stitching ragged holes between the runner's shoulder blades and slamming him against the door, face-first.

Because the door was hung to open inward, they weren't required to drag his corpse aside, but simply stepped across it as they cleared the threshold, searching for Kabir in the warren of cubicles that lay before them. Heads poked out of half a dozen open doorways, as they stepped into the corridor, but only one of those who faced them had a weapon in his hand.

The Arab seemed almost to have forgotten he was armed—no soldier, this one—and in any other circumstances, Bolan might have offered him a chance to drop the gun and save himself. There was no time for mercy at the moment, though, and Bolan shot him in the face, a burst from somewhere close to point-blank range that slammed his target backward, out of view.

Kabir's office was the last in line, the only one of seven that was fitted with a door, to grant some privacy. The door was certainly a status symbol, but the only thing it meant to Bolan at the moment was concealment, and the supposition that his target had to be on alert by now, perhaps already armed and waiting to defend himself.

Unless...

"The fire escape," he said, and cleared the final distance in a sprint that left Kordiyeh behind. It was a risky move, he knew, but Bolan gave the door a flying kick that slammed it open, back against the wall. He had the office covered as he followed through, sweeping from left to right, before he locked on to Kabir's silhouette, already scrambling through the open window, clinging to the metal staircase bolted to the outer wall.

To shoot or not to shoot? The Libyan made a tempting target with the light behind him, but his execution wasn't Bolan's primary concern—nor was he up for a protracted chase through streets and alleyways.

Bolan made his choice in a heartbeat, squeezing off an automatic burst that raked the left side of the window-dowframe but left Kabir unscathed. The Libyan cried out and lost his footing as he tried to duck below the line of fire, thumping downstairs and out of Bolan's view. There was a crash and bitter cursing when he hit the landing, lurching on from there with painful steps to make his limping getaway.

Kordiyeh brushed past Bolan, lining up a shot through the window, ready to fire, when the big American called him off. "Don't bother," he told Kordiyeh. "I'll leave the note and let him read it to whoever pulls his strings. Same difference."

Watching the corridor outside, in case another of

the office workers came up with a weapon, Bolan drew an envelope from his pocket and dropped it on Kabir's desk. It would be waiting for him, if and when the Libyan came back. If he didn't return, then someone else would ultimately read the message, and the word would get around.

No sweat.

As they were leaving, moving past the cubicles with young men huddled in them, crouched beneath their desks, Bolan reached underneath his jacket, palmed a smoke grenade and freed the pin. He dropped it in the middle of the narrow hallway, sputtering and fuming as he made his way back into the reception room. A little something extra for the Libyan contingent to contend with, just in case they harbored any thoughts of smuggling out their dead without involving the authorities. A visit from the Algiers fire brigade would keep them on their toes.

It was shaping up to be a halfway decent day.

CHAPTER FIVE

Physically, Nabi Ulmalhama was a small man. He stood no more than five foot three, and after one humiliating incident involving elevator shoes, he had refused to blaspheme by complaining of the limitations God had imposed upon him. Everywhere he went Ulmalhama saw beggars, the homeless and people with loathsome diseases. Some of them had seen their families massacred. And some, if they but knew it when they gazed upon the little man, were looking at the architect of their domestic tragedy.

What he would always lack in height, Nabi Ulmalhama had determined to replace with power and influence. For that he had required a cause, and it was handed to him on a blood-flecked platter in his twenty-seventh year. With the eleventh-hour ban on scheduled national elections in Algeria, the outbreak of a civil war was virtually guaranteed. Ulmalhama had already joined the Islamic Salvation Front, impressing the founders with his energy and zeal. He rose through the ranks accordingly, and when the original FIS leaders died in a surprise military raid on their top-secret headquarters—following an anonymous telephone tip to their whereabouts—Nabi Ulmalhama was the natural choice to lead.

Life had been sweet since then, as the terrorist measured such things. There had been ample opportunity for him to lash out at his enemies, a yearning he had nurtured since his final spurt of growth ran out at age fourteen. The rest of the world had continued to grow, even Nabi's friends looking down on him, but things had changed in that regard. The men and women who once mocked or pitied Ulmalhama feared him now, and rightly so. He had the power to make them suffer, make their loved ones disappear, or even snatch away their worthless lives.

As leader of the FIS, Ulmalhama had dictated a stronger, more dynamic course of action for the future. Not that the FIS had ever been peaceful; far from it. But before he took the helm, its violence had been sporadic, almost aimless: a sniping here, a bombing there, earnest discussion of a ransom kidnapping campaign that never came to pass. Most of the urban skirmishing had been with members of the GIA or the smaller Movement of the Islamic State. In Nabi Ulmalhama's eyes, it was apparent that their main energy should be directed against their primary target: the ruling regime in Algiers.

Since that time, the assassination of policemen, soldiers and public officials had nearly quadrupled, other dissident groups following Ulmalhama's lead and pretending the idea was theirs. No matter. Even with the new direction of its war, the FIS still found time to strike at various competing militias. In some cases, the internecine conflict arose from doctrinal or ideological differences; other feuds were spawned by simple jealousy, greed or a bitter clash of personalities. Whatever the cause, leaders and members of the GIA and other smaller groups had been conditioned to expect no mercy if the FIS emerged victorious.

Two days earlier, Ulmalhama would have used the word "when," in place of "if," but circumstances changed with bewildering speed in wartime. Yesterday, his troops had been amply armed and funded by their ideological brothers in Tehran. This day, when he dialed Wasim Ruholla's office number, there was only a recorded voice advising him the number had been taken out of service. Ulmalhama didn't know exactly what that meant, but he was troubled by the thought of losing his Iranian support. Scanning swiftly through his recent memory, he could think of nothing he had done or said that should have offended Ruholla. Of course, there was no telling with Iranians.

Assuming that he had committed some real or imaginary infraction of unwritten rules...so what? Ulmalhama was a charmer, when he had to be, and he could win over Ruholla, given half a chance. Should flattery fail to do the trick, he could always try bribery.

The soft knock on his study door distracted Ulmalhama from his train of thought, and he was frowning as he turned in that direction. "Yes?"

Mohammed Zeroual, his second in command, entered and closed the door behind him. There was trouble in his face, dejection in his posture. Where he often slouched a bit to make his superior seem taller, this time he appeared to have a heavy burden draped across his shoulders.

"What is wrong, Mohammed?"

"I spoke to Moneybags, just now," his number two replied, using their private name for the Iranian, Wasim Ruholla.

"And?" It was like pulling camel's teeth, sometimes, to get a story from Mohammed, but it did no good to rush him, since he had a mental quirk that made him tell a tale straight through, from the beginning, without any shortcuts along the way.

"He called from home," Zeroual said. "That is, I mean, the penthouse at the Salomé Hotel."

"I know where Wasim lives."

"Of course." Distracted by the interruption, Zeroual frowned for a moment, recovering his place, and then continued. "Someone has attacked his office. It is on the radio. They mention six or seven dead."

"Who is responsible?"

Zerouel shrugged. "Two men. They were not recognized. One Arab, possibly a native. The other was a white man, European or American."

"What language did he speak?" Ulmalhama demanded.

"Moneybags says English, but he could be wrong. He's never been across the Med, much less to the United States."

That was a well-known fact, yet it seemed to Ulmalhama that he would be foolish to ignore a warning from the man who paid so many of his bills. Ruholla might, indeed, be wrong about the second gunman's nationality, but that wasn't the most oppressive problem bearing down on Ulmalhama at the moment.

Someone had attacked the FIS paymaster, thus incurring wrath from the organization *and* from Tehran. Which meant the raiders had to be either very confident or totally insane. Whichever it turned out to be, Ulmalhama saw further trouble on the way. He couldn't manage to convince himself that this raid would turn out to be a one-time-only incident.

"Alert the troops," he said. "I must consider where and how we should retaliate."

HASSAN FILALI HAD survived to reach the ripe old age of forty-one by taking infinite precautions where his safety was concerned. The fact that he was still alive, more than a dozen years since he began work as a full-time contract agent for the CIA, left no doubt that he knew his business and could take care of himself in almost any situation. His enemies were legion in Algiers, but none of them—at least, none of the ones who still drew breath—knew that the man they hunted was Hassan Filali. From his beginnings as a humble sneak thief, he had grown into an artful master of diversion and deceit.

Which went a long way toward explaining why Hassan Filali had checked into a cheap Algiers hotel that morning with a sweet, young houri on his arm. The fat clerk winked and leered, accepting Filali's payment for three hours in advance with a respectful smile. A man who could maintain himself with such a woman for three hours was indeed a man of substance, and deserved respect.

The clerk had watched them go upstairs, already lost in wishful-thinking fantasies, wherein he took the stranger's part and satisfied the woman in a dozen ways that made her gasp and beg for more. He couldn't know that once they were inside the shabby room, Filali would produce a roll of bills and pay the woman what she had agreed on for a strictly hands-off twenty minutes of her time. She would be leaving through the back of the hotel, unnoticed by the lech at the front desk. Filali sat and waited by himself, sipping occasionally from a silver flask that he extracted from an inner pocket of his tailored jacket.

So engaged and fortified, he waited patiently for the American who called himself Belasko.

He had no fear that the tall man would be followed by police—or by killers from the GIA or FIS. Belasko was a man who plainly knew his business, and he wouldn't hesitate to kill if he believed that he was being tailed. Filali recognized a stone-cold killer when he saw one. After all, he had been rubbing shoulders with them every day since he was eight or nine years old.

Filali was too young to join the fighting when his people rose against the French, securing their freedom only after years of blood and suffering, in 1962. His father had been killed, his only sister raped and thus rendered unfit for marriage, but the war was over and the colonists had fled before the rebels thought Filali old enough to be trusted with a gun.

For all the suffering his family had endured, he hated Frenchmen with a passion that eclipsed all other feelings, but his hate didn't extend to other whites or

Westerners at large. Indeed, Filali recognized that his nation's break with the United States in 1967, shifting toward a military and political alliance with the now-defunct Soviet Union, had been a grave mistake, retarding progress in Algeria, subjugating the welfare of the country and its people to ill-conceived political rhetoric. By 1988, there were bloody riots in Algiers, protesting economic hardship, and the new constitution was approved a year later, clearing the way for a multiparty system of government.

But that wasn't the end. General elections had been scheduled for January 1992, with Islamic fundamentalists expected to sweep the slate. The election, in fact, had been canceled, and there had been mayhem ever since, government troops and their mercenary supporters ranged against a motley group of dissident militias, each pledged to seize power and remodel Algeria in its own theocratic image.

For himself, Filali wanted no part of the zealots. He had seen how the ayatollahs tried to turn back the clock in Iran, how the fanatics of the Taliban wrought havoc in Afghanistan. There was an element within Algeria that wanted much the same—a barricade of civil laws that echoed the Koran, forbidding earthly pleasure in all forms and cruelly subjugating those who disagreed. When he had been approached by a recruiter from the U.S. Embassy, enticed with money and the promise of a hero's life if he would help the Central Intelligence Agency keep tabs on "the crazies," he had readily agreed.

There had been moments of adventure, granted—and he took the money that was offered to him, knowing he had earned it—but Filali never once believed he was a hero. There were times when he felt like a patriot, however, and for him it was enough.

The soft knock on the door to his hotel room jarred Filali from his reverie. He reached inside his jacket, stowing the flask and drawing the vintage TT-33 semiautomatic pistol that he carried with him at all times. It was the Tokarev, long since replaced in Russian military service by the smaller, less powerful Makarov, but Filali appreciated the older weapon's robust simplicity: no safety catch, a simple 8-round magazine that could, if called upon to do so, chamber 7.63 mm Mauser rounds in addition to the standard 7.62 mm Soviet ammo.

Filali had killed two men with this pistol, and had frightened off several others who meant him grievous harm. While newer weapons were available at decent prices in Algiers, he felt a certain loyalty to the two-pound chunk of metal in his fist.

"Come in," Filali said in English. What else could he say? The door wasn't equipped with any kind of peephole that would warn him of an enemy outside, and he couldn't have fled the room in any case, since it possessed no window, no back door. It was, in fact, no better than a dingy, furnished cave.

The door swung open to reveal his Yankee contact, Mike Belasko, standing on the threshold by himself. There was no weapon in the tall man's hands, and so Filali put away his Tokarev. He rose to greet him with a handshake, after the American had closed and locked the door behind him.

"Expecting company?" Bolan asked, his eyes darting to the pistol bulge beneath Filali's jacket.

"I expect the unexpected," the Algerian responded. "I am like your Boy Scouts, yes? Always prepared."

"I hope you came prepared with information. We've already been through half the targets from your first list, and the others won't last long."

"Indeed," Filali said, "they might no longer be available. You have disturbed the equilibrium of your opponents, but they are long accustomed to adversity and setbacks. They will not stand idly by and wait for you to pick them off."

"I'm counting on it," Bolan replied. "I'll need backup targets, names and faces of subordinates...and anything you've got on Malik al-Salaam."

"He is American."

"You'd think so, from his birth certificate and passport," Bolan stated, "but you couldn't prove it by the company he keeps."

Filali knew all about that "company"—well, much about it, anyway—and he didn't mind sharing what he knew with the American. Belasko was already overmatched, even with help from Gholomreza Kordiyeh. It was a minor miracle that either one of them was still alive.

"Malik regards himself as an ambassador of unity to Muslim people everywhere," Filali said. "His arrogance is such that he believes he might somehow unite the several factions that have fought one another bitterly for centuries, and forge from them a strong, united front against the unbelievers of the world."

"So, how's he doing?"

"Spokesmen for the militias speak to him," Filali said, "but always separately. He has not found a way to break down their mistrust and hatred, much less forge them into one."

"But, if he does…" Bolan left the statement hanging, incomplete.

Filali filled the morbid silence for him. "If he does, the West may face an enemy unrivaled since the time of the Crusades."

"WHAT DO YOU MEAN, we still know nothing?"

There was no disguising the explosive anger that had overwhelmed Houari Boudiaf upon receiving news of the attack in Libya, now heated almost to the detonation point at learning of the raid against the offices of Asem Kabir. The field commander of the Armed Islamic Group was livid, spitting out his words as if they tasted foul and he couldn't abide them in his mouth.

If looks could kill, Arif Boumedienne concluded, Boudiaf would have long since fried him to a cinder where he stood.

"I have pursued the usual inquiries," said Boumedienne, and got no further in his statement before being interrupted once again.

"The *usual* inquiries?" Now the man's tone was mocking his lieutenant's choice of words. "Perhaps you would explain to me exactly what you find so usual about the situation, eh, Arif?"

"I simply meant—"

"Our most secure facility has been destroyed in

Libya, beneath Khaddafi's very nose. Now, in Algiers—our own backyard, Arif—Khaddafi's emissary to the Armed Islamic Group is nearly murdered, and we cannot even name the men responsible, much less inflict the punishment they deserve. I do not find the situation usual, Arif. I do not find it tolerable.''

"No." To say more, at the moment, would have been inviting physical assault, if not a bullet from the Browning automatic Boudiaf was wearing on his belt.

"We're in agreement then, I take it," Boudiaf went on, "that certain extraordinary measures must be taken to resolve the present difficulty?"

"Yes, of course."

"And first, before such measures can be taken," Boudiaf continued, "it is necessary to identify the enemy."

Boumedienne knew it was risky saying anything at all, just now, but he had never lied to Boudiaf before, and he saw nothing to be gained from starting now. He let the silence stretch between them for a moment, almost painfully, before he said, "That might be difficult."

"I disagree," Boudiaf replied, without the screaming tantrum Arif had expected. "It is evident to me that these attacks have been conducted by an enemy who hates us and who wishes us destroyed at any cost. It is apparent that they are the work of Nabi Ulmalhama and the Islamic Salvation Front."

Boumedienne had seen it coming, but the statement still surprised him, even so. There was a certain primal logic to it, but he could as easily have named three other groups, at least, that would have been delighted to attack the GIA. More to the point, the ruling party in Algiers detested *all* the dissident militias, and wasn't above employing mercenary death squads to destroy them—or to terrorize civilians thought to be supporters of the revolution.

No. Boumedienne believed his longtime friend was leaping to an insupportable conclusion...but it could be all his life was worth to disagree with him just now.

"I'll check it out," he said, in what he hoped was a placating tone of voice. "We still have two or three men in the FIS, despite the purges. One of them can no doubt tell us whether Nabi is responsible."

"By all means, seek the confirmation," Boudiaf agreed. "But in the meantime, we cannot afford to wait while more and more of our loyal soldiers are destroyed. If we do not retaliate and show our strength at once, we might not have another chance. Are we agreed, Arif?"

"Of course." The trick was sounding like he meant it, even when, in truth, he harbored major doubts about the wisdom of an escalating war against the hard-core soldiers of the Islamic Salvation Front. If GIA soldiers were zealots, those of the FIS were nothing less than superfanatics, committed to the notion that a death in battle, waging war on infidels, assured them of an automatic place in Paradise. If they were finally victorious...

"They need a lesson," Boudiaf said. "We need to teach them that such actions have a price. This is a job, I think, for the Anointed Ones."

Boumedienne could scarcely have been more surprised if Boudiaf had declared his intention to call for help from God. The Anointed Ones were the elite force of the Armed Islamic Group, handpicked specifically to serve as bodyguards for Boudiaf—or, in the alternative, to carry out the most difficult assignments. They were specially drilled and trained, but there was more to it than that, more than a simple matter of skill that produced the haughty attitude of the Anointed Ones. Each member of the team had lost at least one member of his family—more often, several—to the violence that had plagued Algeria for nearly a decade. Some had lost parents or grandparents in the war of liberation from French colonial rule. And each had pledged to spend his life in the pursuit of sweet revenge under the guidance of the GIA's commanding officer.

It was one thing, in Boumedienne's mind, to battle the party in power, while simultaneously fighting bloody skirmishes with fellow rebels over power or some obscure point of Muslim theology; it was quite another to unleash the Anointed Ones. Infighting, the eternal—often sanguinary—struggle for preeminence of place, had been a constant fact of life throughout the Muslim Middle East for centuries. So had it always been; so would it always be.

Mobilizing the Anointed Ones, by contrast, was tantamount to arming a doomsday machine.

He almost objected to Boudiaf's command, but he wasn't a stupid man. His commander was distraught, and rightly so. He was enraged by the insults and losses they had suffered. He hungered for revenge.

And more important still, Boudiaf was in command.

Boumedienne would do as he was told, unleash the dogs of war and hope for the best. It would mean bloodshed, but Algerians were used to that. There would be fewer of them living by this time tomorrow to peruse the media reports of new atrocities. It would be bloody business as usual in Algiers and in the countryside.

Boumedienne could only hope that it wasn't a grave mistake.

MALIK AL-SALAAM WAS troubled. As the self-styled new prophet of Islam, he had planned his tour of the Middle East and Africa as a series of triumphs, his cool head and healing touch bringing peace of a sort to a region long tortured by strife, civil war and terrorism. Al-Salaam had convinced himself that he, and he alone, had the power to repair burnt bridges and unite the Islamic world in a jihad against its greater enemies.

One problem, though: it wasn't working out.

Back in the old days, when he had been Rodney Allen Tuggle in Detroit, no such ambitious plan would have occurred to him. Al-Salaam thanked God every day for the imagination and initiative he had discovered within himself, and for the great stride his Islamic Brotherhood had made, so far. He wasn't satisfied—far from it—but experience had taught him that anything was possible, if you believed in God and were willing to cut through all the legalistic bullshit in pursuit of righteous goals.

Al-Salaam had, quite fittingly, chosen a goal for himself that others believed impossible. He would unite the Muslim leaders of the world, regardless of their differences and personal antagonism, forging their armies into a single massive unit, faced off against the unbelievers of the West.

And if he should profit in the meantime, pocketing donations from Tripoli, Baghdad or Tehran…what of it? Christian leaders in America had long since forgotten the text of Matthew 19:24, apparently believing that a camel *and* a new Mercedes-Benz convertible could fit quite nicely through a needle's eye, with room to spare for thousand-dollar suits and hair styled to the point where it resembled nothing quite so much as a grotesque fright wig.

Tuggle had grown up hungry, and he had vowed to escape from poverty at any cost. The first attempt had drawn him deep into a life of crime, but God had arrived to save him and present him with a mission for the world at large.

Jihad.

He had been meeting for the past six days with Muslim leaders in Algiers, trying to sell his plan for unity and holy war against the infidels. Unfortunately, while the population of Algeria was ninety-odd percent Muslim, the ruling government was hopelessly at odds with the fundamentalist spokesmen who more closely mirrored Malik al-Salaam's vision, and the fundamentalists themselves were fighting daily, killing one another over trifles. To al-Salaam, the turmoil in Algeria was more discouraging than the long-running conflict between Iran and Iraq. In the latter case, at least the majority of citizens in each country were more or less united, ready to confront an outside threat. Algerians, meanwhile, were so busy killing one another that he believed they would have failed to notice an American invasion of Morocco, right next door.

He meant to change all that, and soon. The only problem lay in calculating how he should proceed.

Since his arrival in Algiers, al-Salaam had been in contact with both Wasim Ruholla and Asem Kabir. Tehran and Tripoli had provided letters of introduction to their respective agents in strife-torn Algiers, each regime expressing hope that Malik al-Salaam could somehow use his influence to stop the slaughter. In their hearts, he realized, the men in charge of each regime still harbored schemes to dominate Algeria by means of puppet rulers, but al-Salaam himself had other plans.

Unfortunately, both Ruholla and Kabir had come under attack within the past few hours, each man narrowly escaping with his life. The leaders of the GIA and FIS were predictably blaming each other, arming for another round of internecine mayhem, but al-Salaam had a different take on the problem. Long familiar with the posturing of self-styled revolutionaries, he believed that he could spot fake indignation from a mile away, as when provocative behavior brought retaliation from an enemy, but the provocateur feigned wide-eyed innocence. This day, viewing reactions from the leaders of the GIA and FIS, he believed that the latest explosion of violence had honestly surprised both sides.

Which meant there was another hand at work behind the scenes.

If he was going to restore a modicum of peace between the Muslim brethren of Algeria—more to the point, if he was going to unite them in support of his own grand design—Malik al-Salaam would first have to identify the common enemy, then search him out and help the locals neutralize the threat. It would be no easy task, particularly for a stranger in Algiers, but there was one point in his favor, even so.

Malik al-Salaam believed the latest acts of violence were committed—or, at least, inspired—by someone from outside, a foreigner possessed of nerve and arrogance enough to meddle in Algerian affairs. Around the time al-Salaam was born, that would have meant the French, but they had pulled up stakes and fled Algiers a generation earlier. Today, they were consumed with problems of their own—not least among them the offensive attitude on nuclear testing which had made them virtual pariahs in the world community.

The British? Al-Salaam dismissed the thought almost before it had a chance to take form in his mind. For all their posturing as "world leaders," the Britons had been steadily declining in influence since the 1950s. Today, their "empire" was restricted to the slaughterhouse of Northern Ireland and a handful of islands scattered around the globe. London's interest in Algeria was academic, at best, and Britain's leaders seemed more concerned with the foibles of the royal family than outside events.

Which left the United States.

It was no secret that the present rulers of Algeria enjoyed American support, both political and financial. All the talk about "human rights" aside, no American president in the past two decades had taken any decisive action to limit the abuses practiced in democracy's name. More to the point, America's temper on the subject of terrorism—and particularly terrorism carried out by operatives from the Middle East—made it likely, in Malik al-Salaam's opinion, that some covert arm of Washington's imperial establishment might reach across the sea to chastise those who threatened a client state. The recent deaths of embassy officials in Algiers would provide the perfect excuse, but the action was still sub-rosa, doubtless conducted behind a screen of plausible deniability.

It mattered little to al-Salaam whether the action had been planned and carried out by agents of the CIA, the NSA, military intelligence or some group which he had never heard of. They were all the same to him: imperialist pigs who lorded over nonwhite and non-Christian peoples like the slave masters of old.

It was his mission to destroy them all, and he was looking forward to the moment when his goal would be achieved.

But he would have to make that journey one step at a time.

Algeria would be the perfect testing ground. If he could weld the dissident militias into a cohesive fighting force, he had a decent chance. If not, well, there were other nations waiting for a prophet to enlighten them and lead them out of darkness.

CHAPTER SIX

Sixty-odd miles northeast of Algiers, facing across the Mediterranean Sea toward the Spanish-owned Balearic Islands, the city of Tizi-Ouzu has a population barely one-quarter that of the Algerian capital. Founded as a shipping port, Tizi-Ouzu fulfills the same function today, existing primarily as a point of contact between land and sea. Its major stock-in-trade has varied over time—where slaves once trod the piers in chains, illicit drugs and weapons are consigned to sturdy crates, with phony bills of lading—but the purpose and the soul of Tizi-Ouzu have survived the passage of centuries with little significant change.

Bolan was drawn to Tizi-Ouzu for another reason, altogether unrelated to commerce or tourism. He was looking for the headquarters of the Islamic Salvation Front.

It would have been an hour's drive and then some, from Algiers. The major coastal roads were fairly well maintained, but it wasn't fear of potholes that convinced Bolan he should fly instead of driving overland. Algeria was, in effect, a combat zone, and it was bound to get worse before it got better. And while there was no particular reason for government soldiers to stop a specific vehicle at random, emergency roadblocks were commonplace, compounding infernal delays with the very real risk of a face-off with lawful authorities. The searchers probably wouldn't have been police, per se—and thus wouldn't have been shielded, if push came to shove, by Bolan's personal pledge to avoid killing lawmen—but the last thing he needed at the moment was public exposure, a manhunt with himself as the quarry.

Gholomreza Kordiyeh had readily agreed with Bolan's urge to fly. More to the point, he had supplied the pilot and the wings—or rotors, in the present case. The helicopter was an old Aérospatiale SA-315B Lama, with seating for five on board. Its pilot was a dwarfish, feisty Berber named Ari or Ali. Bolan couldn't have sworn which it was if his life had depended on the answer.

As it was, his life depended in large part upon the little Berber's flying skills.

The Lama cruised at seventy-five miles per hour, and the pilot had Bolan on the ground in Tizi-Ouzu forty minutes after takeoff. Accompanied by Kordiyeh again—his combination guide, interpreter and backup gunner—Bolan worked out the distance from their landing zone to the target, informing the pilot that they would meet him for the pickup in forty-five minutes. If they missed the scheduled rendezvous, the odds were excellent that they wouldn't be coming back at all.

The earlier disguise of business suits and briefcases

had been replaced by native garb, each man attired in a roomy burnoose that concealed his street clothes, weapons slung from combat rigging and most of his face. At a casual glance, they could pass for a pair of locals, but Bolan had drawn the line at sandals, opting for a well-worn pair of boots instead. The harness that he wore beneath his robe, with easy access through the slits on either side, supported a Z-84 submachine gun, the CZ-75 pistol, and more of the Russian anti-personnel grenades. Kordiyeh was similarly armed, but nothing showed beneath their outer garments.

It was a brisk eight-minute walk from the LZ to FIS headquarters on a narrow side street, well back from the center of town. The operation was disguised behind a rundown storefront, two scowling guerrillas staked out the entryway to discourage any would-be customers from going inside. The goons wore baggy shirts that might conceal handguns or compact SMGs, and they were checking out the new arrivals as Bolan and Kordiyeh drew closer.

"On three," Bolan said, and his companion grunted assent. Ten paces farther on he spoke again. "One."

The shooters seemed as if they were beginning to relax, as Bolan slipped a hand inside his robe and found the Z-84's pistol grip. Still watching, one of them leaned back, his shoulders and one foot braced on the wall behind him. Neither of them made a move toward hidden weapons.

"Two."

Six paces closer, and the FIS guerrillas would be near enough to hear him when he spoke the final word. By that time, Bolan hoped, it would be too late for the men to reach their pistols.

"Three!"

The Z-84s had suppressors attached, but their snuffling reports still sounded loud to Bolan in the almost eerie stillness of the street. He saw their human targets jerking, twitching, spouting crimson as they crumpled to the sidewalk. A stray round from one of their SMGs drilled the window where a display of outdated household appliances stood gathering dust. The crack of breaking glass was answered by a shout of alarm from somewhere inside.

Time to move.

They rushed the door together, Kordiyeh a step or two ahead of Bolan, both men swallowed up a heartbeat later, lost to sight.

MUSA HAMIR WAS PROUD that he had been selected to strike the first blow on behalf of the Armed Islamic Group against their enemies in the so-called Islamic Salvation Front. It mattered not at all to him that he was being asked to slaughter fellow Muslims. Members of the FIS were nothing more than traitors to their faith, as far as Hamir was concerned. If they had been truly committed to the struggle for freedom, instead of their own aggrandizement, they would have joined the GIA to start with, and there would have been no need to punish them today.

It never once occurred to him that soldiers of the FIS might view him and his colleagues in the same disparaging way. How could it, when Hamir had God on his side? If he wasn't beloved of God, how could he have qualified to lead a strike force of Anointed Ones?

The first of several targets was a low-life tavern in the Casbah district, not far removed from the spot where the American spies had been shot a few days earlier. Hamir saw no connection between that event and his mission of vengeance. The FIS traitors had chosen to assault his GIA comrades without provocation, killing several and causing grave embarrassment for the rest. For that, they would be punished, even unto death.

Hamir and his warriors were packed into an old four-door Citroën sedan, preferring brief discomfort to the risks entailed in bringing along a second car. Hamir was in the shotgun seat, Hakim behind the steering wheel, with Sayyid, Muddamar and Azzam crowded in the back. Each man except Hakim was carrying an AKSU assault rifle, with the handgun of his choice for backup. As the driver, forced to remain with the car, Hakim carried a Model 61 Skorpion machine pistol in his lap, spare magazines in a brown paper bag on the floor beneath his seat.

"Here," Hakim said, as he braked and nosed the Citroën to the curb outside a green-painted facade that cried out for a touch-up. The tavern was closed at that hour, but Hamir wasn't deceived by the apparent inactivity. He did his homework and was well aware that several members of the FIS were constantly in residence upstairs, where they shared quarters with the whores and generally disgraced themselves in God's eyes.

Their day of reckoning had come at last.

Hamir half turned in his seat, hearing the springs groan, and jabbed a finger at Hakim and Sayyid. "You watch the front," he said, "and deal with anyone attempting to escape that way. Azzam and Muddamar, you come with me."

They left the car and moved along a filthy alley, single file, making no effort to conceal their weapons now. This was the Casbah, and no one who lived there was likely to summon police. Then again, if the authorities arrived unexpectedly, well, it was as easy to kill a man in uniform as one in a burnoose. Hamir wasn't averse to striking two enemies at once, if the opportunity should present itself.

The tavern's back door was locked from within, but a jimmy zealously applied resolved that problem in a matter of seconds. Leading the way inside, Hamir was alert to any resistance, half expecting a clamorous alarm, but no one seemed to notice their unauthorized entry. After checking out the storeroom, a rank-smelling kitchen and the tavern proper—all deserted—Hamir led his commandos to the staircase and ascended to the floor above.

Four doors awaited them, two on either side of a poorly lighted hallway, perhaps thirty feet in length. The rooms would be small and rarely cleaned—all but claustrophobic, by the time a bed, a dresser and a chair were squeezed inside—but Hamir and his raiders weren't concerned with the decor. It was the occupants they wanted, and Hamir had no way of determining which rooms were occupied without examining each one in turn.

Or all at once, save one.

"Azzam," he said, and pointed to the nearest door. His finger moved to indicate a second door, as he said, "Muddamar." Hamir himself staked out the third door, leaving one unguarded in a move that was as unavoidable as it was perilous.

"With me," he said. And added, though it was already understood, "No witnesses."

The three commandos kicked their doors in unison, on Hamir's signal, though Azzam required a second try to get it right. By that time, Hamir was standing over a rumpled, filthy bed, his AKSU leveled at the sleepy, startled faces of a naked man and woman, dingy sheets pushed down around their hips.

Disgust and rage welled up inside, poured out through the muzzle of his short Kalashnikov. He watched the bodies spasm, lunging as if they desired to couple one last time before they died, the sheets around them flushing deep red as their lives spilled away.

Hamir stepped back to check the hallway, just in time to see another naked man emerging from the fourth bedroom. He had a pistol in his right hand, while the left was balled into a fist and digging crusty sleep out of his eyes.

Too late.

A short burst from Hamir's assault rifle raked the young man's chest and slammed him back against the doorjamb, blood from his ragged exit wounds smearing the beige paint behind him as he slumped to the floor.

Hamir reached the open doorway in time to catch a slender girl scrambling out of bed, stooping to re-

trieve her clothing from the floor. She raised her eyes
to meet the gaze of Death, and might have screamed
if he had given her the chance. Another burst from
ten feet out, and she was finished, sprawled across the
rumpled bed and leaking life like a deflated blow-up
doll.

It was a job well done, Hamir told himself, as they
ran back downstairs and out through the alley to the
waiting Citroën, the first of many blows that would
be struck against his enemies this day. Others would
strike, as well, but he had led the way, and he was
far from finished, yet.

In fact, he thought, the best was yet to come.

FROM TIZI-OUZU, Ari-Ali flew them on to Stif, another hour and fifteen minutes southeast of their last
destination. Forty miles inland, Stif had no view of
the Mediterranean, but it *did* have a GIA arsenal
stashed in a World War II-vintage warehouse on the
outskirts of town. The pilot set them down within a
quarter mile of the target, at an airpark used for short-
range cargo flights. Bolan found an old car waiting
for them, with a bearded driver at the wheel.

"One of my men," Kordiyeh told him, and they
readjusted their hardware under their burnooses, as
they climbed into the back.

As Bolan understood it, Kordiyeh's group was a
nameless, loose-knit alliance of native Algerians—a
number of military veterans among them—who resented the way fanatics had turned their homeland
into a shooting gallery and who were determined to
put things right if they could. Bolan wasn't entirely

sure that Gholomreza Kordiyeh was the group's over-all leader or how the chain of command was arranged, and he had no intention of asking. For his purposes, it was enough to have committed allies in a hostile land, all the better that they were competent both in combat and logistics.

From all appearances, the warehouse might have been abandoned, but Kordiyeh assured him it wasn't. The stock of arms, ammunition and explosives on hand was unpredictable from one day to the next, but Libyan support for the GIA included cash and military hardware, the latter smuggled in piecemeal, in shipments ranging from half a dozen rifles to truck-loads of ammo and plastic explosives.

They drove past the warehouse, pulled around behind another one that truly was deserted, and the driver dropped them off. He had his orders: wait ten minutes—or until he heard the sounds of gunfire—and then make another pass at a safe distance. If the warehouse blew and they were still inside, it was his job to spread the word and get the message back to Washington by one means or another.

Bolan and Kordiyeh had made some adjustments to their combat gear, replacing the Russian frag grenades with four fist-sized plastique charges apiece. The plastique was wrapped in waxed paper and duct tape, with peel-and-stick adhesive on one side. Plastique was stable to a fault: you could play handball with it, even burn it, if no detonator was attached. The timers, with their blasting caps, were carried separately, in lieu of tempting fate.

As they approached the warehouse from the north,

Bolan was on alert for sentries, but there seemed to be none posted anywhere on the perimeter. With all that had transpired since the previous night's raid across the border, he couldn't account for such apparent negligence, but neither would he look a gift horse in the mouth. If his opponents chose to make it easy for him, that was their mistake, and he would gladly take advantage of the oversight.

They reached the warehouse loading platform unopposed, and mounted concrete steps that had begun to crumble at the edges, showing their age. There was a large door for unloading cargo, closed and doubly secured with a brace of shiny new padlocks, together with a standard door for personnel. That door was also locked, but Kordiyeh produced a set of picks from under his burnoose and went to work, while Bolan watched his back. It took the better part of sixty seconds, but he beat the lock, and both men had their submachine guns ready as they eased their way inside.

It was stuffy and hot in the warehouse, with an odor that included equal parts of dust, machine oil and fried meat. They passed a vacant alcove that appeared to be a makeshift office and turned left into the warehouse proper. It was sixty feet by thirty, give or take, with ample floor space ranged around three stacks of wooden crates to Bolan's left. He couldn't read the labels printed on the crates and had no interest in translating them. If his information was correct, the only cargo moving through this warehouse in the past five years was military hardware, bound for field detachments of the GIA. Whatever had been packed inside the crates—explosives, firearms, ammunition or replacement parts for weapons—it was all fair game.

The warehouse security detail consisted of two men dressed in matching denim shirts and pants. They sat together at a folding table, one with his back to the new arrivals, the other facing them, absorbed in a game of dominoes. Their AKMs were propped against the nearest wall, just out of reach, but Bolan had no doubt that one or both of them were also packing side arms.

As the thought took shape in Bolan's mind, the shooter facing him raised his eyes and blinked twice. He blurted out a warning to his friend, the second man wasting precious time on a glance across his shoulder, while the first made a lunge for his rifle.

It was too little and too late. Bolan shot them both from fifteen feet away, the table collapsing under Number Two's weight as bullets slammed him forward, facedown in the middle of the tumbling dominoes. Number One's outstretched hand was within an inch or two of his weapon, when a rising burst of Parabellum manglers ripped across his upper chest and throat. He hit the concrete floor with a little woof of air escaping from his lungs, and didn't move again.

A rapid scan revealed no further guards, and the two warriors set to work with a will, palming plastique charges and stripping the adhesive, affixing the charges to various crates, positioned for maximum damage. The timers were set for five minutes, their explosive probes deftly inserted through slits in the waxed paper sealing each block of plastique. Bolan held one of his back, attaching it to the large door of the loading bay as they were leaving, with the timer set for ninety seconds.

They were back inside their car and half a block away before the first charge blew, the others firing off in quick succession, like a string of giant firecrackers. The charges triggered something bigger, setting off a chain reaction that would all but level the warehouse, leaving a heap of smoking rubble in its place.

Not bad, Bolan thought, as they drove back toward the airpark, where the pilot was waiting for them with the Lama refueled. He checked his watch and saw that it was early yet—at least, in terms of abstract time.

The clock had stopped for those he left behind.

For others he had yet to meet—and for the Executioner himself—it was already ticking past the point of no return.

THEY DOUBLED BACK from Stif to Bou Saâda, one hundred miles to the southwest and farther inland, nestled in the foothills of the rugged Atlas Mountains. It was yet a smaller town than any they had visited so far, but still had close to one hundred thousand residents, so that the helicopter's landing at an airpark north of town didn't become a mass community event.

For Kordiyeh, this was the risky part. He had been born a few miles outside Bou Saâda, had grown up there, and while he wasn't famous in the town by any means, he stood a greater chance of being recognized by old acquaintances than in Algiers or any of the other cities they had visited so far.

It was a good thing, he decided, that their visit would be brief and its result chaotic. Few of those who knew him as a youth in Bou Saâda would know him with a submachine gun in his hands and cold death in his eyes.

One fear he didn't have, as they alighted from the Lama, was the dread of being seen by any members of his family. They had been wiped out years ago by killers he was never able to identify, their brutal passing all the reason Kordiyeh required for working overtime, risking his own life, to defeat the various fanatics who had turned his homeland into hell on earth.

Their target in Bou Saâda was yet another FIS facility. It seemed that Mike Belasko was intent on stirring up a war between the FIS and GIA. It made a fair amount of sense to Kordiyeh: sit back and let the bastards kill each other, thinning the ranks and weakening both sides before the final deathblow was delivered. He had no quarrel with the tactic if the killing was confined to members of the radical militias and didn't extend to random, helpless targets in the streets or in the countryside.

If it came down to that, he would be forced to reevaluate his contact with Belasko and Hassan Filali, maybe strike out on his own and try another angle of attack.

He hoped it wouldn't come to that. Belasko was a formidable enemy, all by himself, and Kordiyeh didn't enjoy the thought of waging war against him— much less with the CIA and all of the United States to back him up.

Their target in Bou Saâda was an FIS indoctrination school, where new recruits and certain sympathetic civic officers were taught the Muslim gospel as interpreted and edited by Nabi Ulmalhama. There was still enough of the Koran in what they heard from Nabi's handpicked teachers that the average Muslim might convince himself—albeit with an effort, sometimes with assistance from the strong-arm soldiers of the FIS—that he had formerly misunderstood the message of the prophet as revealed in the Koran. Where once he had believed in peace and tolerance, the student now discovered that the sacred scriptures called for unrelenting, everlasting war against the infidels—who were, of course, identified and singled out by Nabi Ulmalhama and his chosen spokesmen. When the nation had been purged with fire and blood, once Ulmalhama and the FIS had been installed to rule Algeria, the cleansing inquisition would begin. When it was finished, those who dared to disagree with Nabi and his minions would, presumably, have vanished from the earth.

The ''school'' was situated on the third and fourth floors of an old hotel, located in the northern quarter of Bou Saâda. Kordiyeh had made arrangements for a car to meet them at the airpark, but he paid off the driver this time and took the wheel himself. It was a short drive, seven minutes by his wristwatch, and he parked behind the hotel near a rusted garbage bin where a slat-ribbed cat was picking through the trash in search of cast-off meat or vermin.

They wore the same costumes that had already served them well, his burnoose giving off a vaguely smoky scent, now, from the action of his SMG. It made no difference, since anyone who ventured close enough to smell him would be dead before he recognized the odor, but it made Kordiyeh feel as if he carried death not only on his hidden combat harness, but within his very soul, the essence of destruction leaking from his pores.

They went in through the back, bypassed the registration desk and any watchers in the lobby, ignoring the elevator this time and making directly for the service stairs. Despite their haste, they took care with the noise they made, not clomping up the stairs, but moving stealthily, their Z-84s out and ready, with suppressors in place. Five flights, and they were just short of the penultimate landing when Kordiyeh heard the rasping hiss of a match, his nostrils flaring to the sharp aroma of tobacco smoke.

Belasko had already recognized the danger. There was someone on the landing just above them, but important questions still remained. Was it an enemy, a lookout for the FIS academy, or simply a hotel custodian, stealing time from his drudge work for a smoke? More to the point, if the service stairs were guarded, how many guards would be assigned, and how would they be armed?

A quick glance from the tall American told Kordiyeh what he already knew: the only way to answer any of those questions was to take the leap, reveal themselves and see what happened next. If it turned out to be a loafing janitor, they could persuade him to keep silent, one way or another. If the stairs were guarded, then the sentries had to be dealt with, swiftly and decisively.

Belasko pointed to himself, suggesting that he take the lead, but Kordiyeh shook his head, miming speech with his left hand, while the right gripped his Z-84, white-knuckled. In the event that they encountered a civilian, he would have to do the talking, and that meant he had to take the lead.

He mounted the last three steps on the balls of his feet, taking special care to make no noise. Belasko was one long stride behind him as Kordiyeh reached the landing, pivoting to face the young man on the next landing above.

And he was no custodian; that much was evident from the submachine gun he carried, suspended from one shoulder by a sling rigged out of twine.

The FIS sentry was startled, gagging on the smoke that he had drawn into his lungs a heartbeat earlier. A hacking cough expelled the cigarette from his mouth, spinning downstairs toward Kordiyeh's face, while the young man reached for the weapon dangling at his hip.

Kordiyeh sidestepped the flying butt and fired without raising his own submachine gun to aim. His first two rounds were low, a thigh shot and a bad hit to the groin, but as his target slumped, the others found their mark, tattooing a bloody diagonal line across the young man's chest. The target tumbled backward, never having reached the trigger of his SMG, the weapon clattering beside him as he fell.

They had to drag him clear before the door could open inward, and Belasko launched him headfirst down the stairs, to clear the path of their retreat. They both had weapons ready as Belasko reached for the doorknob, twisted it and swung the gray steel door aside.

Nothing.

When they weren't immediately greeted by a hail of fire, they edged into the corridor. It stretched off to their right, with seven doors on either side, staggered, so that no open door would face directly toward another. Roughly half of them were open, and from the sounds of droning voices, Kordiyeh decided that at least some of the classes were in session.

They had worked out the plan in advance, using a rough floor plan, and neither of them hesitated now. Palming fragmentation grenades, each warrior chose an open doorway—Belasko on the left, Kordiyeh on the right—and lobbed their charges into the sea of voices. Moving on, they each tossed one more lethal egg before the first two detonated at their backs.

The chanting turned to screams and curses, cries of panic mingled in, as some of the new recruits lost their nerve in the baptism of fire. Survivors of the detonations, some wounded and others merely shaken, spilled into the corridor, while those from unscathed classrooms joined them in a rush. One moment, Kordiyeh and Belasko had the hallway to themselves; the next, they were surrounded by perhaps four dozen radicals.

The obvious solution was to open fire on anything that moved.

Standing almost back-to-back, they cut loose with their submachine guns, savaging their startled, mostly

unarmed targets. It was slaughter, too intense to last
before the would-be desert warriors died or broke and
ran, but Kordiyeh was on his second magazine before
he felt Belasko tugging at his shirt.

"Come on! We're out of time."

It was their turn to run, and as he put the slaughterhouse behind him, Kordiyeh could still hear
screaming in his head. The shrill sounds followed him
outside into the sunlight, and he wondered for a heartbeat whether they would ever let him rest in peace
again.

CHAPTER SEVEN

Musa Hamir was pleased with what his soldiers had achieved so far, but there was still much work to do. He had been tasked to punish heretics, and while that job could never truly be completed in a sinful world, at least the relatively narrow focus of his orders on specific members of the FIS would make the present task more feasible.

Three strikes so far, and each time the Anointed Ones left blood and death behind them. They had managed to achieve complete surprise with their first two targets, and even the third, with shock waves spreading through the ranks of the Islamic Salvation Front, had found their adversaries disorganized, ill prepared to defend themselves. Hakim had suffered a flesh wound from a lucky pistol shot, it was true, but he didn't complain about his injury, and they had already stanched the flow of blood from the shallow gash beneath his arm.

Their next target promised to be more difficult, but Hamir had faith in himself and his soldiers. Above all else, he had faith in God, believing that he would smile upon his loyal defenders and present them with another victory. If one or more of them should fall in the attempt, Hamir drew consolation from the fact that any warrior sacrificed in a jihad was guaranteed an honored place in Paradise.

The target was an arms cache of the FIS, located in a small house on the outskirts of Algiers. The arsenal's location was supposed to be a secret, but such things were difficult to hide for any length of time, particularly in a teeming city where a brutal internecine war had dragged on for the best part of a decade. Secrets were uncovered, sometimes leaked at once, more often held for ransom, but it seemed to Hamir that they were always revealed in the end.

Because a major arms cache was important to the FIS, he knew that it would have been well guarded even before his commander unleashed the Anointed Ones. With news of the latest attacks now spreading like wildfire through Algiers, the normal guard might be doubled or tripled, soldiers prepared to sacrifice themselves in defending the tools of their trade. It scarcely mattered, though, because Hamir was doggedly determined to fulfill his mission.

Failure was unthinkable.

Azzam was driving when they reached the target, allowing Hakim to rest in the back, with Muddamar and Sayyid. Hamir called the car to a halt well back from the house, half turning in his seat to repeat the instructions his team already knew by heart. They offered no complaint about the repetition, each man chiming in on cue as he was grilled about his part in the assault. When they piled out of the car, weapons barely concealed under loose-fitting jackets, Hamir felt the adrenaline rush kick in, his favorite thing about combat—except, of course, for leaving footprints in the fresh blood of his slaughtered enemies.

All five would be involved in this attack, their automatic weapons primed and ready as they left the vehicle behind them, moving swiftly toward the house. As agreed beforehand, Hakim and Muddamar broke off to cover the rear, Azzam in front, scuttling ahead of the group to find a vantage point at the northeast corner of the house, while Sayyid and Hamir approached from the southeast. When they commenced the attack, Hamir believed it would be difficult, if not impossible, for any of the enemy inside to slip away unseen.

When they didn't draw fire on the approach, Hamir took heart and knew their mission had been truly blessed by God. Moving boldly toward the drab front door, once painted blue but faded now to something more like gray, unmindful of the windows where the heavy curtains hung unmoving, he mounted two concrete steps, leveled his Kalashnikov and fired a burst to clear the double locks that he could see. A swift kick snapped the hidden chain inside and slammed the door back with sufficient force to make it strike the inner wall.

Incredibly, it seemed that he had taken his intended victims by surprise, although they had their weapons close to hand. Two young men of the FIS were bolting upright from a swaybacked sofa, reaching for a pistol and a submachine gun on the battered coffee table, when Hamir unleashed another burst of automatic fire and cut them both down where they stood.

His mind dismissed them even as they crumpled to the floor, blood spurting from their lethal wounds.

He heard a racket coming from what looked to be a bedroom on his left, and swung in that direction as another young man cleared the open doorway, brandishing an AKM assault rifle. The stream of death erupting from Hamir's Kalashnikov ripped through the moving target, painting crimson abstracts on the wall behind him as the FIS commando staggered, stumbled, fell. Still firing, Hamir put another short burst through the doorway where his adversary had appeared, and heard a startled cry as someone else ducked backward out of range.

A burst of automatic fire behind him made Hamir glance backward, just in time to see Sayyid administer a close-range coup de grâce to another fallen enemy. This one had emerged from the kitchen, away to Hamir's right, and Sayyid was edging through that doorway when staccato pistol fire reached out to stop him, rocking him back on his heels for a moment, before he went all the way down.

Hamir forgot about the man or men behind him in the bedroom. Moving swiftly toward the kitchen doorway, firing one-handed with the AKSU as he went, Hamir unclipped a fragmentation grenade from his belt, pulled the pin with his teeth like some old movie star and felt a jolt of pain from his incisors before he made the pitch. Stepping sharply to his left, beyond the line of fire for any shrapnel, he was already facing back toward the bedroom when his grenade went off in the tiny kitchen.

Screams behind him and angry curses in front, not

one enemy but two, charging out of the bedroom with SMGs blazing.

Hamir killed them both in their tracks and went in search of more.

THE AÉROSPATIALE Lama carried Bolan and Kordiyeh from Bou Saâda to Sidi bel Abbès. They touched down on another strip that passed for modern only in the context of the present time and place, Ari-Ali taxiing the plane to park it in the shadow of an ancient, rusting Quonset hut. This time the transport waiting for them was a car so small that Bolan had to squeeze in with his knees almost against his chest, the hardware underneath his burnoose gouging him painfully. Kordiyeh wedged himself behind the steering wheel and twisted the ignition key, grappling with a stubborn stick shift as they pulled away from the strip.

Sidi bel Abbès was GIA territory, which wasn't to say that other factions in Algeria's ongoing civil war wouldn't be found in the area. Instead of shopping aimlessly for targets, though, the Executioner preferred to take advantage of his escort's expertise and make the most of their available time.

The GIA regional commander for Sidi bel Abbès was an ex-convict named Abed Lufti, converted to revolutionary politics after serving five years on a robbery charge. The self-described warrior for God was suspected of instigating various massacres in the countryside around Sidi bel Abbès, most recently the midnight slaughter that had wiped out seven families in an outlying village believed friendly to the rival Movement of the Islamic State—MEA. None of the victims—who included thirteen children aged ten and younger—were armed when raiders swept through their homes with axes, machetes and butcher knives, leaving grisly carnage behind. Thus far, Lufti had managed to avoid arrest because he kept his own hands clean and farmed out the killing to others, while nailing down firm alibis for himself before the fact.

But Lufti had run out of time. Unknown to the butcher of women and children, he had an unscheduled date with Mack Bolan.

The butcher of Sidi bel Abbès lived in a modest home with a woman seven years his junior, alleged to be his wife, and half a dozen bodyguards assigned to keep him breathing. They were competent enough, all seasoned killers, but they had grown lax on sentry duty from the absence of a challenge during recent years. Bolan was counting on their laid-back apathy to offer him an opening, the killing room that he would need to drive a stake through Lufti's rotten heart.

They left the tiny car two hundred yards from Lufti's house, parked behind a bakery closed for repairs, and covered the rest of the distance on foot. Traditional garb hid their weapons and the better part of Bolan's face, a deliberate slouch compensating for his unusual height. As they approached Lufti's sanctuary, Kordiyeh spoke softly from the corner of his mouth, lips barely moving.

"This one is the devil," he remarked. "A monster. Kill him slowly, if you have the chance, or else leave him to me."

"Anger's a luxury," Bolan reminded his companion. "I'll take him any way I can, without sacrificing the mission."

"Of course." There was a tightness in the Algerian's voice that reaffirmed his displeasure at the notion of a swift and easy death for Abed Lufti. Before Bolan could assure the man *any* kind of death, however, they would have to place themselves within striking range.

A low wall surrounded Lufti's house, barely waist-high, but still enough to warn off trespassers and give defenders adequate cover if they chose to fight on the perimeter. Two guards were visible as Bolan and Kordiyeh approached, seated together on the porch, robed in twilight. Neither man made any effort to conceal the Russian assault rifles propped against the stucco wall behind them, within easy reach.

"We need an edge," Bolan said, almost whispering.

On cue, Kordiyeh raised his left hand in greeting to the men, as if they were comrades long familiar with one another. The two stared back at him, one frowning slightly, glancing over at his sidekick for some sign of recognition. It wasn't much of a diversion, granted, but with any luck at all...

As one, Bolan and Kordiyeh drew their Z-84 submachine guns with stout suppressors attached, each choosing a target on instinct, without need for spoken agreement. Bolan took the lookout on the right, Kordiyeh his companion on the left. Two short and nearly silent bursts from forty feet out dumped the guerrillas from their wicker chairs and left them stretched out on the porch in spreading pools of crimson.

Bolan and Kordiyeh vaulted the wall and rushed toward the house, halfway there when a third lookout blundered around the east corner, busy lighting a cigarette, his AK-47 slung across one shoulder, muzzle down. Bolan shot him on the run, saw the gunner's denim shirt ripple with the impact of 9 mm Parabellum shockers. The young man went down as if poleaxed, his face slamming into the rough dirt that passed for a lawn outside Lufti's home.

Bolan was still moving toward the house in a sprint when one of the front windows shattered, the muzzle of a Kalashnikov assault rifle thrusting into view. Both warriors saw it at the same instant, dodging in opposite directions before the unseen shooter let fly. Bolan hammered back with a rising burst from his Z-84, bullets splintering the windowframe and plucking at the heavy draperies. Kordiyeh was dodging like a broken-field runner as rifle slugs chewed up the dirt at his heels.

The Executioner's bullets found the rifleman then, punching him over backward, still unseen in the flesh as his Kalashnikov's muzzle snagged the draperies and brought them down on top of him, a billowing shroud. In the moment of silence that followed, before all hell broke loose, Bolan palmed a frag grenade, jerked the pin and lobbed the bomb through the windowframe vacated by his late assailant. Someone raised a warning shout within before it blew, glass spewing from the other windows as the shock wave hit.

Kordiyeh reached the front door before Bolan, firing through it for effect, then threw himself against it from a running start. Bolan was close behind him as he cleared the threshold, his own weapon angled toward the ceiling, careful to avoid a fatal accident.

He saw three shooters down, one near the window, two more crumpled near the center of the room, both of the latter bleeding from a multitude of wounds. He couldn't tell if they had fallen to his frag grenade or Kordiyeh's gunfire, and it made no difference to the end result. In this scenario, as in so many others, dead was dead.

Pistol fire exploded from the entrance to a hallway leading off to Bolan's left and to the rear of Lufti's home. He fanned a burst in that direction, more to make the shooter dance and spoil his aim than from a realistic hope of scoring, and the follow-through took Bolan toward the gunner's hideaway, preferring to attack in lieu of fighting a defensive action here, on hostile ground.

Bolan had never seen Abed Lufti, but he had Kordiyeh's description of the man and it matched the figure ducking out of sight into a bedroom down the hallway. He fired the last rounds from his Z-84's magazine, but it was too little and too late, blasting divots from the plaster wall and ceiling, while his target waddled out of sight.

The soldier cursed as he fed the SMG a fresh magazine. He could lose Lufti here if there was a convenient back door, or even a window large enough to accommodate the man's bulk. Conversely, if his quarry lay in wait, Bolan could blunder through the door ahead and spill his own blood, lose it all in a case of terminal haste.

He split the difference, hearing Kordiyeh behind him as he primed and pitched another hand grenade. The fuse was good for six seconds, but it felt like forever as he pressed against the wall, knowing every second wasted gave his prey a better chance of slipping through the net. The detonation, when it came, was music to his ringing ears.

Bolan waited for the shrapnel storm to pass, then ducked through swirling smoke, half crouching as he scanned the room with slitted eyes. A sluggish, awkward movement near the window helped him focus, drawing him toward the broke figure of his quarry.

Lufti lay sprawled on his back, one leg twisted beneath him, arms outflung. No, make that *arm* outflung. The left, in fact, while Lufti's right had been sheared off an inch or two above the elbow, somehow landing draped across the cushion of a nearby chair. Bright jets of blood were spilling from the tattered stump, marking the beat of Lufti's failing heart, the output pooling on the wooden floor beneath his prostrate form.

The butcher's lips were moving, but if they produced a sound, it was too faint to register with Bolan's ears. He *did* hear Kordiyeh move up beside him, saw the Algerian raise his SMG, aiming down the barrel at Lufti, then watched him lower the weapon again, without firing.

"It is better this way," Kordiyeh remarked. "Let him die like the pig he is."

Bolan wasn't inclined to argue as they put that house of death behind them and began the walk back to their waiting vehicle.

"WHO DARES to challenge us this way?" Ulmalhama asked, pacing back and forth across the narrow study in his home.

The question was rhetorical, but Mohammed Zeroual was ready with an answer, regardless. "The GIA," he said. "Who else?"

"They go too far, this time," his leader said. "We have a reputation to protect among the people. If we let ourselves be made to seem ridiculous, support will melt away."

And that was only a part of the problem, Zeroual thought to himself. Appearances were one thing, but a series of assaults such as the FIS had lately suffered, wiping out men and material resources, could destroy the group in fact, as well as in the public eye. What value did a reputation have if there was no one left alive to carry it?

Zeroual kept the gloomy thoughts to himself, responding with what he hoped was the proper tone of enthusiastic optimism. "It is not too late, Nabi," he replied. "We can still strike back."

"And so we shall," the leader of the Islamic Salvation Front promised. "Boudiaf and his lackeys have betrayed themselves, this time. A reckoning is overdue, and we shall have it, in the name of God!"

Zeroual considered himself a devout Muslim—indeed, he couldn't have served as second in command of the FIS had he been otherwise—but even so, he wasn't altogether convinced that they could count on God for material assistance in the present crisis. Jews and Christians were fond of saying that God helped those who first helped themselves, and Zeroual suspected that to be a major truth. Only when they struck back with decisive, killing force would he be pleased.

"What order shall I give, Nabi?" he inquired.

His lifelong friend and nominal superior stopped pacing, stood before him with his shoulders squared, spine rigid, hands curled into fists and clasped behind his back. When Ulmalhama spoke again, his voice was cold and sharp, like tempered steel. "I want our soldiers fully mobilized," he said. "No man shall be excused for any reason short of death. We must retaliate against the GIA on every front, repay them tenfold for their treachery this day. God will not be satisfied while any of the traitors are alive."

Nor would he, Mohammed Zeroual nearly said, but he caught himself in time and kept the words penned up behind his teeth. It was enough, for now, to simply be the messenger, command the troops in Nabi's name and see the enemy destroyed. His own day would come soon enough. And when it arrived, Mohammed Zeroual promised himself, he would be ready, waiting to fulfill his destiny.

THE FLIGHT to Mestghanem, a hundred miles northeast of Sidi bel Abbès, brought them nearly full circle back to Algiers. There was one more stop to make, however, before they returned to the capital, and while Kordiyeh had argued briefly, weakly, against pushing their luck, he now admitted to himself that he had been infected with Belasko's enthusiasm, the thrill of the hunt.

No, that wasn't correct, he thought. The tall American clearly took no pleasure in killing, as sport hunters did, and he made no effort to dress up his actions with sociopolitical jargon. Belasko saw a need and acted on it, even when the moment called for him to risk his life and spill the blood of others. At the moment, his needs, his mission, coincided with Kordiyeh's. In other circumstances, the Algerian realized, Belasko might have been hunting *him*.

The prospect brought a queasy feeling to his stomach, as if he had drunk sour milk or eaten tainted meat. He had so many enemies already—men and women who would kill him with a smile and laugh about it later with their cronies—that the thought of one more hunter, one more gun, should not have been intimidating.

But it was.

He was glad that Belasko was on his side, guessing that he wasn't the first to hold that view. Confidence and fear, after all, were sometimes reverse sides of the same coin, and Belasko was adept at inspiring both.

Their target in Mestghanem was a safehouse operated by the GIA for fugitive killers. Algeria's internal chaos helped to conceal a multitude of sins and sinners, but situations still arose from time to time where a specific terrorist or triggerman was publicly identified. In such cases, when the pressure from police became too great, a soldier could be made to disappear, removed from danger of arrest while comrades dealt with any stubborn prosecution witnesses. At any given time, the safehouse in Mestghanem housed between thirty and forty-five men.

"Sounds more like a safe*hotel*," Bolan had remarked with a smile, on hearing Kordiyeh's description of the operation. "Funny the authorities can't find it."

"Those who live and work in Mestghanem are sometimes less concerned with crimes committed in the capital or elsewhere," Kordiyeh explained. "It might be in their own best interest to ignore such visitors to their community."

His companion understood that part of it with no more said, the deadly mix of terrorism and corruption, soldiers and policemen who were either frightened off a case or paid to look the other way while killers used Mestghanem as a home away from home.

But they would find no sanctuary from the wrath descending on them now. Kordiyeh only hoped the two of them would be enough to do the job.

They had a better car in Mestghanem, more legroom for the two of them, less rattling underneath the hood when Kordiyeh turned the ignition key. Still clad in Bedouin garb, they had exchanged their smoky, blood-flecked burnooses for new ones while airborne, seeking to present a more normal appearance on arrival. They carried the same weapons, albeit quickly cleaned and oiled, restocked with fresh ammunition and grenades.

The safehouse at Mestghanem had once been a rich Frenchman's villa, in the bad old days when Algeria was deemed "an integral part of France." Bloody revolution had changed all that, sent the Frenchmen packing at last, but how much else had really changed? Sometimes Kordiyeh suspected that killing had become a habit in his homeland, an addiction that no social changes or apparent victories for the people would ever defeat.

But he had made a start, at least. He had done that much, and there was more yet to do.

They drove past the target and turned on the next side street, away from the main avenue. Half a mile farther, the side road lost itself in trees and twilight, an unpaved track to nowhere. The sun was going down and it would soon be dark. Behind them, in his mirrors, Kordiyeh could see dim light reflected from the streets and homes of Mestghanem, like the penumbra of a distant forest fire.

"This should be far enough," Bolan said, and Kordiyeh edged off the narrow track as far as possible, into the trees. The dome light had no bulb in place, and they were cloaked in darkness as they stepped out of the car. Bolan was the first to notice that their robes seemed almost luminescent in the night. He slipped his off and loosely folded it, draping it across the back of his seat.

"That's better."

Kordiyeh agreed. Dark shirts and trousers were more suitable for hunting after nightfall, their weapons more readily accessible without a burnoose in the way. Of course, they couldn't walk the streets of Mestghanem as they were, but that had never been the plan.

They went in through the trees, approaching the villa from the rear. No guards were posted in the woods—an oversight, in Kordiyeh's opinion, but he offered up a prayer of thanks for the negligence of his enemies. The villa's outer wall was six feet high, with shards of broken glass embedded in concrete on top, but no one from the GIA had sense enough to trim the overhanging trees. A shinny and a leap put them inside the wall ten minutes after they had left their car behind.

The first guard they encountered was a lazy young man who wore his AK-47 slung across his back like a guitar, its muzzle pointing vaguely toward the neighborhood of his right heel. He had no hope of reaching it, much less of getting off a shot, as Belasko stepped in close behind him, slid an arm around the sentry's neck and twisted sharply, separating vertebrae with an audible crunch.

Kordiyeh relieved the dead man of his rifle and spare magazines, moving on as the big American led the way. They met a second lookout moments later. He was older than the first, but no more cautious, sitting on a tree stump smoking, with his rifle on the ground beside him. Kordiyeh swung the liberated Kalashnikov with all his weight behind it, strong arms absorbing the jolt as wooden stock met human skull, stepping in to finish it with another stroke once his adversary was down.

They met no opposition on their last fifty yards to the villa, stopping at the tree line for a final look around the grounds. There were no dogs, no floodlights and no other sentries visible.

"Grenades," Bolan said, unclipping one of the green spheres from his belt as he spoke, drawing the safety pin and letting it fall to the ground at his feet.

Kordiyeh did likewise, his first full glimpse of the villa telling him that it would be madness for them to actually go inside. A man—two men—could be cut off and trapped in the warren of unfamiliar corridors and rooms, cornered and killed without great difficulty when the odds were a dozen or better to one. The American's way allowed at least some hope of getting out alive in the confusion caused by their attack.

The villa was ablaze with lights as they approached, some kind of gathering in progress on the ground floor in what seemed to be a spacious dining room. They were within a dozen paces of the broad, bright window when a shouted challenge rang in Kordiyeh's ears. He spun toward the sound automatically, grenade clutched in his right hand, ready for the pitch, his left hand wrapped around the Z-84 submachine gun.

This lookout fell somewhere between the other two in age, and he was obviously more alert than either of his dead companions, having spotted the intruders before they saw him. Still, he seemed uncertain, shouting when he should have been shooting, calling out to the strangers instead of cutting them down on sight with the AK he carried.

It was a lapse that would cost him his life.

Kordiyeh fired without thinking, instinct taking over as he squeezed the SMG's trigger, half a dozen rounds smacking into his target's chest and abdomen. Even before the dying man collapsed, a crash of glass behind him marked the flight of Belasko's hand grenade through the dining room window. Kordiyeh wheeled back toward the house and pitched his own grenade toward the startled, angry faces ranged around the banquet table, following the American's example as he ducked in preparation for the blast.

And came up firing, even as the shock waves whipped around him, cordite sharp and strong in his nostrils. Gripping the SMG in his left hand, the AK-47 in his right, he braced both weapons tight against his hips and blazed away on full-auto like something from an American gangster movie, raking the smoky shambles of the dining room from right to left and back again, spewing death at an identical 600 rounds per minute.

The guns ran dry together, but it took a moment for Kordiyeh to notice, fingers clenched around both triggers, white-knuckled, as if he expected the weapons to somehow reload and resume firing on their own. He flinched when Belasko laid a firm hand on his shoulder, and the villa's dining room swam into focus, blood and shattered furniture with corpses lying scattered in the mess.

"We're done," he said, and led him toward the car.

CHAPTER EIGHT

Malik al-Salaam had expected his Middle Eastern tour to produce fireworks back home in the States, in florid headlines and perhaps in Congress, but nothing had prepared him for the carnage that had suddenly erupted in Algeria. The violence both excited and intimidated him. Since adolescence, he had dreamed of something similar occurring in America, with the combatants cast in black and white, with the oppressed minority emerging triumphant from the cathartic bloodbath. In grim reality, however, al-Salaam had always known his dream was an impossibility as long as the majority of armed Americans were white.

The so-called Third World offered greater opportunities, exemplified by China, Vietnam and sundry states in Africa and Latin America. It was in the Middle East, though, where Muslim peoples had first learned to use their power effectively, with one hand on the nozzle that controlled crude oil production and the other gripping a Kalashnikov. There were problems, of course, with Israel's continued survival as a nation ranking high among them, but the real stumbling block to Muslim unity was the Arab people themselves. Historic squabbling over water rights and such had evolved into missile-rattling border disputes, armed invasions, terror chased by counterterror, and a stony silence over the negotiating table. If the Muslim folk were ever able to unite, their righteous anger would sweep all before them, cleansing a polluted earth in the name of God.

That, at least in part, was the reason for al-Salaam's world tour, which had so far kept him out of the States for two months. The other reason for his journey—still well hidden from the jackals of the media, he hoped—was a teenaged girl in hometown Detroit, who had recently found herself in the family way. Denise, her name was, and al-Salaam was prepared to swear on a stack of Korans that she didn't resemble any other fifteen-year-old girl in his experience. The baby growing in her womb might not be his—indeed, he had no scientific proof of its existence, yet—but it was surely possible, and that fact by itself could doom his ministry, reduce him to the status of an outcast mired in shame and poverty.

His trip abroad was meant to change all that, give his employees time to break down Denise's story, or break Denise herself, if it should come to that. Reflecting on the old days when a challenge to the prophet meant banishment, even execution for the challenger, al-Salaam almost wished that he wasn't so intent on changing the world.

At the moment, however, he had more important matters on his mind than Denise in Detroit, with her long, silky legs. His Muslim brothers were killing each other at a frenzied pace in Algeria, the warring sides supported—if not actually incited—by sponsors in two more Islamic states. More to the point, since al-Salaam craved financial support from both countries, Iran and Libya, he would have to tread very softly indeed, as he tried to negotiate a truce.

Simply ignoring the problem, allowing the bloodshed to run its natural course in Algeria, had never been an option from the day he arrived. His global peace-and-unity tour would degenerate into mockery if al-Salaam made no effort to quell the bloodshed that was carried out under his nose. The Western media would label him a hypocrite and worse, but the most telling judgment would come from his Muslim brethren. They would soon desert him if he didn't try to ease their suffering, but he would have to find a means of intervention that avoided angering the very fat cats he had cultivated for so long.

Two of those potential sponsors for the Islamic Brotherhood were with him even now, glaring daggers at each other from opposite sides of his hotel room.

"My thanks to both of you for coming," he began, the break in silence earning him a glare from Asem Kabir and a grimace from Wasim Ruholla. At least they didn't curse him. It was something.

"You know my mission," he resumed, when no one else saw fit to speak. Of course they knew his mission, since al-Salaam had already tapped both their wallets for hefty donations to the Islamic Brotherhood, negotiating clandestine deals for military hardware on the side. "I hope to foster unity among the people of our faith around the world."

"Then you must first dispose of traitors," said Ruholla. "You must purge the ranks of hypocrites and heretics, undo their treachery."

"What this one says," Kabir snapped, an index finger pointing, "is the truth, for once. When you begin the cleanup, start with him."

"Son of a goat!" Ruholla blurted.

"Whoreson!" Kabir stated calmly.

"Enough!" Al-Salaam was surprised by the strength of his own voice, cutting through their mutual insults like a blade through warm butter. "Haven't you both wasted time enough, money enough, attempting to humiliate each other? Have you lost sight of the enemies you share in common?"

Both of his guests were silent for a moment, staring at him. He could almost hear the machinery clanking inside their skulls.

Ruholla spoke first. "Common enemies? Which common enemies?" he demanded.

"I know my enemies on sight," Kabir responded. "They reveal themselves by sending men to kill men."

"Dung-heap bastard liar!"

"Spawn of sewer rats!"

"Be quiet, fools!"

His shout surprised them both, and while they glared in fury, neither interrupted al-Salaam as he resumed speaking.

"You suspect each other of treachery and worse," he said, watching the two moneymen scowl darkly. "You each believe the other has sought to undermine

your strategic position in Algeria, even urged thugs
to kill you. Am I right?''

Both nodded, muttering, his signal to continue.

"And for all I know," al-Salaam added, "you
might both be perfectly correct."

That startled both of them, nailed their attention.
From the expressions on their surly faces, an observer
might have said that neither man believed his own
accusations, neither took them seriously before hearing them repeated by another's tongue.

"However," al-Salaam interjected, before they
could launch another round of insults and name-
calling, "I would like to propose an alternative scenario for your consideration. One, I think, which
might explain recent events without suggesting
treachery to God's holy cause on either side."

He had them now, could feel it in his gut, the way
he knew an audience was hooked back home when
he began to rant against the whites in general and
Jews in particular, blaming every misfortune of the
black community from slavery to AIDS on some vast,
more-or-less monolithic conspiracy hatched by
scheming blue-eyed devils.

"I suggest," al-Salaam went on, "that perhaps you
have each been deliberately misled, cast against each
other by an unseen guiding hand, much as actors in
a play are guided in performance of their roles. It is
a possibility, I think, that both of you and those you
have chosen to assist in the ongoing struggle against
the oppressive state have been manipulated, used, as
part of a design not yet revealed in full."

"You believe this?" the Libyan asked.

"It is a possibility. In the United States, when I was still a child, the fascist Federal Bureau of Investigation issued threats to several black nationalist groups, always in the name of a competing organization, to stir up hatred and violence among brothers who should have worked together for the common good. They were successful in some cases. Lives were lost, political careers destroyed."

"I know your FBI," Ruholla said. "They do not operate outside the United States."

"Which only leaves the Central Intelligence Agency, the National Security Council, Military Intelligence or some group so secretive that even its initials are unknown. Then again," al-Salaam said, pausing for effect, "the guiding hand behind these matters might not be American at all. You have a history of conflict with the French, arrogant racists that they are, and your own government—illegitimate though it may be—is not entirely without skills or resources."

"If you are right," Kabir said, "and I say *if*, then what are we to do?"

"It's not for me to say," he replied, turning suddenly coy.

"Your theory does make sense," Ruholla said, reluctantly. "I think you must have thought it through, in terms of a solution."

"Since you ask me," al-Salaam allowed, "the first step must be to restrain the armies you support. Do everything within your power and influence to stop them killing one another in the streets, at least for now. Today, they act on impulse, hungry for revenge, but they have made no real attempt to single out the men responsible for their initial losses. If I am mistaken in my thinking, they will still have ample time to slaughter one another, after I am proved wrong. For now, they must be stopped."

"Easily said," the Libyan proclaimed.

"But not so easy to accomplish," the Iranian decreed.

"Indeed, it might be difficult, especially where blood has now been spilled on top of blood. Today, there are more grievances to be avenged than yesterday. Each passing hour makes the task more challenging, even for strong men like yourselves."

His guests accepted the flattery as their due without demur. Ruholla was first to respond, eyes flashing as he spoke. "I will talk to Nabi Ulmalhama. He can be unreasonable at times, but as you say, I am not without influence here." The expression on Ruholla's face had gone from sour to smug, denoting the shift in his mood.

"And I will speak to Houari Boudiaf," Kabir chimed in. His expression and tone of voice made it clear that he resented Ruholla's beating him to the punch. Still, he would put the best face on it that he could. "The GIA depends on Tripoli for its support. I am confident I will be taken seriously."

"Excellent." Al-Salaam allowed himself a smile that beamed toward both his guests. "And in the meantime," he continued, "we must lay our strategy against the common foe."

NABI ULMALHAMA WAS beside himself with anger, slamming down the telephone receiver with sufficient force to send a small vase and its single flower tumbling from the table to the floor. He stared in dumb rage at the shards of china, then began to stamp them underfoot, pulverizing the debris, while his lips drew back in a silent snarl.

"No word?" Mohammed Zeroual inquired, when the tantrum appeared to have run its course.

"No contact," the FIS leader corrected his second in command. "I have words aplenty, all empty promises of action, but our soldiers cannot seem to find the enemy, no matter where they look." A sudden bark of caustic laughter made it sound as if the man were choking on a bone. "Deliciously ironic, is it not, Mohammed? *They* can find *us* easily enough, it seems, but we cannot find them."

"There have been strikes against the GIA," Zeroual reminded him. "Our contacts in the military have confirmed this."

"Oh, indeed, there have been strikes," the furious guerrilla leader said. "I have no doubt of that. But who has carried out these raids, Mohammed? Can you tell me that? I speak to our lieutenants in the field, and none of them know anything about the targets raided. None of them has the imagination to concoct a lie and claim the action for themselves. Such idiots I am surrounded by! Fools and incompetents!"

Ignoring the implied slur to himself, Zeroual replied, "I ask myself, who benefits from these attacks upon our enemies?"

"A better question," Ulmalhama told his right-hand man, "is who *does not?* There must be half a dozen paramilitary groups, at least, who hate the GIA as much as we do. The MEA, for instance, or the AIS. And then again, there is of course the state itself.''

''You think the military would do something of this sort?'' Zeroual was unable to hide his surprise at the notion.

''Something like what?'' his superior challenged in a tone dripping with sarcasm. ''Something like an unprovoked attack? The ambush murder of unsuspecting victims? Surely not *our* government, Mohammed!''

Embarrassed, Zeroual tried to redeem himself. ''I simply meant—''

''I know what you meant,'' Ulmalhama snapped, then seemed to mellow slightly in the time it took Zeroual to close his mouth. ''If truth be told, I do not believe the state has done this, either. Oh, they have the means and malice to attack us, never fear. But if they were responsible, they would be crowing of their victory throughout the land. I think this must be…someone else.''

''But who?''

''If I knew that, Mohammed, then the bastards would be dead by now—or wishing that they were.'' The cutting edge had returned to Ulmalhama's voice, eyes glinting as he spoke. ''It is our task to find the man or men responsible. But in the meantime, there would also seem to be no doubt that members of the GIA have been attacked by someone they believe to be affiliated with our movement. It is possible—indeed, I take the case as proved—that they have retaliated against us in that belief. Regardless of their guilt in the initial incidents, it troubles me that our men on the street have been unable to respond in kind.''

"But if your theory is correct, our troubles would be worse, in that event."

"I disagree," Ulmalhama replied. "If we are supposed to be an army, then we must be able to defend ourselves *and* launch offensive strikes against our enemies. Today, our weakness has been shown in both respects. Whatever caused the GIA to move against us, right or wrong, they should be on their knees by now, begging forgiveness, pleading for their lives."

"Should we continue searching for them, then?" Zeroual asked.

"Of course, continue! They are out there, hunting down our soldiers even as we speak! Would you prefer to run and hide like some frightened child?"

Zeroual swallowed the insult without responding directly. When he spoke, his tone was brittle and correct. "It shall be as you order, Nabi."

"As I order, yes." A mirthless smile convulsed Ulmalhama's lips, vanishing as swiftly as it had appeared. "And with results, this time, if that is not too much to ask."

"The troops will be advised of your concern," Zeroual replied, and turned to leave the room.

Ulmalhama watched him go, a frown replacing the brief, twisted smile. He demanded much of his second in command, and Zeroual hadn't failed him yet. This latest fiasco wasn't Mohammed's failure, either, though by virtue of his rank and office he was technically responsible for seeing to it that his commander's wishes were carried out by soldiers of the rank and file. Their showing on the streets thus far had been pathetic, worse than laughable, and it could only serve to encourage further violence from their rivals, if a better showing wasn't made...and soon.

Uncertainty brought out the worst in Nabi Ulmalhama. He wasn't a man who enjoyed being made the object of sport, much less of ridicule. It pained him physically that he had thus far been unable to retaliate against his enemies, whomever they might be. His bone-deep hatred for the GIA and Houari Boudiaf wasn't erased by the suspicion that his own group and the GIA had both been victimized by an unknown enemy who wanted them to fight for reasons yet unknown. His soldiers should have punished any raiders from the GIA and *then* moved on to find the man or men responsible for the original attacks. In that way, honor was secured and maintained against all challengers, against all odds.

Whoever was responsible for the present diversion, Ulmalhama understood that only one leader could finally emerge from the ongoing struggle in Algeria. It might take years, yet, for the issue to be suitably resolved. Then again, there was always the chance for a stroke that would finish some part of the game in record time, eliminate a deadly adversary and leave the way clear to final victory.

Nabi Ulmalhama was counting on it.

Whatever happened next, whoever was to blame for his present distress, he would win in the end. He had convinced himself that it was God's will, no less.

"I FEEL THAT WE—that is, my country—has been very generous and understanding with the GIA." Kabir spoke politely in clipped, measured tones, but his courtesy was a facade. Houari Boudiaf could sense the Libyan's anger, simmering just beneath the surface of his dark and homely face.

"Colonel Khaddafi has indeed been generous," the leader of the GIA replied, making it clear that he didn't confuse the master with his errand boy.

If Kabir detected the not-so-subtle insult, he let it pass. "We have not, I believe, attempted to control the GIA or usurp your authority as field commander."

Again, it wasn't a question. Boudiaf could have pointed out the fact that arms and money never came from any source without at least *some* strings attached. He might have pointed out that Libya—more precisely her despotic ruler—had designs on Algeria and clearly hoped to gain influence, if not territory, from his support of the GIA's revolt against the ruling junta in Algiers, but once again, the rebel leader bit his tongue. Instead, he told Kabir, "I make my own decisions for the GIA, it is true."

Another slap, and this one definitely registered. If it was possible to see the angry color rise in such a swarthy face, Boudiaf would have said Kabir was blushing. However, there was a tightening of jaw muscles, a clenching of teeth, a narrowing of eyes. Kabir's bristling caterpillar brows had nearly merged above his beak of a nose, new wrinkles forming on his broad forehead, almost as if the brain inside were struggling to emerge.

"It might be," said the Libyan paymaster, "that

your decisions of late have been...let us say, misguided."

"And which decisions might those be?" Boudiaf inquired, taunting his guest with a crooked half-smile.

"You have initiated violent contact with the Islamic Salvation Front," Kabir replied. "Perhaps with other rival groups, as well."

"You have been sadly misinformed, my friend," the GIA commander said. "In fact, you have somehow reversed the sequence of events. The FIS attacked my people first, inflicting grievous casualties. The first assault, you might recall, was carried out in Libya, your own backyard."

"So you have said." Kabir was clearly skeptical, the frown etched into his face as if with a carving knife.

"You deny the attack on our Libyan base camp?" Boudiaf felt his smile slipping and fought to hold it in place. "Your own soldiers—the colonel's own men—examined the scene, if I am not mistaken."

"No one doubts that the attack occurred as you describe. A question has arisen, though, as to the factual identity of those responsible."

Boudiaf blinked once before he caught himself. The smile was lost beyond recall, but he could still preserve a poker face, albeit with an effort. "I am afraid I do not understand," he told the Libyan.

"It is really quite simple," Kabir replied. "We now have reason to suspect the FIS was not responsible for the attack. You have, perhaps, launched retaliatory strikes against the wrong target."

Boudiaf was bristling now, his stomach roiling.

The thought of such a critical mistake was almost as repulsive to him as the notion of Kabir second-guessing his tactics in the field. "If not the FIS," he answered stiffly, "then who?"

"Outsiders, perhaps," the Libyan replied. "Someone who would support the present government by indirect means, allowing enemies of the state to neutralize each other. Someone, perhaps, from the West."

"The French?"

It was Boudiaf's first and most logical guess. For all its hideous repression, despite the token fealty to Islam, Algeria's ruling party was supported—some said owned—by French politicians in Paris. It was almost as if, having once been expelled from the African nation that they arrogantly deemed "an integral part" of their own decadent nation, the French now sought to maintain their control from afar, using any means from arms and foreign aid to that vague commodity dubbed moral support. That continuing involvement in Algerian affairs had led various rebel factions, the GIA and FIS included, to carry out strikes on French soil. Bombs had rocked the Paris Métro more than once, and drive-by shootings weren't unknown. The previous year, an incident planned to coincide with the Cannes Film Festival had been scuttled with hours to spare, via cooperation by the Sûreté and Interpol.

"The French, perhaps," Kabir said. "God knows they are arrogant enough, defying even the United States with their insistence on nuclear testing. There are, of course, some alternate possibilities."

Boudiaf could feel his anger tugging at its leash, already frayed, about to snap. It was an effort to refrain from shouting at the Libyan. "If you have knowledge of some plot against the GIA, against Algeria," he said, "I must assume that you would make it known to me."

"The very purpose of my visit," Kabir said, his tone edging dangerously close to mockery. "In fact, I have but recently spoken with a major foreign sponsor of the FIS about your current difficulties. We were joined by a visitor from the United States."

Boudiaf knew the Iranian, Wasim Ruholla, who bankrolled the FIS on behalf of Tehran and the black-robed ayatollahs. More than once he had considered killing Ruholla, slamming the door on Iranian influence in Algeria, but caution had always stayed his hand. The Tehran regime was softening, and Boudiaf had worried that any direct conflict might put steel in their backbones, could somehow rebound against him and ruin everything.

Boudiaf knew Wasim Ruholla, but this talk of an American...what could it mean? What visitor? There were no American diplomats or politicians presently touring Algiers, and none would have met with Kabir if they were. Libya was an outlaw state in American eyes, pledged to the funding of terrorism, providing safe haven for the Lockerbie bombers and other notorious killers. A meeting, even covert, with the likes of Kabir—himself involved in illegal subversion—would be unthinkable in the present circumstances. Worse yet, from an American point of view, it would be political suicide. But who, then, was this American visitor Kabir described? Did he even exist?

A possible answer occurred to Boudiaf, and he felt his stomach clench once more. Could it be?

"The black gangster?" he asked, incredulous.

Kabir stiffened in his easy chair, the corners of his mouth dragged down another quarter inch or so, as if by gravity. "Malik al-Salaam is a brother in God," the Libyan replied. "He has repented of his crimes and has been punished for them—rather harshly, one might say—by the racist state. If anything, his background makes him all the more valuable in our present situation. His insight might be critical."

"In what respect?" Boudiaf asked.

"He knows the workings of American intelligence," Kabir said. "Indeed, he has been shadowed and harassed for years, himself, by the American FBI and CIA, along with other agencies. He is familiar with their usual techniques."

"And how, if I may ask, does this pertain to the attack on my soldiers in Libya? What has it to do with the raids in Algiers and elsewhere?"

"Brother Malik suggests that the Americans might be responsible. If not the CIA itself, perhaps some other agency unknown to us. It would not be the first time the Great Satan manipulated affairs in a sovereign nation where greater influence is desired."

Much like Kabir's precious colonel, Boudiaf thought, but kept it to himself. Instead, he asked the Libyan, "What evidence is offered in support of this idea?"

"Brother Malik reminds us that the Great Satan has

long experience in covering his tracks.'' Kabir's eyes flashed with zealotry as he spoke. ''He believes that with cooperation from both sides, your present difficulty with the FIS could be resolved, the guiding hand of those responsible exposed. With his experience—''

''And how,'' Boudiaf cut in, ''does this American expect to be rewarded for his help, assuming that his judgment is correct?''

''Such criticism is unworthy,'' the Libyan said.

''If I am mistaken, I apologize.'' The crooked smile was back. Boudiaf could feel it, didn't need to check the mirror. ''I assume it has occurred to you and those you serve that Brother Malik may himself be serving as an agent of America, sent here to meddle in Algerian affairs?''

''I deem that most unlikely.''

''And Tripoli?'' the GIA commander pressed.

''There is no disagreement. All concerned agree that we—that you—should actively investigate the possibility of outside agitators.''

''While the FIS continues to attack my men?'' There could be no mistake about the anger in Boudiaf's tone. The mocking smile was well and truly lost.

''Brother Malik and I discussed the problem with Wasim Ruholla,'' the Libyan said. ''He has agreed to speak with his contacts in the FIS and seek an equitable resolution. In the meantime—''

''In the meantime,'' Boudiaf interrupted his sponsor, ''I have comrades dying in the streets of Algiers, and in other towns. I will not place more lives in jeopardy by ordering a cease-fire while the FIS is still on the attack.''

''But the Americans—''

''If they exist,'' the GIA commander said, ''I will be pleased to kill them, also. No doubt, Brother Malik can help identify the men responsible, with his experience. It should not take him long. You will, of course, forgive me if I take such steps as may be needed to defend my soldiers in the meantime.''

''Your response is noted,'' Kabir stated. ''I will inform Tripoli of your decision.''

''I can ask no more,'' Boudiaf replied, already on his feet, ushering his guest toward the door. He had a war to fight, on more than one front it now appeared, and he was wasting precious time.

Americans? Perhaps, he told himself, but it would make no difference to the end result. With God on his side, what enemy could stand against Boudiaf?

CHAPTER NINE

A pistol bullet struck the wall near Bolan's head, perhaps ten inches off the mark, and tiny chunks of plaster stung his cheek like shrapnel from a Lilliputian hand grenade. He cursed on reflex, knowing it was wasted breath, but ducked at the same time, reacting by instinct. The shooter's second round would have drilled him through the face, but as it was, the Executioner hunkered down below the line of fire, his Z-84 stuttering through the foot-long suppressor attached to its muzzle.

Downrange, the Algerian gunman was correcting his aim once again, going for the bull's-eye this time, when a 3-round burst of Parabellum slugs tore through his scrawny chest and dropped him on his backside. Bolan's adversary sat there for a moment, staring at the Executioner with a dazed expression on his face before he toppled backward in a widening pool of his own blood.

The raid had gone according to plan for about thirty seconds, not counting the approach to their target through narrow backstreets, all smelling their age. Kordiyeh had fingered a block of apartments on the western fringe of the Casbah district, where FIS fugitives in flight were allowed to rest before they vanished into the wider safehouse network, away from Algiers. Without a man inside, it was impossible to know how many guns were present going in—the place would sleep up to a dozen in relative comfort, Kordiyeh said; perhaps eighteen if they stacked them like children at camp—but Bolan was prepared to buck the odds. His luck was holding, so far, and he meant to stretch it all he could.

He wasn't sure exactly what went wrong, as there was no time to assess the matter while Bolan and Kordiyeh were fighting for their lives. One moment they were entering the block of flats, proceeding up the narrow, filthy stairs; the next, all hell broke loose, with tenants shouting, cursing the intruders, some of them well armed and itching for a chance to use their hardware.

It was chaos for a moment when the members of the home team started shooting. Men, women and children scattered at the first sounds of gunfire, some retreating to their tiny flats, others streaming down the stairs and breaking for the nearest exit. The rush initially provided cover for Bolan and Kordiyeh, the FIS killers apparently reluctant to fire on their immediate neighbors. Bolan, for his part, was equally loath to kill or maim civilians, but he had a slim advantage in the present circumstances. Except for Gholomreza Kordiyeh, every person noted with a weapon in hand was fair game.

Bolan's Z-84 SMG lacked selective fire capabilities, but he was proficient enough with the Spanish

Uzi look-alike to avoid raking the crowd. He had already dropped two shooters, against Kordiyeh's one and a half—the second guy wounded by moving—when the press of flesh surrounding him evaporated. One moment, he was being jostled right and left; the next, it seemed, he had the stairwell nearly to himself, except for Kordiyeh and their assailants. The crowd was siphoned off like water going down a drain, some vanishing behind slamming doors, others spilling out into the darkened street.

Their escape added an extra sense of urgency to Bolan's situation, with the knowledge that police would be arriving soon. It hardly mattered if the fleeing tenants summoned help or not. With all the racket going on inside the small apartment block, it would be difficult for any passerby to ignore the firefight in progress.

As the dying shooter toppled backward, Bolan made a break to gain the third-floor landing, his original destination when the probe began. He had an armed frag grenade in hand as he reached the landing, spun and lobbed it down the hallway past the body of his latest kill toward a clutch of FIS guerrillas milling about in excitement and confusion.

One of them saw death coming, shouted a warning to his comrades and broke for the nearest cover, but 9 mm Parabellum rounds from Bolan's SMG were already slicing through the muddled ranks, one of them clipping the runner's spine and dropping him facedown on the carpet, a heartbeat before the grenade went off. This time it *was* shrapnel zinging through the air around Bolan, pitting the walls, but his enemies absorbed the worst of it, reduced to crumpled caricatures of humanity.

Even then, his grenade and gunfire didn't clear the hallway entirely, more FIS shooters leaning out to snipe at him from the relative security of their individual doorways, some zigzaging from room to room in search of a better vantage point. Bolan caught one of the latter halfway across no-man's-land, within a few strides of a waiting open door. A short burst from Bolan's subgun cut the runner's legs from under him and pitched him into an awkward dive, arms raised belatedly to spare his head from crushing impact with the nearest wall.

It nearly worked, and the guy was still conscious, clearly in pain, as he flopped over on his back, fumbling for something clipped to his belt. Bolan lined up his kill shot, and the wounded man's grenade was airborne, wobbling toward the Executioner and dropping its safety spoon along the way.

The big American nailed his man with another short burst, this one to the head, and flung himself out of the frag grenade's path. No time for clomping down the stairs and trading fire with enemies en route, so he hopped aboard the banister, sliding smoothly, swiftly, on the wood polished over time by so many sweaty palms. Bolan called out a warning to Kordiyeh as he swept past, the Algerian startled, retreating as quickly as he could.

Dust and smoke enveloped the third-floor landing as the grenade exploded. Shrapnel sprayed in all directions, but Bolan missed the worst of it, feeling something sting his biceps as he tumbled off the banister and hit the floor one flight below. Kordiyeh wasn't as fortunate. A gash opened at his hairline, streaming blood down the left side of his face, but he was up and moving as a new storm of gunfire broke around them.

"It's a wrap," Bolan said, as his ally caught up with him. "We're out of here."

"A wise decision, I believe." There was a quick flash of teeth, a smile tinged with crimson, as Bolan retreated, Kordiyeh following him down and out into the street.

There were more targets on the list, perhaps less well protected, and Bolan had made his point with this one. The worst still lay in store for old Algiers.

The Executioner was blitzing on.

MUSTAFA HIBARI WAS nervous. He wouldn't have admitted as much to a living soul, especially his fellow warriors of the Armed Islamic Group, but he couldn't deceive himself. At first, when he had listened to reports of the attacks the GIA had suffered over the past twenty-four hours, Hibari had been keyed up, excited, anxious for an opportunity to prove himself in battle. As a twenty-year-old recruit, lately finished his basic training, he had yet to participate in any GIA activity beyond the distribution of leaflets denouncing the state. Still, he had trained for combat like all other members of the group, and he was anxious to strike a blow on behalf of his faith.

His ardor had subsided, though, with the passage of time, as one report of carnage followed another, each story raising the GIA body count, none relating any progress toward the identification or destruction of their faceless enemies. It was rumored that the Anointed Ones had been unleashed by the GIA's leaders, but there were only vague rumors of the flying squad's success, while each new radio bulletin seemed to make matters worse, reporting more losses of GIA men and material.

It was all too much, and Hibari, for his part, had been secretly relieved when he was selected for guard duty that morning, driven to a warehouse on the outskirts of Algiers where he and half a dozen other fresh recruits around his own age were assigned to watch the building, keep it safe until they were relieved sometime later in the day. For all he knew, they might be stranded there for hours, even well into tomorrow.

Which, all things considered, gave Hibari no cause for complaint.

He was ashamed at the relief he felt when he had learned that he would not be sent to prowl the backstreets of Algiers in search of enemies who had already killed so many of his comrades. It was cowardice, perhaps, and he had joined the others in halfhearted protests, pleading weakly for a chance to join the hunt, but in his heart there was no sadness when his plea for recognition was refused. All soldiers served the cause, he had been told, including those who walked a lonely post and kept the movement's precious military hardware safe. What could Hibari do under the circumstances but accept his duty with a show of disappointment that was mostly sham?

Still, it was boring, sitting on the warehouse loading dock, his Skorpion machine pistol beside him, concealed inside a plastic shopping bag. Hibari didn't recognize the name of the store inscribed on the bag, cared nothing for what it had once contained, whether clothing, groceries or office supplies. This day, it held the Skorpion and three spare magazines, in case his assignment came to more than sitting on his backside and watching cars go by.

Not even many cars, he thought, since the commercial neighborhood had no full-time residents, and economic hard times had emptied nearly a full block of warehouses on either side of the one he was assigned to watch. Hibari wondered what was inside the warehouse, what was so precious that it required six guards with automatic weapons, but the wondering was merely a mind game, something to amuse himself and help pass the time. If his superiors wanted him to know what he was guarding, they would tell him; it wasn't for him to ask, much less to risk a look inside the place.

At least it was relatively cool at his post, the temperature dropping as it always did after sundown, no matter how scorching the daytime hours might be. There was a small light on the loading dock, but Hibari sat at the opposite end, unwilling to make himself a target if he could somehow minimize the risk. He couldn't see the others, stationed at intervals around the large warehouse, and wondered what harm there would be if he left the loading dock for a few moments, just to find one of his comrades, determine that all was in order.

The thought made him anxious, conjuring bizarre images of his fellow sentries being picked off, one by one, knifed or garroted by ninja-type prowlers until Hibari was alone at his post, oblivious to the carnage around him. How did he know that the warehouse was safe? From his lonely post facing the street, how could he be sure that its contents hadn't already been unloaded through another exit, spirited away into the night?

The anxiety was foolish, childlike, but once it took root in his mind, Hibari found it impossible to shake. Moments later, he grew conscious of the pressure in his loins, a typical nervous reaction to worry that made him crave a urinal—or at the very least a darkened corner where he would not be observed. Hibari stalled for several more moments until he felt that he could wait no longer. Grumbling darkly in his self-disgust, he scrambled to his feet, bent to retrieve the plastic shopping bag that held his Skorpion, wincing as the bag made a loud, telltale crinkling sound.

So much for stealth. If there were any watchers in the outer shadows and they hadn't seen him yet, his stirring and the racket from the shopping bag would help them zero in. Hibari half expected to be shot at any moment, chiding himself for cowardice when no bullets flew out of the darkness to find him.

Where to urinate? One option was to leave the loading dock, but that meant walking back to the other end, beneath the lonely lightbulb in its painted metal cage, and descending the short flight of steps. From there, he could have walked around the corner into even deeper shadows...but what if one of the other sentries had noticed him, reporting him for dereliction of his duty?

At last, Hibari decided he would urinate from the loading dock itself, but that posed another problem. His faded denim pants were fitted with a button fly that needed both hands to unfasten it, and every move he made produced more noise, the plastic bag slung from his left wrist hissing and rattling like a saw-scaled viper in the night. Disgusted and embarrassed, Hibari stooped to set the bag at his feet, still four buttons short of ultimate relief.

And he was bending over, backside toward the warehouse, when the world exploded around him.

One moment, Hibari was stooped at the waist, head between his knees, and the next he was airborne, hurtling through a clumsy somersault, propelled by a hot draft like the very breath of Hell. The blast itself was loud enough to deafen him, creating a feeling in his head as if large cotton wads had been rammed into both ears, brutally, perhaps on the tips of steel rods. Hibari struck the pavement on his back some twenty feet from the loading dock, landing with force enough to drive the breath from his lungs and momentarily paralyze his diaphragm.

It felt like drowning, but he struggled to his hands and knees, head dangling limply, as he retched and tried to catch his breath. In front of him, the warehouse was in flames, smoke boiling up from the inferno, whipped this way and that by a sudden, shifting wind. At the heart of the blaze, smaller explosions were going off by the hundreds, but Hibari couldn't hear them, kneeling on the asphalt that was suddenly as bright and hot as if the noonday sun were overhead.

He reached for the Skorpion, instinctively, then realized that he had lost it in the blast, releasing the bag from his hand mere seconds before the explosion. Groping behind him, he found the German P-5 self-loading pistol still snug inside his waistband, its imprint etched on his back when he fell. Hibari drew the gun and held it in his trembling hand, thumbing off the safety even as he wondered what on earth he hoped to do with it.

What had happened to the warehouse? Was the explosion spontaneous, or had saboteurs managed to infiltrate the building, plant their charges despite the presence of half a dozen guards? It seemed impossible, but Hibari wasn't prepared to rule out any explanation yet, before he had a chance to collect his wits.

Still dizzy and nauseous, he tottered to his feet, holding the P-5 pistol in front of him like some kind of talisman to ward off evil spirits. Part of his mind was already racing ahead, trying on explanations of his failure for size, wondering if he would be punished for the loss of the warehouse. At the same time, another quarter of his brain was taking inventory of the body it served, logging pain signals, testing muscles and bones, each in turn. As far as Hibari could tell, short of possibly perforated eardrums, nothing was broken or otherwise critically damaged. His equilibrium was rocky, but a few more seconds on his feet took care of that. With the initial dizziness, so passed away his first wave of nausea, replaced by a leaden feeling in his stomach, as if he had bolted down a meal without taking time to chew it properly.

Internal bleeding?

Hibari shrugged off the fear and concentrated on the warehouse, squinting against the bright flames and cloying smoke, moving slowly counterclockwise around the shattered building in his search for surviving friends or lurking enemies.

At his first glimpse of a figure moving through the smoke and firelight, Hibari froze in his tracks, wobbling slightly as he raised his P-5 in both hands. He couldn't recognize the figure, with the firelight behind it, but it seemed too large for any of the men assigned with him to watch the warehouse. Still, Hibari held his fire, fearing a deadly mistake, in case his bleary eyes were playing tricks on him.

A few more yards...

He saw the dull wink of a muzzle-flash, barely visible in the glare of the burning warehouse, and before Hibari could react, an iron fist punched him in the chest. He went down, sprawling, painfully aware that he had lost his pistol when he fell. It took another moment to realize what had happened, that he had really been shot, and then the pain found him, searing like a white-hot poker rammed into his lung.

Incredible, Hibari thought, that with such pain, he couldn't find the strength or breath to scream.

His pain was fading by the time the shadow-figure towered over him, his killer's face invisible, cloaked in darkness. Hibari regretted that he wouldn't at least glimpse the face of the man who had taken his life, but what did it matter, after all?

He had done his duty as best he could, and the reward of Paradise would be his.

It was almost enough to make Hibari smile, as he

closed his eyes and let the darkness swallow him whole.

THE SHRAPNEL WOUNDS that Kordiyeh had suffered when the warehouse blew reminded him of wasp stings. They were painful but superficial, the worst of them a graze beneath one arm that had ruined his shirt before he stopped the bleeding. The wounds weren't debilitating, though, despite the scattered, nagging pains that flared anew each time he moved. It was a soldier's lot to suffer, and his intuition told him that the worst still lay ahead.

Belasko had taken some flesh wounds, as well, but he had cleaned them with disinfectant, bandaged them with sticking plaster, and apparently forgotten about them. From the stoic expression on his face, a casual observer might have thought he was immune to pain.

The next target on their slowly dwindling hit list was a temporary radio station maintained by the Islamic Salvation Front. The station had been outlawed because of its outspoken support for FIS terrorist activities, but that didn't prevent it from beaming propaganda messages throughout Algiers and the surrounding territory. Hunted like rats, the station's operators relocated their equipment every three or four days, broadcasting at irregular, unscheduled times. Unlike some terrorist groups, the FIS didn't give advance warning of its actions to spare innocent bystanders, but the pirate station was quick to claim credit for various atrocities after the fact.

Kordiyeh had been aware of the FIS radio station from its inception almost five years earlier, but he—

like the police and military—had never been able to pin it down. Now, thanks to Belasko's contact from the CIA, they had been favored with a one-night-only address. If they missed their chance that evening, the crew and its equipment would be gone, moved on to another address, perhaps this time outside the city proper.

The plan was slightly different this time. It went beyond what the Americans called search and destroy, into the realm of something Belasko termed "psy-war." Inside the breast pocket of his new shirt, safe and secure with the flap buttoned, Kordiyeh carried a single piece of notebook paper, folded into quarters. Covering one side of the paper, written in his own precise script, was the message he and Belasko had joined forces to compose. If it was possible—assuming he survived the raid, and the pirate station's broadcasting equipment was still intact when the smoke cleared—Kordiyeh would read that message on the air.

Before it came to that, however, they still had to verify the address, deal with any lookouts and the station's crew, all without disabling the radio equipment. If and when that sequence of events had fallen into line without mishap, then Kordiyeh would have himself an audience.

"The corner house," he told Bolan, peering through the fly-specked windshield as he drove. "That should be it."

"Should be," Bolan echoed, sounding neither critical nor pleased.

"It is the address you were given," Kordiyeh assured him. "Beyond that..."

He left the rest unsaid, no point in repeating his initial skepticism about the American's mercenary source. They hadn't been betrayed thus far, and his uneasiness about Hassan Filali had receded, for the most part, into irritating background noise, a dull itching at the back of his brain. Surely, if the man were going to sell them out, the trap should have sprung before this.

They parked a half-block from the private home, few cars on the street at this hour despite the relative affluence of the neighborhood. Those homeowners who had both cars and garages kept the former locked securely in the latter when their vehicles weren't in use. Auto thefts by members of the various insurgent bands were so common that police hardly bothered to investigate complaints, more often logging license plates and engine numbers in their files, then waiting for the missing cars to turn up stripped for parts or twisted into smoking wreckage by explosives. Those without garages, if they owned a vehicle, were more likely to park it in the backyard, out of sight from the street, perhaps with the battery or the distributor cap removed to frustrate thieves.

In place of native garb, this time, they both wore loose-fitting sport coats over shirts and slacks. Kordiyeh's Z-84 submachine gun was hidden by his jacket, three spare magazines straining the inside pocket, his pistol tucked into the waistband of his pants, in back. He hoped that he could draw it quickly, if the need arose.

The house showed signs of occupancy: lighted windows at the rear, an old Mercedes-Benz sedan parked in the narrow driveway, its nose toward the street for a quick getaway. There was no sign of lookouts posted in the yard, no movement of the draperies that covered windows at the front of the house, but they took no chances, veering off the crudely patched sidewalk and across a dark yard two doors down. They circled to the rear of the structure, alert for any sign of sentries or dogs. They met no opposition by the time they reached the backyard, where flimsy curtains spilled yellow glare into the night.

Standing well back from the windows, Kordiyeh could still make out the shape of men inside. He counted three around the kitchen table, marveling that even hunted as they were they took no greater care to guard themselves against spies. It would have been ridiculously easy to fire through the window or lob a grenade, but the two men had agreed to spare the radio equipment if possible—at least, until they had completed their own unscheduled broadcast.

"Quick and clean," the American reminded him, Kordiyeh merely nodding in response. Both men had their weapons ready as they moved toward the back door, almost shoulder to shoulder. Kordiyeh took the lead in the last few yards, hoisting one foot at the penultimate moment, slamming the door with a mighty kick above and slightly left of the knob. He was rewarded by a snap of metal, woodwork splintering, and the door flew open, Kordiyeh charging inside with his companion close behind him.

There were four men, not three, in the kitchen. He

had missed one from his vantage point outside, standing beside the sink and sipping water from a plain glass jar. Incredibly, none of the FIS guerrillas had weapons close at hand, although Kordiyeh saw the rifles waiting for them, standing upright in corners just beyond reach.

After the first shock of surprise, the gunners scattered, each man lunging for a weapon. The broadcaster was hampered by a bulky set of headphones, and Kordiyeh ignored him for the moment, swinging first toward the man who was already on his feet, craning toward an automatic rifle near the stove. A burst from Kordiyeh's Z-84 opened the rebel's chest and slammed him back against the counter, a dazed expression on his face as his legs betrayed him, turned to rubber, and he collapsed to the floor.

Swinging back toward the table, he saw one of the shooters take a burst from Belasko's SMG between the shoulder blades, pitched forward with a heavy thump against the nearest wall. The dead or dying soldier left a bright red smear behind him as he fell, but Kordiyeh ignored it, looking for a live one.

Number three was on his feet and moving swiftly, actually had one hand around the barrel of an AKM assault rifle, when Kordiyeh hit him with half a dozen Parabellum rounds. The target seemed to stumble, tripping on some obstacle that no one else could see, and went down in a heap, the rifle pinned beneath him as he fell. Where Kordiyeh's full-metal-jacket rounds had pierced him through and through, the stucco wall was marked with crimson spray.

Bolan took the fourth and final man, still fumbling

with his headphones when a short burst to the chest slammed him over backward, chair and all collapsing to the kitchen floor. Ironically, his fall dislodged the headphones, left them dangling by their slim cord from the table's edge.

"Your turn," Bolan said, stepping aside to give him room.

Kordiyeh stepped around the dead man, scooped up the headphones and slipped them on. He grimaced at the feel of someone else's perspiration on his skin: a dead man's sweat. He checked the radio transmitter, found the channel open, dead air humming as he fumbled in his pocket for the folded slip of paper.

Seconds later, seated in the corpse's chair, the paper spread in front of him, Kordiyeh began to read aloud. He felt Belasko watching him and shrugged it off, caught up in talking to the night.

IT WAS A FLUKE, Malik al-Salaam told himself later, that he happened to turn on his radio at just that moment, tuned to just that channel in time to catch the final moments of the pirate broadcast. In fact, luck had little to do with it, since al-Salaam made a practice of keeping up with dissident Muslim activity wherever he traveled. The Islamic Salvation Front was well-known for its pirate radio broadcasts, and he was hoping to catch one that evening, perhaps even hear his own name mentioned as a mediator in the latest outbreak of violence.

What he heard, instead, was something very different.

The voice was calm, well-modulated, all the more

surprising in view of its message. Al-Salaam had expected one of the patented FIS attacks on the ruling Algerian government, perhaps some reference to the recent street violence, but he was wholly unprepared for the evening's message. After brief preliminaries, the usual praise for God that prefaced and concluded every broadcast, there was a sudden babble of startled—frightened?—voices, followed by a moment of dead air. When the broadcast resumed, there was a new hand on the microphone, a richer, deeper voice in al-Salaam's ears.

"My brothers, hear me in the name of God," said the new announcer. "You have been betrayed. False prophets have deceived you, used you in pursuit of power and glory for themselves, against the will of the divine. Your wives and children have been sacrificed by men who care nothing for you or your homeland. The Islamic Salvation Front and the Armed Islamic Group are, both alike, unworthy of your trust. Those who perpetuate the cycle of terror shall not win God's favor, but instead earn everlasting condemnation. They will not see Paradise. For God's sake, in God's name, lay down your arms and let the killing cease!"

Malik al-Salaam could scarcely believe his ears, although the strange voice spoke precisely, without hesitation. The message was so alien to his experience, virtually unprecedented, that it left him speechless. He wondered if Houari Boudiaf and Nabi Ulmalhama were listening, and knew what their reaction would be if they were. Ulmalhama, the FIS leader, would be livid, screaming for the heads of those who had bitched up the broadcast. Boudiaf, for his part, would doubtless be amused by the discomfiture of his enemies in the FIS, but mention of his own group in the broadcast was bound to have him chewing the carpet, as well. He would try to blame Ulmalhama and the FIS for his embarrassment, even though the Islamic Salvation Front had been attacked on its own radio broadcast, and al-Salaam could almost feel another round of mayhem coming on.

Was that, in fact, the purpose of the broadcast, after all? Granted, the basic message had been standard fare—peace and brotherhood for all—but it was hard to believe that the man or men responsible wouldn't anticipate exacerbation of ill feelings between the chief combatants of the GIA and FIS. Considering the violence that had rocked Algiers and other coastal cities in the past twenty-four hours, the radio bulletin would be akin to dousing a wildfire with gasoline.

The good news was that *he* hadn't been mentioned, either by name or by implication, while the faceless broadcaster was running down his list of so-called traitors to Islam. Malik al-Salaam had caught himself holding his breath while the disembodied voice was speaking, fearful that some passing mention of foreign interlopers would pin a bull's-eye squarely on his back. Al-Salaam had done his groundwork with the Iranian and Libyan sponsors of Algeria's long civil war, easing himself into the role of divinely blessed peacemaker, but it could all fall apart in a flash if leaders of the GIA and/or the FIS refused to play ball. As long as the rebels were killing one another in the streets instead of concentrating on their common enemy in government, the revolutionary cause was weakened—and Malik al-Salaam fell short of his personal goals.

The former Rodney Allen Tuggle of Detroit had plans in mind for the nation that had first given him life, then turned that life into a nightmare of drugs, crime and dark nights in prison. He blamed himself for nothing that had happened, though he did take credit—shared with God, naturally—for turning his wasted life around. In al-Salaam's view, there was a debt remaining to be settled with Amerikkka, and it could only be repaid in white man's blood.

But he would never see that debt collected, never come into the glory he deserved, unless he could first build a larger following for himself, secure cash and arms for his struggle from the devout Muslim states of Central Asia. Any major setback, at this point, might well prove fatal to his grand design.

Al-Salaam wasn't prepared to let that happen, not if he had anything to say about it.

And he did.

Scowling, he switched off the radio and reached for the telephone.

CHAPTER TEN

Hassan Filali knew what he was looking for; the question was, where to find it exactly. Spying, as a trade, consisted primarily of voyeurism, eavesdropping and listening to rumors by the hour, sifting through the urban legends, lies, exaggerations, wishful thinking, to discover pearls of truth. Sometimes informants didn't even know that they were lying; they would simply pass along a bit of gossip, maybe adding tidbits of their own—perhaps unconsciously—and took it for the gospel truth.

Such difficulties were particularly common with subversive groups and individuals, outcasts or the religious or political fringe who required inflated membership statistics and fabricated victories to make themselves appear significant, help them stand out in the crowd. It wasn't, Filali knew from long experience, simply a matter of exaggerating numbers, claiming a thousand disciples where barely one hundred existed. Tough talk demanded action, and Filali was accustomed to deception in that realm, as well. He had seen as many as three terrorist groups claim credit for bombing a commercial aircraft downed by wind shear, and final exposition of the disaster's true cause produced wails of a CIA cover-up. He shuddered to think of how many would-be assassins would fire off crudely written confessions when the present aging Pope at last went on to his reward.

That evening, however, Filali was seeking a special informant, one who cut through the daydreams and confabulations, reporting hard facts that, thus far, at least, had proved one-hundred-percent reliable. The man's name was Yacoub Jabbar, and while he claimed to be Egyptian, Filali had done some quiet digging on the side, determining that Jabbar came from Lebanon, where he had narrowly escaped imprisonment by the Israeli occupying forces for dealing military hardware to Palestinian resistance fighters. His business was much the same in Algeria, supplying various private militias with anything from pistols to rocket launchers, but he also doled out information...for a price.

Jabbar's rules were simple: he would never talk to the police, but otherwise, as a nonpartisan outsider, he would sell whatever crucial information he possessed to the highest bidder—without betraying himself in the process, of course. If he had lately sold a shipment of Kalashnikovs to the Islamic Salvation Front, for example, Jabbar might report that this or that lieutenant of Mohammed Zeroual had recently taken possession of new military hardware. Should a terrorist attack closely follow the sale, Jabbar might go so far as to venture a guess at the shooter's identity, or at least name the group responsible. And, while he wasn't above betraying his best customers,

Jabbar made it crystal clear that he, himself, should be immune to betrayal.

Filali was aware of two young men, both local thugs, who had tried to blackmail Jabbar with threats of exposure as a tout some eighteen months after Jabbar first arrived in Algiers. Their demand was not extravagant, considering Jabbar's rumored wealth and the fact that his life was on the line, but the arms dealer chose not to pay. Instead, within twenty-four hours of first contact, the young extortionists were found hanging by their heels from a lamppost in the Casbah district. Cause of death was listed as exsanguination from the multitude of wounds each body had sustained in what appeared to be a torture session lasting several hours.

Both young thugs were mutilated—prior to death, the medical examiner reported—in a manner normally reserved by paramilitary groups for traitors and police informants. Thus, authorities were left to speculate on which Algerian militia was responsible...assuming that they cared enough to ask at all. Jabbar, meanwhile, reminded certain valued customers that he wasn't a man to trifle with, implying that he might have plied the blade himself.

To prove his point, he kept a grim set of before-and-after Polaroid instant photos.

Requesting information from Yacoub Jabbar was normally a last resort for Filali, not only for the cost, but knowing as he did that any contact with Jabbar entailed a fair degree of risk. There was at least a fifty-fifty chance that some official agency was watching Jabbar at any given hour of the day or night, trying to identify his clients, but the greater risk came from Jabbar himself. Simply stated, he was among the least trustworthy persons in Algiers. A handful of money might loosen his tongue, but the cost of his silence was higher, a perpetual debt with no firm guarantees, which Filali sought to minimize by restricting his use of Jabbar as a source.

Still, in the do-or-die, now-or-never spirit of the past twenty-four hours, with all hell breaking loose in Algiers and the worst yet to come, Filali deemed that a special interview was justified. No, make that critical. If he was going to contribute something more to the present campaign, Filali required more information—the currency of names and notions that was Yacoub Jabbar's secondary stock-in-trade.

Finding Jabbar in Algiers wasn't difficult, unless you carried a badge or appeared short of cash. Filali met neither of those criteria; in fact, his several meetings with Jabbar over the past two years established him as a client in his own right—not a VIP, of course, but someone worthy of respect. He would, if nothing else, be granted leave to ask his questions. Beyond that point...

As usual, Filali traveled eastward from his home on foot until he reached the outskirts of the Casbah district. There, he found a ''blind'' beggar wearing a turban, loincloth and new sunglasses, endlessly shaking a crude wooden bowl as if it were a tambourine, making tuneless music with the coins inside. Filali covered the loose change with two crisp bills of large denomination.

The ''blind'' man noted his contribution and

peeked quickly at Filali over the rim of his shades. "May God bless you tenfold for your generosity," the beggar said.

"I need to find the Fox."

It was a label, not surprisingly, that Yacoub Jabbar had chosen for himself, claiming the tag was a hold-over from his days with Egyptian military intelligence, playing fox-and-hounds with the Mossad and CIA. Sometimes, Filali thought Jabbar should call himself the Housefly, since he always seemed to know what everyone was doing in Algiers.

The beggar made a show of acting puzzled, stopping short of removing his turban to scratch the balding pate beneath. At last, when he had milked the moment for all it was worth, he suggested a possible hour and address where Jabbar might be found. Suggestion was the closest this wretch ever came to a positive statement, thus avoiding any discussion of money-back guarantees.

Filali ignored the beggar's raised eyebrow, a silent suggestion that the information delivered was worth more money than he had already paid. As he made his slow, cautious way toward the rendezvous, still with the best part of ninety minutes to kill, Filali had no doubt that his inquiry would be reported to Jabbar, his scheduled appointment neatly filed in the arms dealer's memory bank. There had been no discussion of price, but Filali carried more cash than he was likely to need: more, in fact, than the sought-after information was probably worth.

And because he carried so much money, he also carried a gun.

Going armed went against his better judgment, but Algiers—indeed, the country at large—was a madhouse these days. All manner of criminals were cashing in on the long civil war by any means available, from extortion and black marketeering to smash-and-grab robberies. If word got around that Hassan Filali was bound for a meeting with the Fox with cash in his pockets, he would be a prime target for mugging.

But the gun on his hip wasn't primarily intended for thieves. In fact, Filali was more concerned about the Fox himself, professional acquaintance that he was. A man who played all sides against the middle for his own personal profit might do anything, including robbery, if he thought that he could get away with it. Filali, for his part, didn't mind parting with the cash if he got his money's worth.

And, truth be told, the self-styled Fox wasn't Filali's foremost worry. If he obtained the desired information, he would be exchanging one risk for a greater—leaping from the frying pan into the fire, as his American contact might say.

The gun was for his enemies. And if it seemed that they might capture him, Filali meant to save one bullet for himself.

"SO FAR, SO GOOD," Mack Bolan said.

He sat with Gholomreza Kordiyeh in a small, sparsely furnished apartment. They faced each other across a wobbly kitchen table, cleaning, oiling and reloading their Z-84 submachine guns. Both men understood their rest stop was a breather, nothing more, a chance to double-check their hardware and take stock of their achievements so far, while the enemy panicked and ran in circles, looking for targets.

"The FIS and GIA each blame the other for their losses, as you planned," Kordiyeh said. He had touched base with several of his people in Algiers and elsewhere, listening for aftershocks and rumbles of activity. "There have reportedly been counterstrikes by the Anointed Ones—an elite GIA unit—against FIS targets, but someone is also trying to make peace between the factions, even as we speak."

"Who's that?"

"An American," Kordiyeh replied. "A black man, I am told. He calls himself Malik al-Salaam and pretends to be the prophet's new voice on earth."

Bolan had to smile at that, although there was no warmth in his expression, no amusement in his eyes. He had been waiting for the itinerant rabble-rouser to surface, wondering lately if al-Salaam might not choose to bypass the chaos in Algiers and go in search of friendlier climates. The Detroit native's decision to meddle in Bolan's war answered any remaining questions about his involvement in the politics of prejudice.

And it also made him fair game.

"I know who he is," Bolan said, and left it at that. He didn't plan to make a move on Malik al-Salaam at once. The Islamic Brotherhood's leader was alone in Algiers, except for a handful of bodyguards who followed him everywhere, and he presented no more than a nuisance in the broader carnage that had rocked Algeria for most of a decade. There would be time enough to take him out if he crossed Bolan's path directly, or if he forged a visible alliance with one side or the other to enhance his own position locally and in the States.

"It will be difficult for him to calm Houari Boudiaf, I think," Kordiyeh said. "With Nabi Ulmalhama, it might be impossible. The FIS has taken many casualties without inflicting any damage to balance the books. A cease-fire at this point would look too much like a surrender, I believe. Ulmalhama's men must at least draw blood before they can afford to make peace."

More power to them, Bolan thought, as long as they didn't take it out on innocent civilians. "Maybe we can help them out," he said. "Direct them to a couple of the targets on our list and let them do the work."

His ally smiled at that. "I have a telephone number. They will be suspicious of any calls at this juncture, but rage and curiosity might get the better of them. Once they have confirmed the information, strikes are sure to follow."

"The more, the merrier," Bolan said. Noting the grimace on Kordiyeh's face, he softened his tone a bit and added, "This has to be rough, like calling air strikes in on your home town."

"I was not born in Algiers," Kordiyeh replied, "but it is all the same. My country has been torn apart by violence for so long, so many people killed, that it is difficult to summon memories of peace. Sometimes it is required—how do you say?—to cauterize a wound, or else the injured man will bleed to death. My country has been bleeding for a decade now from self-inflicted wounds. We cannot blame the French, although they do support the government in power. Frenchmen do not control the GIA and FIS, or any of the smaller private armies. They are not responsible for the bloodshed that wipes whole towns and villages off the map. We do these things to ourselves."

"Not all of you," the Executioner reminded him. "You're working overtime to stop the war."

"By slaughtering my countrymen." Kordiyeh's tone was bitter, weighted with self-condemnation. "I tell myself that it is justified because the men I kill are men of violence who have murdered women and children. Even so, I must ask myself whether I am any different from those we hunt. How many widows and orphans have I made today? How far do the ends justify the means?"

It was a question Bolan had confronted the first time he served in combat, as a teenager, and it had come back to haunt him when he brought his war home, first against the American Mafia, later branching out to include all manner of human predators on the agenda. He could only answer the question for himself, in his own terms, but he offered that much to his comrade.

"I believe a man has the right to defend himself," he said, "and a duty to defend those less capable than himself. That isn't limited to family and friends, or even to specific human beings. I believe a man is duty-bound to stand up for concepts and principles within the limits of his personal ability. Honor, justice, liberty—they're not just words, unless we choose to turn our backs on what they stand for."

"But the killing…"

"There are predators within the human race, the same as any other species," Bolan said. "The difference is that while an animal will kill for food or to defend itself, the human predators endanger everyone they meet. It's not enough to recognize them and keep out of their way. That may eliminate the risk to me, but only at the price of passing it to someone else— most likely someone who's less able to defend himself. I share the blame, if the next man in line takes a beating intended for me."

"So much blood."

"Force is the only language predators understand," Bolan answered. "Sometimes the law can't handle it, or won't. I believe each person is entitled—make that obligated—to kill, if no other means is available to prevent an atrocity."

"And afterward?" Kordiyeh spoke with the voice of a warrior who had already answered that question for himself, but who still hopes there may be an escape hatch.

"Afterward," the Executioner replied, "you live with it. I have my share of nightmares, but at least they're mine. I didn't hand them off to someone else."

He knew it wasn't much, as pep talks went, but Kordiyeh appeared to draw some meager comfort from it, nodding thoughtfully as he began to reassemble his newly cleaned Z-84 SMG. There was no tremor in his hands, no hesitation as he put the compact weapon back in operating form.

"We are not finished yet," he said at last.

"Not yet," Bolan acknowledged, "but we're getting there."

"I wish to thank you," Kordiyeh said, "for all that you have done to help my country and my people."

"That's not necessary," Bolan told him.

"I believe it is. And only God knows if I will have another chance."

Bolan wasn't a superstitious man, but still he said, "Don't borrow trouble for yourself. The single best weapon you have is confidence. The other side is losing theirs. With any luck, we'll have them on the ropes this time tomorrow."

There was no need to explain what would become of them if they ran out of luck. Kordiyeh was a soldier at war in his own homeland, and he had seen enough corpses to know that "death with dignity" had no meaning in combat. Death was always ugly, always squalid, always miserable. The most a frontline soldier could hope for, short of victory or reinforcements, was a quick and relatively painless end.

Bolan, for his part, wasn't prepared to welcome Death just yet. He meant to go down fighting, if it came to that, and give the Reaper a brisk run for his money. Those of his enemies who managed to outlast the Executioner would know that they had faced the challenge of their miserable lives.

And none of them would ever be the same again.

YACOUB JABBAR WAS smoking hashish in the back room of a dingy Casbah nightclub when the beggar found him, navigating unfamiliar rooms and doorways very skillfully for one who claimed to have no eyesight. Jabbar recognized the new arrival as a member of that unwashed tribe that served him as a conduit of information from the streets, and welcomed him without inviting the malodorous intruder to sit.

The beggar took off his shades, stuck them in a pocket of his filthy shirt and ran his fingers through a thinning mat of salt-and-pepper hair. His smile was tentative, obsequious, revealing auburn-colored teeth with several gaps in front.

"You have something to tell me." It wasn't a question. Jabbar drew on his water pipe and waited while the beggar fidgeted, scratched himself and worked around to spilling his report.

A man was asking for Yacoub Jabbar. Hassan Filali was his name, a fence of stolen goods and sometime information broker in his own right, known to move among the several Muslim underground militias, never forging obvious alliances with any single one. Filali had paid well for an appointment with Yacoub Jabbar—a meeting that the reeking beggar, all apologies and false humility, now hoped Jabbar would willingly affirm.

Why not?

He made a show of pondering the problem, frowning as he took another long hit from the water pipe, then nodded grudgingly, as if committing to some tiresome chore that he couldn't escape. The beggar bobbed his head in gratitude but didn't leave. Jabbar knew he was waiting for a tip, his second payoff for a job that cost him nothing, but he didn't plan to make it easy on this fraud who didn't seem to understand the use of soap.

"What are you waiting for?" Jabbar demanded, frowning like a man who found a cockroach floating in his coffee.

"Um, I thought, that is, I mean to say, perhaps the information might be worth a few dinars, to one so generous," the beggar stammered.

"You've been paid already, by Hassan Filali. You weren't lying to me when you told that story, I suppose?"

"No, sir!" It was good to see a sudden pang of fear distort the beggar's swarthy face. The eyes that could not see when he was begging on the street now sought a rapid exit from the room. "I only meant—"

"You meant to profit twice, at my expense," Jabbar interrupted him. "First, you take money from a stranger and pledge my time without permission, then you ask me to reward you for such gross impertinence."

"I beg your pardon."

"How much did Hassan Filali pay you, then?"

"Ten dinars, sir." He was lying, probably shaving the figure by half or two-thirds. The greasy-looking sweat on his brow told Jabbar that much.

Because the hashish made him mellow, Jabbar decided to be generous. "Give me the ten dinars," he said, "and I make you a present of your life, such as it is."

The sudden flush of relief on the beggar's face told Jabbar that he had been correct about the markdown on his payoff from Hassan Filali. Fifty percent, at least, and probably more. The beggar fished a hand inside one pocket of his threadbare trousers and came out with a jumble of coins. Sorting through them, he extracted two and laid them on the table in front of Jabbar, carefully placing them side by side.

"With your permission, sir...?"

"You may go," Jabbar stated. "And tell no one that we have spoken. Blot Hassan Filali from your mind, or bear the consequences if I hear your story echoed in the street."

"Hassan Filali?" Now the beggar flashed a cunning, crooked smile. "I am afraid that I know no one by that name."

"Maintain your ignorance, and you shall have no cause for fear," Jabbar informed him, waving the beggar off and out of the room.

Alone once more, Jabbar pushed the water pipe away from him and relaxed on his overstuffed cushions. The beggar had presented him with a pretty problem, and he needed his full wits about him in order to deal with it properly.

The meeting with Hassan Filali was no problem, in and of itself. They spoke from time to time, every six or eight weeks on average, exchanging information on the troubles in Algeria, sometimes discussing other topics that related only tangentially to the nation's long civil war. Yacoub Jabbar had known—well, suspected, at least—that Filali was collecting data for someone else, perhaps an outsider, but such matters didn't concern him, as long as he was promptly paid and felt no repercussions from the information he dispensed. A consummate mercenary and proud of it, Jabbar had no personal stake in the violence that ravaged this country, except insofar as he found a way to profit from the carnage.

To that end, he considered the scheduled meeting with Hassan Filali from various viewpoints, seeking the angle of maximum benefit to himself. For starters, Filali would certainly pay him for data transmitted; that was understood from past transactions and taken for granted. On occasion, when they met by chance, Jabbar was satisfied to trade one piece of information for another he didn't possess, but when a customer came asking for him, making an appointment, it was strictly cash-and-carry.

With that much settled in advance, Jabbar turned his thoughts toward parallel means of deriving a profit from his meeting with Filali. It didn't escape him that Filali's request for an appointment—a rare occurrence, in itself—coincided with a nearly unprecedented spate of violence in Algiers and several other cities. From appearances, if they could be trusted, it seemed that the Armed Islamic Group was locked in a death struggle with the Islamic Salvation Front, each band committed to extermination of the other at any cost. Of course, the two private armies had been rivals from their inception, often trading barbs in print and sometimes bullets in the street, but there was nothing in the past to indicate such brutal internecine mayhem in the offing. As an observer of human nature in general, and its dark side in particular, Jabbar had trouble accepting that Filali's sudden request for a meeting was unrelated to the killing in the streets.

The information vendor was suspicious of coincidence.

Only one question remained: if Hassan Filali was somehow involved in the violence, or sought information on someone who was, then who was his sponsor? An adversary of that sponsor would pay well for the names of his enemies in times like these. Jabbar could name his own price for information that would tip the balance of power one way of the other, either to the FIS or to the GIA.

Jabbar imagined a suitcase filled with cash, perhaps with gold. Once or twice, he had even accepted payment in drugs, but the narcotics business was too risky for a novice to break in at the management level, and he had ruled out such payments for the future.

Cash or gold, then...but from whom?

It made a difference, since he only had one opportunity to make the overture, one chance to get it right. If Filali was in league with the GIA, and Jabbar approached them with an offer to sell out Filali, he would be signing his own death warrant. Likewise, if Filali had joined forces with the FIS. It was a matter of determining which side already owned Filali's soul, and which would pay to pick his brain.

The original notion of Filali working for an outside agency came back to Jabbar, demanding his fuller attention. If his first impression was correct, and Filali had a foreign sponsor, maybe someone with a vested interest in the mayhem, then Jabbar's prospects for profit were improved dramatically.

Jabbar could auction Filali off to the highest bidder, once he had Filali in the bag. It might just be the best deal he had made all week.

Jabbar was steady on his feet as he rose from the cushions, barely feeling the hashish now. He had to make some phone calls, double-check his options, but he trusted his instincts.

Of course, he couldn't make a habit of snatching his sources and selling them off like livestock for slaughter, but it should work, just this once.

In fact, he doubted that Hassan Filali would even be missed.

NABI ULMALHAMA had torn his radio out of the wall while the treasonous broadcast was still in progress, missing the brief tirade's conclusion as he hurled the instrument away from him, across his study, smashing it against the doorframe. He was dizzy for a moment with the sudden, overwhelming power of his rage, recoiling as if struck when Mohammed Zeroual laid a hand on his arm. He almost lashed out at the man, but his blurry vision cleared in time to let him recognize his second in command.

"Traitors!" he roared, spittle flying in Zeroual's face. "They will perish for this! Their wives and children and their children's children will be wiped off the face of the earth!"

"Nabi," Zeroual said calmly in a low-pitched voice, "a moment, please. Before we act, a moment to consider something."

"What? Consider what?" the leader of the FIS demanded, trembling with rage.

"What you heard just now, before—" Zeroual gestured toward the scattered radio components "—did it sound like anyone we know?"

The question startled Ulmalhama, forcing him to think beyond the blinding anger. "Anyone we know?" he asked, confused. "Husam al-Din presents the word."

That much was true. Husam al-Din had been selected by default to operate the pirate radio and broadcast propaganda for the FIS, because he had been trained in electronics and he had a striking voice.

The voice—

Zeroual saw recognition dawn on Ulmalhama's face. "You see, then," he confirmed, pronouncing judgment. "Husam began the broadcast, but someone else cut in, somehow. The last bit, the betrayal, was delivered in a different voice."

"You are certain?" Ulmalhama asked, but he already knew the answer. He was certain, and he would have recognized the truth immediately, if his rage hadn't betrayed him, overwhelming common sense.

"There can be no mistaking Husam's voice," his number two replied.

"But someone else..." Ulmalhama's mind was reeling at the prospect. It was almost worse than betrayal by one he had trusted. At least, in that case, he would have known what to do, how to retaliate. "How could this happen? Can they intercept the signal?"

"Anything is possible, but I believe a simpler explanation is available.

"Then share it, by all means." The anger was returning, edging out confusion. Ulmalhama hated it when his subordinate turned coy, forcing him to ask questions instead of simply sharing any information he possessed. One day, perhaps, if Mohammed pushed him too far—

"It would be possible to find out where the broadcast came from," Zeroual replied. "Not easy, I grant you, but possible. Once the transmitter's location was known, the rest would be simple."

"The rest?"

"A determined man or group of men could interrupt the broadcast at its source," Zeroual said. "Kill or disable Husam and his assistants by any means available, and the slayers could present the message of their choice."

It was even worse than treason in the ranks, Ulmalhama realized. Some unknown enemy had the unmitigated gall to murder one of his most valued followers—his minister of propaganda, in effect—and then, on top of that grave insult, heaped the injury of turning Ulmalhama's own equipment against him, broadcasting a message that slandered the Islamic Salvation Front.

True, the unknown interloper had also taken a swipe at the GIA, denouncing both groups with equal venom, but that only confused matters further. Ulmalhama's first choice for a suspect in the treacherous attack, given recent events, would have been someone from the Armed Islamic Group itself, yet why would any soldier of the GIA denounce his own brothers as traitors to God? Wouldn't he have seized the opportunity to praise the GIA, in fact, while heaping scorn upon Ulmalhama's private army?

It simply made no sense. He felt the anger coming

back full-force, compounded by confusion. Any moment now, his head would start to throb with pain.

One thing was clear: he had to avenge his personal embarrassment and the humiliation heaped upon the FIS in this unseemly episode. It was a slight that he couldn't forgive, dared not forget. His soldiers and rivals alike would be waiting and watching to see how he dealt with the insult. They would all expect payment in blood, and he would gladly oblige them.

If only he knew who to blame.

"There might be more to this than meets the eye," Zeroual said, as if reading Ulmalhama's thoughts.

"Explain," he commanded.

"This much is obvious. Someone despises both our movement and the Armed Islamic Group to brand us all as traitors to God. Of course, no one with any common sense will believe such slanderous lies."

Not much, Ulmalhama thought. He had been spoon-feeding identical messages to the people of Algiers for years on end—identical, that was, except in the naming of himself and his followers as godless villains. How many had believed *his* propaganda? Had it all been a colossal waste of time?

"Someone who hates me *and* Houari Boudiaf?" No matter how he tried, Ulmalhama couldn't resist personalizing the insult. "The MEA, perhaps? Some other group that envies our success?"

"Perhaps." Zeroual sounded skeptical. "It has occurred to me, however, that the author of this outrage—and, perhaps, of the attacks that we have suffered recently—may represent another enemy."

It clicked for Ulmalhama, then. The same thing

Wasim Ruholla had suggested, after his meeting with the black man from America. What was his name, again? No matter.

What did matter, at the moment, was the suspicion blossoming in Ulmalhama's mind. He wondered, suddenly, if Ruholla might have been on the right track after all. Perhaps a foreign power—the Americans, for instance—had provoked the recent fireworks between his militia and the Islamic Salvation Front. Was it any coincidence, then, that a self-described American dissident and professed Muslim leader should happen to be in Algiers when the shooting started? One, moreover, who was said to covet favors from Iran and Libya alike?

"The black American," Ulmalhama blurted out. "What is his name?"

Zeroual looked confused for a moment, then understanding dawned in his eyes. "Malik al-Salaam," he replied. "A minister of the Islamic Brotherhood in the United States."

Of course. It all made sense to Ulmalhama, now. He knew enough of American history to remember that the FBI and other intelligence agencies made a habit of infiltrating domestic dissident groups, both right- and left-wing. Sometimes, he recalled, when a group couldn't be infiltrated, a counterfeit rival was created by the government, funded from taxpayers' money, luring members away from the legitimate movement, sidetracking their efforts and energy in hopeless make-work exercises, frequently entrapping them in schemes to break the law, which thereby landed them in prison.

"I would like to meet this Malik al-Salaam," he said, an icy calm suffusing him, damping the heat of his anger. Noting the surprise on Zeroual's face, his superior put on his best plastic smile.

"I think," he told his number two, "that we have much to talk about. Do you not agree?"

CHAPTER ELEVEN

Keeping up the pressure. Turning up the heat.

No matter how you phrased it, part of Bolan's battle strategy had always been to keep his adversaries reeling, staggered by one blow after another, robbing them of rest and a chance to regroup. Squeezing them until something cracked, and they began to fall apart.

It hadn't taken long to spark a fierce shooting war between the rival factions in Algeria. His work was half done for him by the time the Executioner arrived, with years of tension, propaganda and occasional skirmishes laying the powder trail, a fuse that would ignite a deadly conflagration in the streets.

All Bolan really had to do was strike the match.

He could have left it there, could have sat back and watched the soldiers of the GIA and FIS annihilate one another, but he didn't think much of war as a spectator sport. If there were battles to be fought, Bolan preferred the role of a participant.

And so he kept the pressure on.

His target of the moment was a field officer of the Movement of the Islamic State. Thus far, the MEA had not ranked high on Bolan's list of enemies, and his selection of the present mark had nothing to do with equality, spreading the mayhem around. Rather, he was adding spice to the lethal stew that was already simmering, putting a new twist in the convoluted trail of action that had marked the past twenty-four hours.

Perched on a rooftop in downtown Algiers, Bolan was alone with his weapon, an SVD Dragunov sniper rifle provided by Gholomreza Kordiyeh. Through the PSO-1x4 scope, he had picked out his target in an office located across the street and two doors east. Now, all he had to do was watch and wait.

Kordiyeh, for his part, hadn't followed Bolan to the rooftop. He had wanted to come, but his part of the strike was critical. Bolan wouldn't trust it to an underling whom he had never met, much less seen tested under fire.

Not that Kordiyeh had to do any shooting, this time. In fact, all he had to do was make a telephone call. The dialing wasn't difficult, once they obtained the number, but his message—scripted and rehearsed until he knew the words by heart—was everything.

Downrange, the MEA "major" was shuffling some papers, pausing now and then to look at one more closely. He jumped a little when the phone rang, scowling at the show of personal weakness, reaching for the handset to lift it on the second ring.

The office wasn't wired, and there was no tap on the phone line, but Bolan knew what the target was hearing, could almost predict his response. On the other end of the line, Kordiyeh was introducing himself as a spokesman for the Armed Islamic Group, speaking in clipped but proper tones as he accused the MEA of launching violent raids against the GIA. Shock and anger vied for dominance on the target's face, nearly life-sized in the field of Bolan's telescopic sight.

Kordiyeh had learned one thing about the MEA: all incoming calls to the office were monitored, automatically recorded to keep track of threats and warnings, any tips that might be garbled in translation by a careless operator.

Kordiyeh would have gotten to the meat of his message by now, advising the mark that his minutes were numbered. Bolan had the crosshairs centered on his face as the target blinked, half turned toward the window and seemed almost to meet his gaze across five hundred yards of darkness.

The Dragunov was basically an oversized Kalashnikov, some six feet in length, and half of that the slender barrel. It was chambered for the 7.62 mm rimmed cartridge, using the basic Kalashnikov action, simplified to eliminate full-auto fire and smoothed for greater precision in single-shot kills. Fitted with a 10-round box magazine, it had an effective range of more than 800 meters, closing that gap between shooter and target in just under one second.

Bolan held his mark between the target's eyes and stroked the trigger once. Across the street, glass shattered with a crisp, bright sound. His target staggered from the impact of an armor-piercing round that hardly felt the windowpane at all. The entry wound was clean and dark, as if inflicted with a power drill, but when the bullet exited, it took a chunk of skull two inches in diameter, propelling blood and mangled gray matter against the nearest wall.

The man was dead before he dropped the telephone receiver, slumping backward in his chair. It was enough, but Bolan gave him one more, anyway, a clean shot through the shadowed oval of his open mouth. The second round propelled his lifeless target through a half-turn to the left, his body sagging lower, lower, until it was lost from sight.

Another job well done.

If there were operators manning telephones across the street, they would already have reported Kordiyeh's threat, coupled with the target's lack of a response, the strange sounds emanating from his office. If the switchboard was on automatic, there would still be tape to educate whoever found his body in the morning. Either way, it all came out the same.

Bolan had stamped the GIA's signature on this one, inviting the Movement of the Islamic State to join in the violence racking Algiers. Whether the militiamen came out to play was of no real consequence at this point. Bolan had bloodied the waters even further, adding yet another crime to the GIA's tab, presenting yet another group of suspects for his next move against the Armed Islamic Group.

HASSAN FILALI WAS ten minutes early for his meeting with Yacoub Jabbar. It wasn't simply common courtesy that made him come ahead of time, though he was punctual by nature, in defiance of the laid-back attitude that dominated Middle Eastern life. Because Filali was an information merchant in the middle of a three- or four-way civil war, because he served outsiders—specifically, the CIA—his every waking moment, every move he made, was shadowed by concerns about security.

There was no price upon Filali's head, but it would only take one slip, a single lapse in judgment, to put the hounds on his trail. Consulting Jabbar was a risk in itself, but Filali believed he was safe.

As safe, that was, as anyone could claim to be in modern-day Algeria.

The meeting place dictated by the beggar was a smallish tavern in the Casbah district, off the beaten track for all but the most hearty—or foolhardy—tourists. Those who gathered there between sunset and dawn were likely to be criminals, though relatively petty ones. As Filali's eyes adjusted to the murky lamplight, he recognized several faces among those present: two pickpockets, a small-time narcotics dealer and a middle-aged pimp who was said to maintain ties with slave dealers, farther to the south and east.

There was no sign of Jabbar, so he found a table in one corner and settled in to wait. Instead of asking for his order, though, the hostess who approached him simply verified his name, then told Filali that Jabbar would see him now.

Unsettled by the fact that Jabbar was ahead of him and obviously well prepared, Filali trailed the woman through an archway with a beaded curtain, left along a corridor where lights were dim and far between. Filali counted six rooms as they passed, three on a side, before the hostess stopped outside the fourth door on the left. She rapped lightly, waited for the summons, held the door open for Filali, then closed it softly behind him.

"Welcome, my friend!" Jabbar made no attempt to rise from where he sat, arms folded, covering his chest. The smile he wore might have been genuine, but Filali took nothing for granted. Once again, he was glad for the weight of the small pistol in his waistband, pressing tight against his spine.

The men didn't shake hands, for this was principally a Western custom. They traded perfunctory compliments instead, and Filali settled into his chair. There was no offer of refreshments, nothing to delay Filali's getting to the point. He understood that time was money, to himself as well as to Jabbar. He launched into the spiel he had rehearsed, without further preliminary small talk.

"I have been following the recent troubles," he stated. No point in asking if Jabbar had done the same; it went without saying. "There are some points that remain obscure, however."

"And you wish them to be clarified," Jabbar remarked. He wasn't asking, but rather stating a fact. Filali had requested the meeting, hence he needed information from the city's leading unofficial source. Jabbar didn't ask why Filali wanted the information; he would no more seek the names of Filali's clients than he would reveal his own.

"As you say," Filali acknowledged. "If the whereabouts of certain individuals was known, it could be, ah, most lucrative."

Jabbar's face broke into a smile. He understood

such business, dealing in the lives of wanted men. It made no difference that the answer to a simple question could mean life or death to someone he had never met—or even to a friend, if that should be the case. Jabbar would answer, or he would refuse, depending on the price. All else was secondary to an independent operator who had no stake in the outcome of a never-ending civil war.

"These individuals," Jabbar replied, "have many friends who would lament their passing, and who might seek vengeance if they came to any harm."

"I understand," Filali said.

Jabbar wasn't displaying fear over the notion of reprisals from the GIA or FIS. Rather, Filali understood, he had begun negotiation of the selling price by stating the obvious: that his life would be in danger if he shared the information he possessed. Filali knew that in advance, and Jabbar knew he knew it. It was simply part of the negotiating process to establish risk, a foolproof means of driving up the price.

"These men," Jabbar went on, "cherish their privacy. They strive to safeguard it at any cost."

Filali felt the short hairs bristling on his nape. This could be more palaver over money, but he didn't like the predatory smile Jabbar was showing him. It put him in mind of hungry crocodiles.

"The risk, of course, would be considered. We are businessmen," Filali said. "We understand such things."

He instantly regretted the attempt to place himself on common footing with Jabbar. His host was nodding, and the hungry smile was still in place as he replied, "I knew that you would understand, Hassan. It's nothing personal, of course. A simple economic matter, if you will."

Filali heard the door open behind him, bolted from his chair and cursed Jabbar, his right hand darting for the pistol wedged into the small of his back. He made it, grazed the warm steel with his fingertips, half turning as the sound of heavy boots came up behind him in a rush. The wooden stock of a Kalashnikov assault rifle swung toward his face, and there was no time to deflect it, no time to recoil or blunt the stunning impact.

Stretched out on the floor, Filali felt as if a small explosive charge had detonated on the inside of his skull. His whole head felt misshapen, too large for his body, as if it were filled with liquid, like some gross balloon. He tasted blood and tried to spit it out, along with something sharp and flat—a tooth?—that was suddenly stuck to his tongue. Filali couldn't tell if he had been successful in his effort, since his mouth filled up with blood again at once. There seemed to be no stopping it.

He moaned and made a feeble effort to resist as rough hands turned him over, found the pistol that was punishing his kidney, whisked it from his belt and made it disappear. He was defenseless now against his enemies.

The good news was that he was also losing consciousness.

With any luck at all, Filali thought, he might wake up in Paradise, and miss what lay in store for him if he survived.

THE SILENT BEEPER vibrated once, and then again, as Bolan cleared the gangplank of a freighter that flew a Liberian flag, demanding his attention at a moment when he had none to spare. Behind him on the freighter's bridge, three men lay dead, all shot at point-blank range. Two more, both locals, had been cut down trying to defend the cargo in the freighter's hold.

Five dead, and he still wasn't finished with the diesel-powered workhorse known as *Lucky Lady,* painted on her hull in fading cursive script. A weathered paint job was the least of the ship's problems at the moment. Her crew had sampled Bolan's wrath already, and the ship herself was next in line.

Below, with the dead sentries, he had found a shipment of automatic weapons, ammunition and plastic explosives purchased at bargain-basement rates from a needy nation of the former Soviet Bloc. If asked about the shipment at some future date, the vendors could reply with perfect candor that the hardware had been purchased by an agent in Liberia, with end-user certificates and all other mandatory paperwork duly filed in triplicate. Ostensibly, the arms and plastique were intended for use by Liberia's national defense force, a friendly nation with no known links to terrorist activity. Of course, if the buyers had lied, or if the shipment was illegally diverted somehow after leaving its port of embarkation, the suppliers couldn't be held responsible in any way. Nor would they feel obliged to pay back the money.

Business was business, after all.

Bolan had come prepared with plastique of his

own, but after checking out the *Lucky Lady*'s cargo for himself, he saw no need of using up Filali's stock. The detonator he was carrying would work as well on one charge as another. All he had to do was slit the oilcloth covering one block of plastique in the first crate that he opened and insert the blasting cap. The trigger device resembled a small kitchen timer, and he gave himself six minutes—time enough, and then some, to evacuate the ship and clear the blast zone if he wasn't intercepted on the way.

In fact, his luck held…except for the beeper. Bolan deliberately ignored it as he moved along the dock, past other dark and silent freighters, their names inscribed in French or German, Arabic or Spanish, one of them in Greek. He wondered in passing whether any of the rest held secrets like the *Lucky Lady*'s. Drugs, perhaps, or some other contraband bound for Algeria's thriving black market.

A war zone was always good for business, and the profiteers were never far away if there was cordite in the wind.

Two minutes left and counting by Bolan's watch, when he reached the end of the dock and slid into the waiting sedan, with Kordiyeh behind the steering wheel. He still ignored the beeper, even when it shivered on his belt a second time, the callback indicating urgency.

Which meant, in turn, that it could only be bad news.

"Not yet," he said, as Kordiyeh turned the ignition key, prepared to drive away. His comrade killed the engine, sat and waited with him in the darkness, counting down the *Lucky Lady*'s doomsday numbers.

When it blew, they felt the shock wave first, heard it a heartbeat later as the hatches blew, then saw bright plumes of fire erupting from belowdecks, reaching for the stars. The blast was powerful enough to drop a good-sized office building, and it broke the freighter's back, likewise inflicting fatal damage on the ships nosed in on either side. From where he sat, Bolan could hear the rifle ammunition cooking off like popcorn in the distance, losing track of it as the vessel settled, burning to the waterline.

"Okay, let's go."

He checked the beeper only then, when they were moving, and confirmed what he already knew. The callback number was a cutout that would relay Bolan to a secure, scrambled line in the basement of the U.S. Embassy. Since it wasn't the number he had memorized for contacts with Filali, it could only mean that there had been a breakdown in connecting with the local contract agent.

That was bad.

"I need to make a phone call," he told Kordiyeh, "as soon as possible."

"On a secure line?" the Algerian inquired.

"It shouldn't matter," Bolan said.

Without further questions, Kordiyeh drove directly to the nearest good-sized hotel, discharging Bolan near the entrance and bypassing the valet service to park it himself within sight of the doors. Inside the lobby, deserted except for a concierge and the young clerk on the registration desk, Bolan made a bee-line for the public telephone, thumbed in the necessary coins and dialed the cutout number.

Two rings, followed by a click-clack from the hardware at the other end, then two more rings before a male voice answered speaking Arabic. No indication that the man behind the voice was an American, much less a CIA employee at the U.S. Embassy.

"It's Striker," Bolan said, using the standard code name.

"Ah, of course." He heard a Boston accent now, betraying the Company's fondness for Ivy League types. "We have a problem, I'm afraid."

He made no comment, waiting. It was obvious they had a "problem," or he wouldn't have been paged. As for the details, he wasn't about to play the role of supplicant.

"Um, well," the man from Boston said at last, "it seems we've lost our local contact, if you get my drift."

"Define 'lost,'" Bolan said.

"He was supposed to have a meeting scheduled with another information broker," Boston said. "An independent operator called Yacoub Jabbar. We know that much because he left word with a friend—Filali did, I mean. 'If I'm not back by such and such a time, call so-and-so.' You know the drill."

"I do," Bolan confirmed.

"Well, then, long story short, Filali went to keep his date, and never came back home again. He was supposed to check in with his friend by 1930 hours. The friend gave him ninety minutes extra, then he dropped a coin to us. We told him something would be done, if possible."

"And is it?" Bolan asked him.

"Is it...?"

"Possible."

"Officially? No way. We don't spy on our friends, the cultural attaché's office has no role in gathering intelligence, yada yada. As far as the embassy is concerned, we've never heard of Hassan Filali, much less hired him to spy on native dissidents."

Which meant they were cutting him loose, Bolan realized.

Unless...

"I'll need an address for Yacoub Jabbar," he said, "and any background information you can share."

"Of course," Boston said, crisp and business-like, with more than a hint of relief in his tone. "You have a pencil handy?"

"I'll remember it," the Executioner replied.

And so he did.

HASSAN FILALI WOKE to pain. It came at him in dizzy, stomach-churning waves, the nausea only worsened by a stench of vomit that told him he had already soiled himself, even before he regained consciousness.

When he opened his eyes, the first thing he saw was his own hairy chest and paunch, his naked lap, stout thighs. The vista told Filali he was seated in a chair, stark naked, with his head throbbing head slumped forward, chin on chest. His arms had been secured behind him, somehow, fingertips already going numb from where bonds of wire or narrow cord restricted circulation at his wrists. Below, his legs had also been secured to the chair that supported his weight, knees separated by a foot or so. He tried to move one foot, and felt the sticky, hair-pulling sensation of duct tape wrapped around his calves and ankles.

He was helpless. Trapped. Most probably as good as dead.

The only question, now, was whether his abductors would be merciful and kill him swiftly, or elaborate his suffering as part of an interrogation. From the very fact that he was still alive and trussed like a goose bound for the oven, rather than reposing in a ditch somewhere with bullets in his brain, Filali made an educated guess that he couldn't expect an easy death.

So be it, then. He would consider it a test of faith and courage.

"He's awake," said a gruff male voice, emanating from a point somewhere to Filali's left, beyond the scope of his bleary peripheral vision. He remained immobile, hoping that his captors would leave him in peace for a little while longer, but it wasn't to be.

Denim-clad legs shuffled into his visual field, scuffed brown boots on the feet. A hairy-backed hand moved past his face, angling for some target lower down. Filali couldn't help crying out as the stranger pinched one of his nipples between callused thumb and forefinger, giving it a vicious ninety-degree twist.

"I told you he's awake," the same voice said.

In lurching to avoid the painful grip, Filali saw his tormentor's face. It wasn't one he recognized, but the fact that the man wore no mask boded ill for Filali's chances of survival. The bastards didn't care if he knew who they were, and that, in turn, told him that they had no fear of facing vengeance at some later date.

Because he would be dead, unable to reveal their names.

"You're right, as always, Akhmed," said another voice. More cultured than the first, this was, and all the more sinister for that.

A second man moved into Filali's field of vision, and the groggy captive had no trouble recognizing this one. Arif Boumedienne was well-known as the second-ranking officer of the Armed Islamic Group. His name featured prominently in newspaper stories, on arrest warrants—and, some said, on hit lists compiled by government-sanctioned death squads. Still, he remained alive and at large, apparently none the worse for wear. Just now, despite the hour—whatever that was—Boumedienne seemed vigorous and well rested, prepared to go all night without a wink of sleep.

Bad news, Filali told himself.

"So, you've rejoined us," Boumedienne said. "I was worried, for a moment, that Brahim might have struck you too hard. A coma would be inconvenient at the present time."

"For me, as well," Filali replied, although he didn't mean it. At this moment, short of swift and painless death, a coma was the very best escape he could have wished for. Blissful darkness. An escape from pain.

"You have a sense of humor," Boumedienne said. "That's good. It indicates a certain level of intelligence. If you were a retarded oaf, my task would be more arduous...and less rewarding."

Practicing his silence for the time when he would truly need it, any moment now, Filali made no reply.

"You have imagination," Boumedienne said, "and that, ironically, will be my most effective weapon. Tell me—when you've thought about this moment in the past, anticipating capture and interrogation, was it terrible?"

Again, no answer from the man bound to the straight-backed chair.

"Of course it was," Boumedienne answered his own question, scarcely missing a beat. "And yet, you tell yourself that you've imagined the worst of it. Nothing I devise and do to you can possibly exceed your expectations. You have already beaten me, here."

As Boumedienne finished speaking, he raised one hand and tapped a slim index finger against one temple, indicating the mind. Filali, for his part, kept his mouth shut.

"But you're wrong," he went on, as if Filali had, in fact, responded to his words. "Whatever you've devised in terms of torment, I have anticipated and elaborated. My refinements will exceed your wildest dreams...or nightmares."

Filali was perspiring now, although the room was cool, perhaps a basement, earthen walls ideal for soaking up his screams. He considered making some defiant statement, but refrained. His silence, if he only had the strength to hold his tongue, would be defiance enough.

"You have considered all the normal angles of attack," Arif Boumedienne continued, delivering his surmises as statements of fact. "Beatings, electric shock, perhaps the water treatment. Strategic application of flame is often effective. But they all seem so…mundane.

"It is a fact," the GIA guerrilla said, "that most interrogators have no more imagination than their subjects. They begin with the extremities, perhaps the genitalia, or else restrict themselves to body blows that could prove fatal, rather than persuasive. I propose, therefore, to try a new approach. It's not original, I fear." Boumedienne couldn't resist a wicked smile. "In fact, between the two of us, I got the notion from a James Bond novel. May I trust that you will not reveal my source?"

Boumedienne laughed at his own little joke, Filali waiting, trying to suppress the tremors that rippled through his body like aftershocks from an earthquake. Any show of weakness, now, was a betrayal of himself.

"You see," Boumedienne explained, "where most interrogators fail is in forgetting that a strong man, with the proper stimulation, might divorce himself from pain. There is a mental cutoff switch—a breaker fuse, if you prefer—that finally short-circuits pain.

"There is one place, however, that a man cannot escape…because it is the very place he goes away to hide." Boumedienne stood smiling at him for another moment, then he raised one hand and tapped his skull again. "In here. The mind. No man escapes his head...unless, of course, the head is separated from the rest of him."

That brought another self-appreciative laugh. Filali's captor was his own best audience, it seemed. At last, though, he was getting to the point.

"Despite my eagerness to test these methods, you still have a chance to save yourself, Hassan. I know the following—you deal in information for a price, and someone has employed you to report on the activities and movements of the Armed Islamic Group. I mean to know the name of your employer. Neither of us will rest easy, until you have told me what you know."

"I know your father was a camel with the pox," Filali said. "I see it in your face. But there is nothing more."

"Defiance," Boumedienne said. "Most excellent. I hoped you would resist, Hassan. It's good to see you understand the spirit of the game."

A gesture to the hairy one, and Boumedienne's companion stepped out of sight, returning a moment later, pushing a wheeled metal cart in front of him. Atop the car, Filali saw a plastic tray like those found in so many cafeterias. Instead of dishes, though, this tray was filled with shiny surgical instruments, most of them sporting needles, probes or hooks.

"Now, then," his captor said. "Shall we begin?"

BOLAN HAD PLANNED to take Yacoub Jabbar alone, until Kordiyeh reminded him of the potential language barrier. Slipping, he chided himself, accepting his comrade's offer to tag along as an interpreter, in case the target came up short on English skills.

"He will have bodyguards," Kordiyeh warned, as he parked the car in a dark alleyway behind Jabbar's home.

"I only need the one alive," Bolan replied.

They checked their weapons once more out of habit and confirmed that all were fully loaded, sound suppressors in place on the Z-84 submachine guns. It was second nature to the Executioner, the list of mundane chores that went before a killing. Only this time, he required one prisoner alive or the whole exercise would be in vain.

The building was situated in a better neighborhood, which meant police drove through the district several times each day and swept up any beggars who had found their way this far. The homes resembled one another, though without the cookie-cutter similarity of American tract houses. All were done in stucco, most possessing a detached garage for rolling stock. And most of them were dark, this hour of the night.

Most, but not all.

From the appearance of the house, lights showing from one room only, Bolan calculated that the guards were awake, drinking coffee to stay that way, while their employer was most likely in bed, perhaps dreaming of the day's successful transactions.

Bolan didn't know how many guards would be watching Jabbar through the night, but he counted on a minimum of two. Approaching the house, he noted that the lighted window was open perhaps six inches, thin curtains ruffling in the fitful breeze. Up close, he heard male voices engaged in a good-natured argument, the tone familiar from a thousand bivouacs, although the meaning of the words eluded him.

He used the muzzle of his sound suppressor to ease the left-hand curtain back an inch or two, enough for him to scan the room inside. It was the kitchen, with two young men seated at the table, facing each other across a spread of dominoes. Both wore pistols in black shoulder rigs, and the man on Bolan's right was smiling, prepared to celebrate his victory.

But he would never get the chance.

Bolan's Z-84 stuttered twice, short bursts, taking his targets from fifteen feet away, and they hit the floor in tandem, making more noise as they fell than Bolan's gunshots had. Instead of waiting to discover if the noise had roused his prey, he shoved the window open wide and tumbled through it, bringing down the curtains in a swirl about his shoulders.

Unopposed, Bolan moved through the silent house as if he were a tenant long familiar with the floor plan. He found the master bedroom and its light switch, stood looming over the king-sized bed before its solitary occupant came fully awake.

Bolan slapped the information broker twice to get his attention, then showed him the gun. "Do you speak English?" he demanded.

Jabbar was blinking rapidly and *thinking* rapidly, as well. "I do," he said.

"That's good," the Executioner replied. "We need to talk."

CHAPTER TWELVE

Mack Bolan was an expert when it came to rattling cages, stirring up the human predators who were his natural enemies. He had first learned the skill as a young Green Beret, then refined it after he brought his war stateside, matching wits and wills with the grand old men of the Mafia, moving on from there to challenge—and defeat—terrorists of every political and religious persuasion under the sun. Already, in Algiers, he had applied his skill to the Armed Islamic Group and to the rival Islamic Salvation Front, turning one against the other in an all-out shooting war.

But this was different.

This was personal.

Bolan had known Hassan Filali for less than two days, in fact had met him only twice, speaking with him on the telephone twice more for only moments at a time. They couldn't be described as friends, in any true sense of the word.

But that made no difference at all.

They were comrades, at least for the duration of the present mission, and Filali had been kidnapped—perhaps killed, by now—while serving the Central Intelligence Agency. Serving Bolan, in fact, as another set of eyes and ears, another source of vital field intelligence on unfamiliar ground. As a comrade in arms, however briefly, Filali was entitled to the Executioner's protection.

Failing that, he was entitled to revenge.

Jabbar had put the wheels of the kidnapping in motion, reaching out to contacts in the Muslim paramilitary underground when he learned that Filali sought details on the recent violence and was willing to pay hard cash for specific information. According to Jabbar himself, he had contacted members of the GIA and FIS alike. The Armed Islamic Group had outbid their competitors, and so it was arranged for their goons to lift Filali, when he kept a scheduled appointment with Jabbar in the Casbah.

Jabbar had little to say beyond that, and nothing at all to say after Bolan was finished with him. His housekeeper would find the bodies when she came to work and make the necessary, fruitless calls for help. That part of it was done, a portion of the debt repaid in blood.

The information broker had been unable to reveal if Filali was alive or dead. The contract agent had been damaged, but still breathing, when the GIA commandos dragged him through the back door of a seedy Casbah tavern, dumped him in their stolen car and drove away into the night. Beyond that…who could say?

Someone inside the GIA, presumably, and to that end, the Executioner was mounting a campaign designed to shake the information loose, no matter what the cost. By 9:00 a.m., he had already razed two hide-outs in the suburbs of Algiers, where members of the Armed Islamic Group killed time between assignments in the field. He had killed seven men so far that morning, but at each location he left one man coherent and breathing, if not precisely in the best of health. The lucky two were spared to serve as messengers, and each had memorized a simple message for the renegade militia's brass, translated into Arabic by Gholomreza Kordiyeh.

"I want Hassan Filali back alive," the dazed and hurting men were told. "If it's too late for that, I want the men who killed him."

Simple.

All he had to do from that point on was keep the heat cranked up beneath his squirming enemies, repeat the message every time he made another strike against the GIA, and hope that someone at the top knew when to fold a losing hand. If they refused to yield, Bolan would keep the pressure on, keep terrorizing terrorists until he blew their house down, until there was no one from the home team left alive.

Unless they killed him first.

Bolan didn't rule out the possibility, but he refused to let it slow him. No sane combatant was immune to fear, but the successful ones fought on, regardless. Once a soldier made a habit of surrendering to trepidation, he was finished. Each retreat was easier in turn, until running away came naturally. And then, one day, there was nowhere to run. He was faced with the choice of surrender or death—assuming his enemies gave him the option.

Bolan, by contrast, was a master at controlling fear, using that precious energy to power through when things looked blackest, and the odds were seemingly unbeatable.

And he was only getting started in Algiers.

For Bolan's enemies, the worst was yet to come.

KEEP ONE ALIVE.

The American's command was difficult to obey, when the enemy was pouring fire at Kordiyeh from automatic weapons, clearly intent on snuffing his life. He had already shot two men—both corpses, from the look of them—and there were still at least three more behind their barricade of crates and boxes in a corner of the gloomy warehouse, fighting for their lives.

The sound of shots behind him, from the general direction of the warehouse office, told him that Belasko had engaged the other GIA commandos, pinning them down. Or would it prove to be the other way around?

The gunfire died almost as quickly as it had begun, and Kordiyeh risked a backward glance, crouching in the shadow of an ancient forklift, searching for a sign to tell him who had been victorious. No gunmen rushed him from the office, an encouraging sign in itself, but he didn't relax until he saw Belasko on his feet and moving in the small, glass-walled enclosure of the office, obviously checking out the dead.

Keep one alive.

Another rain of bullets from behind the makeshift barricade made Kordiyeh recoil, his shoulders hunched, anticipating lethal impact, but the forklift

shielded him. It would be something else if those he
had engaged decided they should rush him, all of
them firing at once and charging from different directions. He would be lucky just to kill them, then, much
less to take a living prisoner.

There were footsteps behind him, and Kordiyeh
half turned toward the sound, tracking with his Z-84
submachine gun, relaxing as Belasko slid into cover
beside him. It was getting crowded in the narrow
space behind the warehouse vehicle, but Kordiyeh
was glad to have the tall American beside him.

"How many back there?" Bolan asked, jerking his
head in the direction of the crates and boxes serving
as a minifort.

"Three men, I think."

"We need to root them out of there," Bolan said.

"Agreed. What did you have in mind?"

It would have been the time to use a stun grenade,
perhaps, had they possessed nonlethal weapons. As it
was, an antipersonnel grenade employed at such close
quarters would be almost guaranteed to kill. Kordiyeh
was surprised, therefore, when he saw Belasko unclip
one of the apple-green spheres from his belt.

"You wanted one of them alive," he whispered a
reminder to the tall American.

"I'm working on it. When I make the pitch, you
shout a warning in Arabic. With any luck, at least one
of the three will make a break, and we can try to wing
him."

"If they don't?"

Bolan shrugged and flashed a grin. "In that case,"
he replied, "I guess we'll have to leave a note."

Kordiyeh watched as he pulled the grenade's safety pin, cocked his arm and let the bomb fly with an overhand pitch toward the stout wall of boxes and crates. He was dead on target, the high-explosive egg dropping out of sight behind the barrier, as Kordiyeh began to shout in Arabic, "Grenade! Watch out! Grenade!"

The GIA commandos had perhaps five seconds to decide, and two of them were on their feet in half that time, one breaking to the right, the other to the left, both firing wildly as they came. Number three popped up behind the barricade, standing fast, and was leveling his AK-47 toward the forklift when the frag grenade went off, enveloping him in a maelstrom of shrapnel and flame.

Kordiyeh tracked his moving target, the man on the left, and aimed for his legs with the Z-84. Unfortunately for the runner, his return defensive fire came in too close for comfort, striking sparks from the forklift's chassis, causing Kordiyeh to flinch as he squeezed the SMG's trigger. Instead of a precision 3-round burst around knee level, he could feel the submachine gun's muzzle rising, spitting closer to a dozen rounds before he managed to release the trigger.

Dammit!

Twenty feet away, his target might have been a scarecrow toppled from its perch, limp arms and legs splayed in different directions, head cocked at a curious angle. The difference, of course, was that scarecrows didn't bleed, and this one was spilling quarts of crimson on the rough warehouse floor. The young man's eyes were open, glazing as they stared through Kordiyeh and sought the secrets of the universe.

There was no point in checking him for signs of life.

A shorter burst from Belasko's weapon silenced opposition on the right, and Kordiyeh followed the tall American as he broke from cover, moving cautiously toward his fallen opponent. This one was moving, at least from the waist up, though a bullet through the groin, near the midline of his body, seemed to have disrupted signals to his legs. The blood that Kordiyeh saw soaking through his clothes was relatively sparse, and he could only wonder whether more was being spilled inside the body cavity.

Bolan kicked away the fallen soldier's Kalashnikov, relieved him of a side arm and tossed it after the rifle. Next, he took one of the gunner's trembling hands and brought it to the groin wound, pressing it against the bloodstain on his khaki pants.

"Tell him to keep the pressure on," Bolan said, "unless he wants to die before the ambulance arrives."

Kordiyeh translated the order, repeating it before the young man's eyes swam into focus and he gave a jerky little nod. At once, his fingers clamped into the fabric of his trousers, bearing down upon the wound.

"All right, tell him the rest," Bolan ordered, and then repeated it for Kordiyeh, as if his comrade didn't know the words by heart. "I want Hassan Filali back alive. If it's too late for that, I want the men who killed him. Make sure that he has it straight.''

Kordiyeh did as he was told, commanding the wounded man to repeat it twice, satisfied that he would remember the message, even if he failed to grasp its meaning.

"He has it," the Algerian assured Bolan.

"Fair enough. We'll call the ambulance first chance we get. Let's move.''

"The weapons?'' Kordiyeh couldn't help asking, as he nodded toward the stack of crates and boxes.

"The police can work it out within.'' Bolan cocked a thumb in the direction of the wounded man. "He's got no way to call for backup, as it is. The guns aren't going anywhere.''

As they departed from the warehouse, moving toward another target, Kordiyeh was suddenly reminded of a line from an old American movie. He thought it was a comedy, perhaps Mae West, but couldn't say for sure. In any case, his mind had added something to the dialogue, and it wasn't a laughing matter, now.

So many men to kill, he thought. So little time.

"SOMEONE DESIRES your safe release.''

Filali heard the voice, as if from miles away or speaking underwater, and it took a moment for him to recognize the source of the words. Arif Boumedienne was standing over him again, empty-handed this time, with no sign of the dreaded surgical implements.

"Someone?''

Filali didn't think he had spoken aloud, until he

saw Arif Boumedienne bobbing his head in agreement, a deep frown distorting his features. "That's right, Hassan. We have someone concerned enough about your safety that he moves heaven and earth to set you free. Already he has killed Yacoub Jabbar and fifteen of my soldiers. Everywhere, he leaves the same message."

"Message?" This time, it was Filali's own voice that seemed to come from miles away, a faint whisper, barely audible even to his own ears.

"Indeed," Boumedienne replied. "He wants you back alive, or failing that, the men who killed you. Most heroic, is it not? You have a champion, it seems."

Filali's brain could offer no response to that. There had been too much pain. His voice was hoarse from screaming, and his ears were numb from listening to his own shrieks of agony. Besides, he couldn't think of anyone who knew he had been kidnapped or who would have cared, much less assassinating so many men to win his freedom.

"This one interests me, Filali," Boumedienne said. "I wonder if he might be the same man who has caused us so much grief these past two days. His messengers—the ones that he allows to live—report that he speaks English. An American, perhaps, or possibly an Englishman. He has a lackey with him to interpret his demands, but it is clear who gives the orders."

An American. It had to be the one who called himself Belasko, then. Filali knew the U.S. Embassy wouldn't have sent a man to rescue him, assuming they had known he was in danger. That much had been understood before he spent his first paycheck.

"We have established that you deal with the Americans," Boumedienne reminded him. "I wonder if you know this champion of yours, his name, perhaps, or where he might be found. A physical description would be useful to my hunters."

"I have told you everything I know," Filali croaked, and it was almost true. Between the shrieks and sobs, he had revealed the basic details of his contract with the CIA, described the agent from the U.S. Embassy who closed the bargain—though, again, he didn't have a name to share—and sketched the outlines of the plan that had produced so much raw carnage since the raid in Libya two nights earlier. The only secrets he had managed to retain, thus far, had been the name and physical description of Belasko, plus the name of Gholomreza Kordiyeh. He had been on the verge of yielding them, as well, but then Boumedienne had found a new and more insistent pressure point, coherent dialogue reduced at once to ragged screams.

It was the weakness of torture, Filali realized. Victims would fabricate to spare themselves from further suffering, of course, but there were also times when they couldn't respond at all.

"Nothing to say?" Boumedienne inquired.

"Nothing," Filali answered, with an air of weary resignation.

"We must try some new inducements, then," the GIA interrogator said. "You might yet disappoint your champion." A gesture from Boumedienne produced the tray of instruments again, some of them looking slightly tarnished now, marred by suspicious stains.

"Let's see," he told Filali, "if we can loose up your tongue a little more."

THE SENTRY WAS A YOUNG MAN, early twenties from his general appearance, but he wasn't getting any older. At his first sight of Bolan stepping from the shadows, the GIA gunner reached for his Kalashnikov, but he was too slow to compete with one who had survived a thousand confrontations such as this. The silenced SMG in Bolan's grip spit out a burst that stitched neat holes across the shooter's chest and slammed him over in a flopping sprawl. The loudest noise of all came from his AKM, as it went clattering across the patio and vanished into shadow, somewhere off to Bolan's left.

The racket brought another sentry running, this one from inside the house that was the Executioner's most recent target. Gholomreza Kordiyeh had fingered the address of yet another GIA lieutenant, one Akhmet Saddam, and while they didn't know if the man was at home, yet, he had clearly been concerned enough to station guards around the place.

The second lookout was an older man with bushy whiskers straggling almost to his chest. An unkempt beard was viewed as mandatory by some Muslim fundamentalists—in Afghanistan, under the fanatic Taliban regime, men could serve ten days in jail for simply trimming their whiskers—but this one looked more sloppy than devout. His shirttail was pulled out on one side, the shirt itself stained by at least one recent meal, and the laces of his left shoe trailed behind him on the ground.

Bolan saw all that in a flash, before he stroked the Z-84's trigger a second time. His Parabellum manglers caught the gunner waist-high as he blundered into the Executioner's line of fire, and the dying man staggered, stumbled, going down. He did get off a short burst from his own Kalashnikov, but his rounds were wasted, angled skyward as he fell.

Instead of cursing the disturbance that would clearly rouse the neighbors and produce no end of calls to the police, Bolan bypassed the corpses and rounded a corner, hesitating only for an instant as he found the kitchen door ajar. Inside, he followed lights and startled, worried-sounding voices to locate the rest of his prey. A sudden clamor from the far side of the house told him that Kordiyeh was making his entrance on schedule.

Bolan was nearing the harsh sound of voices, narrowing the field to one of two bedrooms before him, when a gunman of indeterminate age emerged from the door on his left. Although he had a pistol in his hand, the new arrival still seemed unprepared for active confrontation with the enemy. He gaped at Bolan, jaw gone slack and working on a warning cry that never quite arrived.

Taking advantage of the shooter's momentary hesitation, Bolan squeezed off a burst that dropped the guy in his tracks, then moved past the body while it still twitched on the floor. He had already used up roughly half a magazine, but there was no time to reload his SMG before he reached the gaping door, where at least three men were still snapping at one another in Arabic. Bolan heard weapons click-clacking into readiness and knew that he couldn't afford to waste another moment now that he had lost the slim advantage of surprise.

He went for it, clearing the threshold in a crouch and taking his targets as they came. In fact, there were four men ranged around a rumpled bed, with extra magazines for their Kalashnikovs and submachine guns scattered across a coverlet, along with stray, loose rounds of ammunition. Bolan wasted no time trying to communicate with any of them, though he hoped to leave one messenger alive.

It wouldn't be the master of the house, however. Bolan recognized Akhmet Saddam from blurry hidden-camera photographs, the chief impression of his face embodied in a thick, black beard, with eyes to match. Saddam was armed with what appeared to be a Spectre submachine gun—the Italian model with a unique 50-round box magazine—but there was no time to check the weapon's pedigree as he swung around and brought its muzzle into line with Bolan's face.

A short burst from the Z-84 broke Saddam's clavicle, took a few whacks at his beard and sheared off a ragged chunk of his lower jaw. The stricken GIA lieutenant toppled backward with a gurgling cry of pain, pinning the scattered extra magazines beneath his bulk.

That still left three, and all of them displayed quick reaction times. The two armed with Kalashnikovs stood close together, one handing a curved magazine to the other as Bolan burst in, which meant one of the rifles was unloaded and inoperative. He sprayed them both with Parabellum rounds and had a vague impression of them tumbling together in a heap, but his attention had already shifted to the fourth and final able-bodied gunner in the room.

They faced each other for a heartbeat, from opposite sides of the bed, before the young Algerian showed what he was made of, the muzzle of his French MAT 49 submachine gun dipping slightly, drifting off-target for a crucial half second.

Bolan saw his opening and took it, hammering a 3-round burst into the young guerrilla's shoulder. The sledgehammer impact spun his target like a dervish, flinging his SMG across the room as nerveless fingers lost their grip. The wounded man slumped to his knees, might have collapsed, except he found the strength to raise his one good arm and catch himself, palm braced unsteadily against the nearest wall. He was still kneeling, head bowed in an attitude of prayer or resignation to impending death, when Kordiyeh burst in.

"All done," he said. "All dead, I'm sad to say."

His tone revealed no sadness, but Bolan had no cause to rebuke him. "I've got a live one. So far, at least."

A cursory examination told them that the wounded youth probably wouldn't bleed to death before police arrived. Once more, the message was delivered, Kordiyeh well able to recite the terms from memory.

"We want Hassan Filali back alive," he told the

dazed gunner, deliberately including himself in the equation. "If it's too late for that, we want the men who killed him. Tell your masters."

Waiting for a feeble nod of understanding, he turned back to Bolan. "He will pass the message on."

"Okay, let's move. We've still got miles to go before we sleep."

"A poem, yes?" Kordiyeh smiled, proud of his knowledge. "Your Walt Whitman."

"Close enough," the Executioner replied.

THE PHONE CALL, when it came, didn't surprise Arif Boumedienne. It stood to reason, after all, that if his enemies were on a rampage in Algiers, demanding Hassan Filali's safe release, they had to have some means of discovering Boumedienne's response to their demands. He wasn't overly concerned about the leak that had disclosed his personal, unlisted number to such lunatics. When he was finished dealing with the present difficulty, there would be no end of time for plugging leaks and punishing the negligent.

He had considered trying to conceal the truth from Houari Boudiaf, but swiftly abandoned the perilous idea. Boumedienne had enough on his plate as it was without going behind Houari's back, perhaps being caught in a lie that would place him under suspicion of treason. Besides, Houari had approved the abduction and interrogation of Hassan Filali. If the plan had backfired to their detriment, at least a portion of the blame lay with the leader of the Armed Islamic Group.

Boumedienne was points ahead, however, in the

fact that he already had a plan to solve their problem and, with any luck at all, eliminate the men who had been savaging their ranks these past two days.

His scheme hinged on the phone call that he knew would come, and so Boumedienne was pleased to hear the caller's voice. First one man, speaking Arabic, who asked Boumedienne if he spoke English. When the chief lieutenant of the GIA replied in the affirmative—a point of pride, his education, even in a system that was weighted heavily against his kind—there was a moment of dead air before another, deeper voice came on the line.

"You have the authority to deal?" the second caller asked.

It took a moment for Boumedienne to understand the idiom—the caller was American; he had no further doubt of that—and then it came to him. "I do," he said.

"You got my message." This time it wasn't a question.

"You were most emphatic."

"It gets worse if you don't deliver," the American informed him. There was no trace of excitement in the tone, none of the bully's trademark bluster. This man was prepared to go on killing endlessly, it seemed, until his demands were met or he ran out of targets.

Boumedienne admired that in a man. "I understand you perfectly."

"Which will it be?" the caller asked.

Another fleeting moment of confusion. "Which...? Ah, yes, I understand. The one you seek is with us.

He was ill, but the prognosis is encouraging. I think he's ready to come home."

No audible relief—indeed, no clear emotion whatsoever—as the grim American replied. "Two hours, on the waterfront," he said. "The far-west end."

A good choice, Boumedienne thought. The Algerine waterfront stretched nearly three miles, end to end. It had been near the eastern end that very evening, where the not-so-*Lucky Lady* had been blown to smithereens—perhaps, he speculated, by the very man to whom he was speaking. The blast site was still crawling with police, which meant a shortage of patrolmen at the far end of the docks.

"Agreed."

"If anything goes wrong, it's down to you," said the American.

Boumedienne could only smile at that. "I am not afraid," he said. "I have every confidence that nothing will go wrong."

CHAPTER THIRTEEN

The aftershocks from Bolan's visit to the *Lucky Lady* had subsided, for the most part, by the time he returned to the waterfront at half-past midnight. Cleanup crews were still on the scene, and would be until the wreckage was hauled away for scrap or towed a few miles out to sea and scuttled. Either way, the authorities had packed it in already, privately convinced that the destruction of one freighter and massive damage to its neighbors meant simply one more insolvable terrorist action in a ten-year series of massacres, bombings and riots.

More critical from Bolan's point of view, the west end of the Algiers waterfront was dead quiet, apparently deserted. That was an illusion, of course: some of the boats moored here were live-aboards, while others, simply passing through, most likely had at least some members of their crews on board. More to the point, however, there were no lights showing, no activity, no parties going on.

The west end of the docks was reserved for private pleasure craft, a relatively small enclave catering to the wealthy of Algiers and occasional wandering yachtsmen from France, Spain, Italy, the Greek archipelago. At this time of night, on a weekday, the west end of the Algiers waterfront was as private as any place in the city, and a good deal more secure than any backstreet in the Casbah district.

Bolan drove the last quarter mile with his headlights off, wishing there was some way to disconnect the taillights before he used the brakes. It was the best he could do, in any case, and the risk of meeting a traffic cop in this place at this hour was considerably less than that of driving into an ambush prepared by the GIA.

Bolan assumed that there would be a trap waiting for him on the waterfront. He had suggested that Kordiyeh remain behind this time, but the Algerian had flatly refused, and the soldier hadn't argued the point. A second gun would come in handy if it fell apart, and it was also possible that he would find himself in need of an interpreter before the night was over.

Expecting a setup, he took what precautions he could. Bolan had scouted the territory, before selecting it for the meet. He had a feel for the best hiding places, the handful of vantage points a sniper might choose, and knew that there was nothing he could do to neutralize them all. It was a gamble going in, and showing up some forty minutes early, with enough hardware to slaughter a brigade, exhausted the range of available precautions.

Given more men, a half-dozen or so, he could have posted his own snipers, covered the docks with interlocking fields of fire, but two men alone would be lucky to get in and out with their lives. As for coming out alive with a hostage…

Bolan had no way of knowing whether Hassan Filali was even still alive. He could have asked to speak with Filali on the telephone, but it would have proved nothing; assuming that Arif Boumedienne didn't have someone standing by who could mimic the captive's voice, it would have been a simple thing to let Filali speak, then kill him when the call was disconnected.

If he had to guess, Bolan would have given Filali no better than fifty-fifty odds of survival, so far, and those numbers would drop like a stone if Boumedienne had any tricks up his sleeve. A botched delivery meant almost certain death for Bolan's contact, and there was no precaution he could take against that possibility.

But if it came to that, and Bolan managed to survive the trap, he could exact revenge. Oh, yes. And nothing that the Armed Islamic Group had thus far suffered in the past two days would hold a candle to the Executioner in vengeance-fury mode.

He backed the car into the darkened space beside a bait shop, switched off the engine and left the key in the ignition. Just in case. An extra fraction of a second in the crunch could mean the difference between life and death. The rental's dome light was already disconnected, Bolan and Kordiyeh sheltered by darkness as they stepped from the car, easing their respective doors shut behind them. In addition to their SMGs and pistols, both men had doubled up on spare magazines and frag grenades, Bolan adding a Heckler & Koch 40 mm Granatpistole grenade launcher to his personal armament, the pockets of his trench coat heavy with high-explosive rounds.

They had chosen their places well in advance, Bolan three doors east of the bait shop, Kordiyeh behind a telephone kiosk opposite the Executioner's niche and several yards farther east. Time had begun to drag and grate on both men's nerves when Bolan saw the headlights coming, two cars running in tandem, approaching slowly from the east.

Show time, he told himself.

ARIF BOUMEDIENNE had briefly considered sending a subordinate to meet the enemy, but his hesitation had evaporated in an instant, his fear of the unknown replaced by grim determination and an understanding of the plaudits that awaited him when he presented Houari Boudiaf with the heads of their recent tormentors.

It went without saying that he had no intention of delivering Hassan Filali to the enemy, much less allowing the American and his lackey to escape unpunished after all the damage they had done. Honor demanded vengeance, and Boumedienne's desire for personal advancement in the front ranks of the revolution called for him to strike the killing blow himself. Not literally, perhaps, but he must at least lead the strike team, preside over the execution of the GIA's most formidable enemies.

With that triumph behind him, Houari could refuse him nothing. In time—and perhaps very soon if the rank and file soldiers blamed Houari's inaction for their recent losses—Boumedienne might even be per-

suaded to replace his present leader at the helm of the
Armed Islamic Group.

It wouldn't, he decided, require much persuasion
at all.

Hassan Filali slouched beside him in the back seat
of the gray Mercedes-Benz, sandwiched between
Boumedienne and one of ten bodyguards he had
brought to the waterfront meeting. That was ten
guards in the cars, exclusive of the four snipers he
had dispatched to the docks an hour ahead of time,
with instructions to cover the area, watch for any traps
and wait for his signal before they opened fire.

Unless, of course, his adversaries had an ambush
of their own in mind. In that case, the shooters had
been instructed to use their own best judgment, pick
their targets carefully and safeguard their commander
at all costs, under penalty of execution if they failed.

His bodyguards in the two cars were armed to the
teeth, each man with an automatic rifle or a submachine gun in addition to his side arm. One man in the
second vehicle carried a Belgian Minimi squad
support weapon, chambered in 5.56 mm, with a
200-round linked belt attached to the machine gun in
a sturdy plastic box. With a cyclic rate of 700 rounds
per minute or higher, the Minimi could provide suppressing fire beyond the capability of any assault rifle
or modern submachine gun.

It would be enough, Boumedienne told himself. It
had to be enough.

As for himself, the strike team leader traveled light,
restricting his personal hardware to a Glock 17 pistol,
the original 9 mm model, fitted with an extended

magazine for greater firepower. As it was, Boumedienne expected to fire only two shots during the engagement: one for Hassan Filali and the other—if he
had the opportunity—to finish off the smug American.

In fact, Boumedienne decided, he would definitely
put a round into the American's brain, even if his
enemy was killed by someone else. A small, symbolic
act, perhaps, but satisfying, nonetheless.

The lead car reached its preselected stopping point,
and the driver braked on cue. He left the engine running and the headlights on, as he had been instructed.
Boumedienne didn't wait for an all-clear signal from
his snipers—they had no direct means of communi-
cation, anyway; the risk of radio transmissions being
intercepted was too great—before he stepped out of
the car, dragging Filali behind him.

The prisoner was capable of standing on his own
two feet, but only just. Concerted forward motion required a helping hand from Boumedienne and the
gunman who flanked Filali on his right. They
marched him along like a drunkard slouched between
two comrades on a pub crawl, head slumped forward,
the ruin of his face barely visible in the shadows.
Filali's hands were bound behind his back, the wrists
secured with loops of wire.

Where he was going, the informer would have little
use for hands.

Boumedienne heard and felt his soldiers fanning
out behind him, as he moved with Filali and his gunman toward the front of the Mercedes into the glare
of the headlights. Somewhere above him, away to his

left, the snipers would have him covered now, waiting for hostile targets to reveal themselves. The thought of other snipers, with their crosshairs fixed upon his body, made the short hairs bristle on his nape.

Be calm, he told himself. Control the situation.

Standing in the spotlight of the point car's high beams, Boumedienne raised his voice to the surrounding darkness. "I am here," he told the night, "as promised. I have brought Hassan Filali, as demanded. Will you show yourself?"

Downrange, some thirty yards in front of him, a shadow stirred, detached itself from darkness and assumed the likeness of a man. Boumedienne couldn't make out the stranger's face, but marked his height as setting him apart from most native Algerians. The figure wore a long coat, hanging almost to his knees, and neither hand was clearly visible.

"The deal was that you let him go."

Boumedienne couldn't mistake that voice. It was the same man who had spoken to him on the telephone, presumably the man—or one of them, at any rate—who had inflicted so much damage on the GIA and the FIS within the past two days. Boumedienne would have applauded him for his attacks on the Islamic Salvation Front, but nothing would excuse the loss and embarrassment this outsider had caused to the GIA.

"We had a bargain, it is true," Boumedienne declared, a sly smile tugging at the corners of his mouth. "Unfortunately for your spy, I have changed my mind."

As the last word passed his lips, Boumedienne

raised the Glock, pressed its muzzle to Filali's skull behind his ear and shot him dead. The echo of the shot was still reverberating from the storefronts to his left, as he shoved the limp body in front of him to block incoming fire, and turned to race back for the cover of his vehicle.

DESPITE HIS conversation with Belasko on their long drive to the docks, his understanding that Boumedienne would probably have some kind of trap in mind, Kordiyeh was still shocked into fleeting immobility by the terrorist's point-blank execution of the hostage. More than anything, he supposed, Kordiyeh was surprised that Boumedienne would pull the trigger himself, place his own life on the line. Unless...

Of course, it *was* a trap, as Belasko had predicted from the start. Filali's corpse had yet to strike the pavement when half a dozen guns opened fire on Belasko, automatics stuttering in the darkness, well-placed sniper rifles cracking from on high, the gunners Kordiyeh had sought—and somehow missed—since they arrived.

Belasko wasn't finished yet, though, dodging through the firestorm as he scuttled back toward cover. Kordiyeh saw something like a bloated pistol in his comrade's hand, the German grenade launcher, its single note an almost childish *plop* in the midst of so much raucous gunfire.

There was nothing childish about the grenade's impact, though. The 40 mm HE round struck the right-front fender of the Mercedes-Benz and detonated with a thunderclap that stung Kordiyeh's ears. He saw the car shudder, slumping to starboard as one of its wheels was sheared off at the axle. The same blast enveloped Boumedienne's nearest gunman in flames, and he crumpled where he stood, arms flapping uselessly, his shrill scream instantly devoured by the fire.

That flash and shriek jarred Kordiyeh out of his momentary shock. He raised his submachine gun, chose a sniper on the rooftop of a nearby seafood restaurant as his first target and brought the shooter down with half a dozen Parabellum rounds. Stone dead before he toppled from the roof, the sniper fell like a rag doll, striking the pavement with a solid, satisfying sound.

Because his SMG still had its sound suppressor attached, Kordiyeh wasn't instantly revealed to his enemies. He still had time to spot a second sniper, this one also firing on Belasko's position, and stitch the crouching figure with a burst that left him stretched out on the flat roof of a shop that sold boating supplies. He was angling toward a third rifleman, hoping for time to make a clean sweep of the snipers, when a burst of automatic fire raked the telephone kiosk beside him, shattering glass and splintering woodwork, causing one of the pay phones to jangle as if from an incoming call.

So much for the advantage of surprise.

Kordiyeh guessed that there were still at least eight to ten weapons firing on the other side, one of them hammering away with long bursts like a regular machine gun. If Boumedienne had brought along that kind of firepower, then he was clearly intent on wiping out his opposition. In this case, Kordiyeh thought, the GIA lieutenant's preparations were equivalent to swatting a wasp with a hammer.

Two wasps, Kordiyeh corrected himself. And both still had their deadly stingers intact.

Defiantly, he unleashed another burst from his Z-84, rewarded with the metallic sound of his bullets striking one of the cars. Which one, he couldn't say, nor did it matter much. Any damage inflicted on his enemies or their transport was better than none, each round he sent their way another gesture of defiance in the face of overwhelming odds.

He still might not survive the night, but Kordiyeh could take some of the bastards with him, at the very least. He could remind them that they didn't speak for all Algerians, and that their reign of terror wasn't unopposed.

It was too late to save Hassan Filali, granted, but one sacrifice wasn't the death of hope.

Cursing the men and guns that pinned him down, Kordiyeh palmed an antipersonnel grenade and yanked the pin, lobbing the bomb downrange toward the scuttling figures of his enemies. He had to duck back under cover, dodging more incoming rounds, but the grenade went off six seconds later and produced another strangled scream.

"Take that!" he shouted at his enemies in Arabic, uncertain whether they could hear him over all the racket from the guns. It made no difference, either way.

He was alive and fighting back.

BOUMEDIENNE HAD EXPECTED return fire from his enemies, if they weren't cut down in the first few seconds of the battle, but the blast that shattered his Mercedes-Benz still came as a surprise. Afterward, as he lay dazed on the pavement, bleeding from a ragged scalp wound and watching one of his men collapse in flames like a burning scarecrow, Boumedienne couldn't have said precisely whether the physical impact of the blast was a greater or lesser shock than the fact that it occurred at all.

One thing he realized even before his head cleared completely, while the automatic weapons were spitting flame and hammering all around him: his chances of a safe retreat had just been cut by half, one of his two vehicles blasted into smoking wreckage where it stood. As for the other car, some of his men were crouched behind the open doors, using them for cover while they dueled with unseen enemies, the stately BMW was taking hits, as well.

Mouthing a curse, Boumedienne began to wriggle on his stomach, like a crippled lizard, dragging himself farther from the firing line, halting in the shadow of the shattered Benz. The flames of the initial blast had mostly died away by then, and while he still smelled burning rubber—maybe hoses, maybe wiring, maybe both—beneath the crumpled hood, the car itself didn't appear to be at risk of any secondary detonation that would fry him where he lay.

Against all odds, the GIA lieutenant found that he had kept his pistol, somehow, clinging to the Glock with fierce, muscle-cramping determination, even when the explosion swept him off his feet and slammed him to the ground. With the metallic clamor of guns all around him, Boumedienne felt a sudden urge to shoot at something, even one of the nearby storefronts, just to be in on the action and to prove his pistol still worked.

Never mind that, he chided himself. The Glock was perfectly reliable—in sand or underwater, if it came to that—and it wouldn't cease to function simply because he fell down. It would serve him as well with the stranger as it had with Hassan Filali, but first, he had to find a target.

The rest of his soldiers apparently had no shortage of shadows to shoot at. The muzzle-flashes from their weapons reminded Boumedienne of summer lightning in the mountains, complete with the thunder it brought. In the shadows where his vision couldn't reach, he heard the storm of bullets raking storefronts, shattering wood and windows, drilling countless holes in stucco walls, and still he had to wonder if the fire-storm would, in fact, eradicate his faceless enemies.

Two of them, at least, were still alive and fighting back. One crouched or lay behind a bullet-riddled telephone kiosk, some forty paces in front of him and away to his right, toward the water. That one had some kind of automatic weapon, possibly a submachine gun with a flash-hider attached, the winking of its muzzle-flashes barely a pinprick of light in comparison to the jagged lightning blazing from the guns of his surviving men.

One shooter on the right, and yet another on Boumedienne's left, sheltered by one of the darkened buildings that faced the docks. In fact, there might have been two gunners hiding there, since different weapons alternated fire from the position, but Boumedienne couldn't be sure. One weapon was an automatic, similar if not identical to the one behind the telephone kiosk.

The other was an infernal device, which had already crippled his Mercedes-Benz. Some kind of grenade launcher, Boumedienne assumed. There was no flash of ignition, no telltale rocket's glare, as from the Russian RPGs or any of the portable antitank weapons presently available through black-market sources. Likewise, the impact of the HE rounds, while stunning and lethal, was altogether less destructive than the normal antitank round, most of those rockets weighing between ten and thirty pounds each.

If it had been an RPG or something similar, Boumedienne realized, his Benz wouldn't merely be crippled, it would have been blown out to sea. At least this way the Mercedes was still good for cover, several of his soldiers crouched behind it, popping up to fire on unseen enemies before they dropped back out of sight again.

Boumedienne was crawling toward the second car, favoring his left side and the sharp pain of at least one broken rib, when the grenade launcher made its distinctive plopping sound once again. Instinctively, the GIA lieutenant hunched his shoulders, cheek pressed to the pavement, one arm raised to shield his face. It would make little difference if the HE round hit close enough, but there was no more he could do with less than two seconds' warning to save himself.

In fact, he caught a break, the grenade sailing over

his head to strike one of the BMW's open doors. The shock wave of its detonation thrust him backward half a foot or so, and deafened him again. It felt as if he had the world's worst hangover, the drumbeat of his agony keeping perfect time with his elevated pulse.

When Boumedienne could see again, he checked the BMW and found that one door had been sheared off at the hinges, the door behind that one slammed shut on the soldier who was using it for cover, jammed with his legs protruding at an awkward angle, twitching spastically. At least three more of Boumedienne's gunners were down, one missing what appeared to be almost three-quarters of his skull. The other two were still alive, lips moving silently.

The GIA lieutenant was thankful for the shell-shocked deafness that kept him from hearing their screams. Small blessings, in the midst of hell on earth.

It was no longer clear, by any means, that he could best his unseen enemies, not with the decimated force at his disposal. Thinking rather quickly for a man who suffered from concussion, fractured ribs and sundry flesh wounds scattered from his hairline to his knees, Boumedienne decided there was still a chance to save himself, at least, whatever should become of those he left behind.

He told himself it wasn't cowardice to run away from certain death. If anything, it was a combat leader's duty to survive and fight another day. If he was criticized for his decision afterward, at least Boumedienne would be alive to face his critics and defend himself.

If he was dead, the same men who despised him

would be free to slander him at will, and none would take his part. Not only his name, but the reputation of the Armed Islamic Group would suffer grievously.

When viewed in that light, fleeing from the trap almost appeared to be an act of selfless courage. He would do it for the movement, after all; give up his ticket into Paradise, out of loyalty to the GIA.

Assuming that he managed to escape.

Teeth clenched against his pain, Boumedienne began to crawl across the blood-drenched killing ground.

THE H&K GRANATPISTOLE was, in effect, a cut-down version of the same M-79 grenade launcher used extensively by American ground troops over the past thirty-eight years, since its introduction in 1961. A single-shot, breech-loading weapon, the 40 mm hand cannon resembled nothing quite so much as an old-fashioned flare gun. Its primary differences were the collapsible shoulder stock and the folding "ladder" sight, which allowed for reasonably accurate fire up to 350 meters. The chunky "pistol" weighed five pounds unloaded, and would chamber the full range of 40 mm military and nonlethal ammunition, ranging from HE and fléchettes to pepper gas.

For the mission at hand, Bolan had carried only HE rounds, desiring maximum punch to help balance the odds. And so far, it appeared, his choice had been the right one.

Both of the GIA vehicles were effectively crippled, one or more tires shredded on each, with substantial engine damage to the Mercedes-Benz, and enough gaping holes in the BMW's left-front fender to suggest its power plant had likewise taken hits. Besides putting the enemy gunners on foot, his first two HE rounds had also taken five or six out of the fight, thus cutting the unhappy numbers by half.

Bolan was still concerned about Kordiyeh, pinned behind the telephone kiosk while incoming fire ripped apart his cover, but the Algerian seemed to be holding his own. If he was hit, it didn't show. He still returned fire with his SMG, though he was doubtless running low on ammunition, and had lobbed a frag grenade downrange some thirty seconds earlier to keep the opposition jumping.

It all came down to scorched-earth tactics now, in Bolan's mind, since the first shot of the firefight had taken out Hassan Filali. There was nothing but revenge to be achieved, and it began with wiping out the present hit team, making sure that none of them escaped. Above all else, he wanted the trigger man who had killed Filali.

Arif Boumedienne, the Armed Islamic Group's exalted second in command.

He was out there, somewhere, in the firelit darkness of the waterfront. He might be dead or wounded, though the Executioner's first HE round had been a trifle off the mark, striking the right-front fender of the Benz, instead of dead center—and thus closer— to Filali's murderer. Boumedienne had gone down when the grenade exploded, all right, but until he saw the body, Bolan had no way of knowing whether he had scored a kill or whether the Algerian had saved himself by dropping to the pavement.

And the only way that Bolan could be sure was by going to see for himself, up close and personal.

He broke open the Granatpistole, extracted the spent cartridge and thumbed another HE round into the smoking breech. As with the larger M-79, he had to cock the hammer, six-shooter-style, in order to prime the weapon. Shifting it to his left hand, Bolan gripped the freshly loaded Z-84 submachine gun in his right, waited briefly for a sudden flurry of incoming fire to subside, then made his move.

There was no reloading his 40 mm launcher on the run, but Bolan made the one shot count, framing the battered BMW over open sights and squeezing off a heartbeat after he rounded the corner. Two or three of the GIA gunners saw him coming, swinging their full-auto weapons around to meet him, but Kordiyeh dropped one adversary in his tracks, and the others had no time to find their mark before Bolan's HE round hit the sedan amidships, rupturing the fuel tank and simultaneously sparking fumes from the spilled gasoline.

A spreading lake of fire enveloped the vehicle and the gunmen hunched behind it, the doomed men trying desperately to scatter, flames already tangled in their clothing, in their hair, trailing behind them as they ran.

Two of them broke for the harbor, and one of them made it, plunging off the pier into darkness with a final parting scream. His sidekick caught a burst from Kordiyeh's Z-84, stumbling through a smoky pirouette before he crumpled to the deck, a smoldering bag of bones.

Three others broke toward the storefronts, toward Bolan's right, but he was ready for them, tracking with his SMG, milking short bursts from the weapon that dropped them in their tracks: one, two, three. A previously unseen gunner rose from hiding, on the far side of the Benz, and started blazing away with some kind of full-sized machine gun, but converging streams of fire from Kordiyeh and Bolan cut him down two seconds later, his last rounds wasted on the sky above.

And that left one.

Boumedienne appeared to know that death was coming for him. He was crawling on his belly like a reptile when Bolan first spotted him, but the sudden lull in gunfire seemed to galvanize the hit team's sole survivor. Bolting to his feet, he was about to run, one hand clutching his side, then thought better of it, turning to face his enemy. He had a pistol in his right hand, muzzle pointed toward the ground.

"It seems you win this round," Boumedienne called out, while Bolan was some fifty feet away and closing. "But you will not win the war. My death is nothing to the movement."

"Well, then, here goes nothing," Bolan said, just loud enough to carry, as he raised his SMG, one-handed, and unloaded half a magazine into Boumedienne.

The dead man vaulted backward, as if yanked by unseen cables, sprawling some ten feet from where he had been standing when he spoke his final words. A tremor rippled through his body, neurons firing off their final burst of energy in vain, but he was long past rising to fight again.

Vengeance.

It left a sour taste in Bolan's mouth, an empty feeling in his soul, but there was more to come. He owed Hassan Filali that, and there was still a mission to accomplish, enemies to be destroyed.

Algiers had yet to feel the full wrath of the Executioner.

But it was coming.

Soon.

CHAPTER FOURTEEN

Slaying the bearer of bad news went out of style among Middle Eastern potentates sometime in the early nineteenth century, but it still required a monumental force of will for Houari Boudiaf to keep from strangling the young man who stood before him, eyes downcast, slender hands fidgeting at his sides.

Boudiaf should have known the young man's name, as surely as he recognized the face. Was it Omar? Perhaps Ali? One of his youthful messengers, at any rate, and one who had reported to him frequently within the past twelve months. A name he should have remembered as well as his own.

So overwhelming was his rage, however, that Boudiaf could scarcely speak, much less resort to small talk and common courtesy. With a few halting words, the young man had come close to unhinging Boudiaf's reason, nearly tipping him over the edge into screaming, homicidal violence, and it was only with mighty effort that the GIA commander held his clenched fists level with his waist, instead of smashing them into the young man's face.

Boumedienne was dead, along with better than a

dozen of Boudiaf's best soldiers. Even as he stood there, fuming in his study, ambulance attendants were picking up bits and pieces of his men on the waterfront, bagging the mangled remains for transport to the city morgue. The captured spy, Hassan Filali, had been killed, as well.

But no other enemies.

It was another clean sweep for his enemies, doubly infuriating to the Armed Islamic Group's commander, since he still had no clear grasp of who those enemies were, why they had selected this particular time to torment him. Should he blame Nabi Ulmalhama and the FIS? Was the American visitor, Malik al-Salaam, somehow involved?

Or was there yet another enemy abroad and stalking his troops in Algiers, as yet unidentified?

Boumedienne had claimed success in his interrogation of Hassan Filali. The worthless peasant was a contract agent for some foreign power, Arif had reported, probably the United States or Great Britain. The man who had demanded Filali's release spoke English on the telephone, Arif said, but without the accent of a Briton. He was most likely American.

Did that prove anything?

Boudiaf wasn't convinced, as yet. Experience had taught him that Americans—some of them mercenaries, others "retired" or "semiretired" from the U.S. intelligence network—were nearly as ubiquitous as Russians in the world of international intrigue, these days. The cold war's end had not only sidelined agents of the former KGB and its Eastern Bloc tentacles. Any number of CIA contract agents, including a small legion of "illegals," had likewise been cut adrift in the new era of glasnost and shriveled budgets. There were Brits and Frenchmen fending for themselves, these days. Some Germans, also; even some Vietnamese.

Times changed, and enemies, but none of that meant anything to Houari Boudiaf, at the moment. He needed action, and quickly, both to calm the rage inside himself and to protect his reputation—already damaged, perhaps beyond repair—as the uncontested leader of Algeria's foremost dissident militia. In his present circumstance, Boudiaf realized, any retaliation, even against the wrong target, was better than standing idle, permitting himself to become a laughingstock.

And if, in fact, he was about to strike without regard to accuracy, why not direct his stroke against the known adversary who vexed him the most? Why not use Arif Boumedienne's death to justify annihilation of the Islamic Salvation Front?

Faceless Americans could wait their turn; he would catch up to them in time. Right now, with Arif and his soldiers dead, Boudiaf was the sole authority on what Hassan Filali had disclosed to his interrogators. If he said Filali had named his employer as Nabi Ulmalhama, who was there to dispute him?

No one, at least, who would survive the next twenty-four hours.

Houari felt himself beginning to relax, the fury slipping from him, as if the floodgate had reversed directions, sucking his rage back into the vortex from whence it came. He had a plan, now. A holy mission, no less. He was about to mount a great jihad.

And if, in fact, he missed Boumedienne a trifle less than he appeared to, if a niggling voice inside him even hinted that the death of his ambitious second in command might be a blessing in disguise, what of it?

Arif was a bona fide martyr to the cause, and his name would serve Houari's surviving troops as a rallying cry in their new offensive. There would be time enough later, when the smoke cleared, for selection of a safer, more subservient subordinate.

First things, first. Before the celebration, they would have to wade through blood.

And if a certain meddling American visitor found himself caught in the cross fire, well, it would be no great loss to the world.

THERE WERE SEVERAL different ways to kill an army. Sometimes, if you took out the leaders, the rank and file fell apart, lost courage and focus, scattered in a panic. Sometimes, though, a dedicated force would fight to the last man, requiring total annihilation to snuff out resistance. In different circumstances, where a siege was practical, there might be no armed engagement at all, the army cut off and starved of its material support.

A thorough warrior by nature, Bolan had decided to apply all three techniques at once in his blitz through Algiers.

Partial decapitation of the Armed Islamic Group had already been achieved with the death of Arif Boumedienne. His lightning strikes over the past two days had likewise depleted the GIA's fighting ranks, although he cherished no illusions that the group was running out of men.

Which brought him to the tertiary angle of attack.

Bolan's next target was the man from Tripoli.

Asem Kabir had escaped with a scare and the loss of some peripheral employees in his first encounter with the Executioner. This time around, Bolan meant to finish the job.

The Libyan's home address in Algiers was well-known, a matter of public record. He didn't live at the embassy, nor—somewhat surprisingly—had his near miss with death prompted him to give up his sumptuous lodgings. Another, wiser man might have gone underground, or even gone home, but Kabir seemed confident of his own invincibility.

Or perhaps he simply trusted his new bodyguards.

Bolan killed the first two of them on his oblique approach to the house, snapping one's neck in a death grip, dropping the second with three silenced rounds from his Z-84 while the lookout was rolling a cigarette.

If they were the best security Kabir could afford, the Libyan was as good as dead.

Bolan met Kordiyeh on the east side of the house, where broad glass doors overlooked a patio and swimming pool. Though small by American standards, the pool was meticulously kept, its bottom an elaborate sunburst mosaic fashioned from bright, one-inch square tiles. The poolside furniture, by contrast to the underwater art, resembled something inexpensive from a Wal-Mart department store catalog.

The guard assigned to watch the patio and pool was dead when Bolan got there, throat gaping darkly in the moonlight. Kordiyeh showed no expression as he stood beside the cooling corpse, his blade already tucked away out of sight. No lights were showing from inside the house. If there were guards awake and on the job in there, they had to be sitting in the dark.

"You have a preference how we do this?" Bolan asked his comrade, whispering.

Kordiyeh thought about it, frowned, and shook his head.

"Straight up the middle then," the Executioner suggested.

Kordiyeh responded with a nod.

They faced the broad glass sliding doors together, didn't bother checking them to see if they were locked. Twin submachine guns sputtered softly through their suppressors, the double stream of Parabellum rounds exploding through plate glass and clearing a path for the two men in black.

Inside, they didn't have to find the light switch. One of Kabir's bodyguards had bolted upright on a stylish sofa when the glass imploded, spraying him with jagged shards, and somehow switched on a lamp, even as he grappled with his pistol in a shoulder rig. The sudden light stabbed Bolan's eyes, but also helped him find his target, squeezing off another burst that put the gunner down before he had a chance to draw.

They swept through the house, found no one in the kitchen or the formal dining room. Another sleepy lookout met them in the parlor, and they left him stretched out on the wooden floor, spilling blood across the Chantilly parquet.

Bolan took the point as they entered a hallway plainly leading to the bedrooms. He kicked in the first door they came to, pumping rounds into a blanket-swaddled figure on the one occupied bed. Kordiyeh, meanwhile, had veered across the hall to sweep a second bedroom, finding both beds empty.

And that left only one.

The master bedroom was situated at the end of the hallway, with extra space set aside for its private bathroom. Kabir was out of bed and struggling with the window sash as they entered, Bolan flicking on the light. It struck him as a replay of their first encounter with the Libyan, except that the man was dressed in silk pajamas this time, midnight blue with golden pinstripes.

The Libyan flicked a glance over his shoulder, gave a breathless cry of panic as he saw their guns and redoubled his hopeless effort to escape through the window. There was no point taunting him, pretending that he had a chance, both gunners hosing rounds into his back at nearly point-blank range.

The chunky corpse was frozen for an instant, crucified against the windowframe, before it toppled backward, almost in slow-motion, Kabir's death grip dragging the curtains down after him, so that they settled over his face and torso like a shroud. From the slack attitude of his body, the amount of crimson soaking through the draperies, it would have been superfluous to check for signs of life.

One down. How many left to go?

The numbers were irrelevant, to Bolan's mind. He had been trained to fight with everything he had, all-out, until the tide of victory was obvious for one side or the other. And he hadn't reached that point, yet, in Algiers.

But it was coming.

He could feel it in his bones.

MALIK AL-SALAAM WAS worried, verging on frightened. He hated the feeling—had spent his whole life, it seemed, struggling toward a position where he would never be frightened of anything, ever again—but there it was, and no mistaking it.

The former Rodney Allen Tuggle of Detroit was scared half to death.

But that was only half, and he had come through worse than this before, when there was less to gain from putting his life on the line. His Middle Eastern tour had been a gamble from the planning stage, viewed by some of his patrons in the Islamic Brotherhood as a needless extravagance, even an exercise of ego; reviled by the honky dinosaurs in Congress as part of some vague conspiracy to overthrow the white man's rule in the States.

They were closer to the truth than they realized, those turkey-wattle rednecks with their white hair plastered into goofy pompadours. If those pathetic old crackers had known even half of what Malik al-Salaam had in mind for the U.S.A., they would have stopped making speeches about him and pooled their illegal slush funds to take out a contract on his life.

Now, here he was in the middle of an Algerian

shooting gallery, caught between feuding factions of
his own Islamic brothers.

It was ironic, one of countless words the former
Rodney Allen Tuggle had memorized in the joint,
reading Mr. Honky Webster's unabridged dictionary
from cover to cover, between prayer sessions and his
study of the Koran. Talking white and thinking white
was close to half the battle in the U.S., one of the
first lessons Malik al-Salaam had picked up from the
Islamic Brotherhood, while he was still inside. Instead
of thinking black and coming off like something from
an old-time minstrel show, the way you did it was to
beat the bastards at their own damn game. You had
to be more erudite, learn how to take the master race's
language and twist it around, tie the damn thing in
knots like a clown making balloon animals.

Of course, it still took time—and money, yes indeed. Finding that money, and the hardware to go
with it, was the first and foremost purpose of his Islamic unity crusade. Now, here he was in the eye of
the storm, rubbing shoulders with the men who made
it happen from Algiers to the Bekaa Valley, and al-
Salaam could feel it slipping through his fingers, all
crumbly and falling apart.

Goddammit to hell!

He had begun to wonder if it was time to split and
find himself a healthier environment. He was welcome in Tehran, perhaps in Baghdad—though, once
again, it wouldn't do for him to rile either host by
seeming to play favorites in that long-standing conflict between Muslim states. Perhaps he should get out
of the Middle East entirely for a while, visit the Tal-

iban brothers in Afghanistan and congratulate them on their recent good works, while the locals cleaned house in Algiers.

There were those in the U.S. who would call his visit to Algiers a failure, of course; some would doubtless brand it a precipitating factor in the recent violence. None of that was Malik al-Salaam's concern. He had become adept at blunting criticism— most of it white criticism, and thus immediately suspect to his followers—from sources as diverse as the liberal Democratic Party and the Christian Coalition. Anytime the honkies of the left and right joined forces to denounce him, they succeeded only in proving his point: that white men stuck together when the chips were down, when brothers of color demanded their slice of the pie.

He could still pull it off, al-Salaam thought. If peace couldn't be restored in Algiers through his efforts, then one side or the other would inevitably pull into the lead. In that event, he thought, there would be no harm in a visitor revising his first estimate of the local situation, casting his lot—and offering his blessing—to the victors. All in the spirit of global Islamic unity, of course.

But in order to bless anyone, he would have to be alive. Short of fleeing the country with his tail between his legs, the next best alternative was to find a safe haven with the group best able to protect him. The most likely victors, as it were.

Or, better yet, with the men who held the purse strings.

Malik al-Salaam's first telephone call was directed

to Asem Kabir. He meant to offer the Libyan fraternal greetings, perhaps wangle a breakfast invitation that would blossom into sanctuary while the in-house fighting sputtered on, but he never got the chance to make his pitch.

It turned out that the Libyan was on his way to hell and gone past taking any calls, much less protecting anyone. Poor bastard hadn't even found a means of protecting himself.

That left Wasim Ruholla, the Iranian. If he was disinclined toward welcoming a houseguest on short notice, then at least he might provide an introduction to the leaders of the Islamic Salvation Front. They, in turn, might take a visiting brother under their collective wing...or, if nothing else, show Malik al-Salaam the safest way to get the hell out of Dodge.

Right now, a hasty exit didn't look too bad at all.

Al-Salaam was scowling, mouthing curses, as he reached for the telephone once more.

WASIM RUHOLLA HAD TAKEN the precaution of abandoning his home for the duration, moving to a penthouse suite in what passed for a three-star hotel in downtown Algiers. He had also doubled his personal bodyguard, sharp-eyed Iranians all, to a total of eight. Between their guns and his selection of a public lodging place, the money handler from Tehran apparently believed that he was safe from any harm.

But he was wrong.

Kordiyeh had made a walk-through of the hotel lobby on his own, examining the layout—exits, elevators, stairs, the uniforms that bellmen wore—before he ducked through a door clearly marked Employees Only. After finding what he wanted, Kordiyeh exited through the rear, without passing the registration desk a second time, and met his American comrade in arms back at the car, one block east.

Bolan examined the maroon blazers, each marked with the hotel's logo where the breast pocket ought to be, and the round pillbox hats, which Kordiyeh assured him were a staple of the hotel bellman's uniform. Neither would fit him well, but the soldier didn't care. Role camouflage had as much to do with attitude and the perception of your audience than any fine details of a particular disguise. If they avoided contact with the hotel's manager and night clerk, if they went in through the back and moved directly to the elevators for a quick ride to the penthouse, they should be all right.

At least until they faced the eight Iranians.

The odds weren't bad, all things considered, but Bolan never took a victory for granted. He had seen enough, lost enough friends and squeaked through enough tight places himself to know that one lucky shot could make the difference between victory and defeat, between life and death. It wouldn't take eight men with automatic weapons to destroy the Executioner if he relaxed his guard or anything went wrong. A teenager with a homemade .22-caliber zip gun could kill as swiftly and efficiently as a professional sniper if he got a clean shot.

Shrugging off the morbid thoughts of death, Bolan cleared the hotel's rear entrance, remaining a cautious yard or so behind Kordiyeh, letting his interpreter lead in case they were stopped by some member of the staff. Bolan didn't want civilians involved in this action, and he wasn't about to shoot a curious bellman or custodian, but he would gladly deal with any minor interference on a nonlethal basis, leave the human obstacle with some bruises and a headache if it meant insuring the mission's success.

One way or another, Wasim Ruholla had to go.

They caught a break and made it to the elevator without incident, unobserved. The hour helped with that, of course, insuring that most—if not all—of the guests were asleep in their beds, energy levels lagging for those on the staff who remained at their beck and call through the long, quiet night. The elevator took them straight up to the penthouse, fourteen floors, without another stop along the way. In passing, Bolan noted that the lighted control board included a thirteenth floor, ignoring the American practice of bowing to superstition and pretending the "unlucky" floor didn't exist.

This night, the Executioner thought, it was the fourteenth floor that was unlucky—either for Ruholla or himself.

The elevator car announced its arrival on fourteen with a muffled but distinctive chime. In daylight, when the maids were busy cleaning, guests checking in and out, room service making its deliveries, the melodic ding would fade into background noise, unnoticed or deliberately ignored by those with other business on their minds. At close to 3:00 a.m., however, when the penthouse floor was like a morgue, the elevator's cheery greeting rang out loud and clear.

Bolan and Kordiyeh both had their hats off and their submachine guns ready when the door hissed open to reveal a swarthy, slender man, one hand inside the jacket of his baggy suit. They waited for the vision of their SMGs to register, in case this proved to be some insomniac businessman reaching for a cigarette, but all doubt was removed with the first glimpse of the pistol in his hand.

Instead of choosing who would fire, each man milked a short burst from his Z-84, the double impact hurling their target backward with destructive force, his body shattering a mirror that was mounted on the wall directly opposite for some reason, as if to let those disembarking from the elevator catch a fresh glimpse of themselves. Between the thump of impact and the sound of breaking glass, Bolan suspected they had given up whatever edge they might have gained from stealth.

Not that it mattered.

Two more of Ruholla's Iranian shooters were waiting for them as they cleared the elevator's threshold, Bolan moving in a combat crouch, Kordiyeh emulating his actions. The gunners were away to Bolan's left, pointing him toward Ruholla's suite, and while both appeared shocked by the sudden death of their comrade, they were recovering quickly, professionally.

One of the sentries had a chunky Desert Eagle semiauto pistol in his hand—it looked like the .357 Magnum model—while the other sported a mini-Uzi, minus sound suppressor. Bolan had no time to consider the irony of Iranian hit men favoring Israeli weapons. He was too busy trying to stay alive as all hell broke loose in the hallway.

Both of the Z-84 SMGs still had their suppressors attached, but it made little difference with the mini-Uzi rattling at them, the big Desert Eagle booming in rapid fire, knocking quarter-sized holes in the walls. Bolan went down firing, hit the carpet with sufficient force to empty his lungs, but it was all about discipline, hanging on to target acquisition and making the shot, even when you couldn't breathe.

His primary mark was the shooter on the left, Mr. Desert Eagle, since they occupied the same side of the corridor. The stout Iranian was very nearly good enough to finish it, his last round zipping past within an inch or two of Bolan's skull before a spray of Parabellum manglers rocked him, pitched him backward, crumpling into an untidy heap.

Bolan was swinging toward his sidekick when Kordiyeh tagged the second shooter. Down on one knee and firing from the hip, Kordiyeh hosed the short machine gunner, bouncing him off the nearest wall, leaving bright crimson smears on the ivory-colored wallpaper.

Surprise was nonexistent now, and time was of the essence. Bolan and Kordiyeh rushed the door of Ruholla's suite, veering off in opposite directions at the last moment before Kordiyeh fired a burst into the doorknob and dead bolt. Bolan followed through with a kick, but the door was barely halfway open, swinging freely, when a burst of automatic fire erupted from inside the penthouse, stitching ragged holes across the door panels, slamming it shut in their faces.

One more time, Bolan thought. There was no alternative entrance, short of heading for the roof and scrambling down the outer wall with climbing gear that they didn't possess—an exercise that would have made them sitting ducks, and which was barred by fleeting time in any case.

It was the door or nothing.

Reaching underneath his tight maroon jacket, Bolan found a frag grenade and armed it, nodding to Kordiyeh as he braced himself for the pitch. This time, it was the Algerian who kicked open the door, ducking back again before the shooters could nail him. Bolan lobbed his charge around the jamb, felt a bullet tug his jacket sleeve before the door slammed shut a second time, now scarred with twice as many bullet holes.

At that, the riddled door helped shield them from a storm of shrapnel when the grenade went off. Bolan was first inside before the smoke cleared, veering to the right, while Kordiyeh, behind him, took the left. One of their adversaries in the main room of the penthouse was stretched out on the deep-pile carpeting, apparently unscathed, except that he was missing half his face. A second shooter, holed by shrapnel in one side, knelt beside a leather-upholstered recliner, reaching for the little Ingram submachine gun he had dropped when he was wounded.

Bolan shot him in the chest before he could reach it, already seeking new targets before the dead man toppled over on his back. As if on cue, a young, slender man stumbled out of the suite's kitchenette, a dazed expression on his face. The AKM assault rifle he carried seemed out of place in his hands, as if he were a child caught playing with his father's gun.

No matter. Bolan dropped him in his tracks without a second thought, without regrets. If he was old enough to carry arms and guard Wasim Ruholla, he was old enough to pay the price of failure.

Six men down, and that left two still unaccounted for, aside from their primary target. The shooters wasted no time in declaring themselves, long bursts from their Kalashnikov rifles erupting from two separate doorways—bedrooms, Bolan thought, unless one of them took his weapon to the washroom with him. The first shots were high and wild, a reaction to chaos rather than firing for effect, but they still came close enough to let Bolan know these two shooters could handle their weapons.

Of course. The moneyman from Tehran wouldn't have summoned amateurs to watch his back.

Once again, Bolan took the nearest shooter as his target, palming another grenade, pitching it overhand toward the dark rectangle of doorway that sheltered his opponent. It bounced off the door going in, and he heard the shooter's startled cry of recognition, even as the other AK raked the parlor with another probing burst.

Downrange, his adversary burst from cover, trying to escape from the grenade. Bolan met him with a rising burst of 9 mm rounds that opened his chest in a splash of scarlet, pitched him backward through the open doorway just as the grenade exploded, its blast enveloping his airborne corpse in smoke and flame.

Kordiyeh, in the meantime, had tossed a grenade

of his own, and he shouted a warning to Bolan a heartbeat before it went off in the other occupied bedroom. Kordiyeh was on his feet and rushing the sniper's nest in a flash, passing where shrapnel had peppered the walls, lunging through the smoky doorway and firing a short burst from his SMG at something he found on the floor beyond Bolan's line of sight.

"Ruholla?" Bolan asked him, rising cautiously from his crouch.

It took a moment for Kordiyeh to respond, craning his neck and peering through a cloud of smoke and plaster dust, but he finally retreated, shaking his head.

One door was still closed and silent off to Bolan's right, flanked by a broad plate-glass window with a panoramic view of downtown Algiers. The two men moved in cautiously, aware of passing time, the danger to themselves if the police arrived while they were still in the hotel, both men determined not to miss the target they had come for.

Bolan kicked the door, expecting gunfire, and was met by sobbing sounds instead, as he flicked on the light. Ruholla huddled in a corner, knees drawn up against his chest. Unlike his Libyan counterpart, Ruholla apparently shunned pajamas, preferring the feel of crisp, clean sheets against his naked skin.

Repulsed by the weeping man yet devoid of pity, committed to fulfillment of his mission, Kordiyeh hurried forward. He sighted down the barrel of his SMG, then looked up at Bolan.

"A lesson to the others, yes?" asked the Algerian. "That's right."

"In that case—"

Without completing his thought, Kordiyeh bent to grab Ruholla by one pudgy arm and started to drag him across the floor. For all his bulk, the Iranian offered no effective resistance, slapping weekly at Kordiyeh's knuckles with his free hand, wailing like a frightened child as he was scuffed across the carpet back to the smoky parlor.

Bolan followed, watching as Kordiyeh dragged his man toward the broad picture window, his intent now crystal clear. From fifteen feet away, Kordiyeh raised his SMG and emptied it, one-handed, taking out a man-sized portion of the window, broken glass cascading into the street below.

"You tell the people God is your master. He directs you when you kill." Kordiyeh's lips were drawn back from his teeth in a snarl, as he addressed Ruholla. "Let us see if he will bear you up on angel's wings."

Ruholla started to scream as his captor jerked him to his feet, kept it up as he was violently propelled across the last few yards of carpet, through the shattered window and into empty space. His naked body almost seemed to linger for a moment, stubbornly denying gravity, but that was an illusion, Bolan realized.

The screaming dwindled to nothing as Ruholla fell.

"We're finished here, I think," Kordiyeh said.

"I'd say that's right," the Executioner replied.

CHAPTER FIFTEEN

Houari Boudiaf was smiling, for once, as he cradled the telephone receiver and moved toward the window, peering through a gap in the curtains to glimpse the first dull gray of the approaching dawn. The call had brought him good news for a change, and from an unexpected source.

The black American who called himself Malik al-Salaam had called personally, apologizing for the hour, tiptoeing cautiously around the reason for his call until Boudiaf made him feel at ease, putting on a facade of false friendship that al-Salaam gobbled up like a cat with warm milk.

In simple terms, what an American would call the bottom line, al-Salaam was afraid for his life. He had been following the violence in Algiers, the body count rising hourly, but after all the killing of the past few days, two deaths had finally pushed him over the edge.

It was the foreigners, of course. They stuck together, oddly, even when they came from different races and nations. In this case, the common bond of Islam was a factor, though Boudiaf frankly questioned any Westerner's devotion to God, regardless of the supplicant's pigmentation. Still, if the charade served his purpose...

Al-Salaam was unnerved by the bloody execution, within the past two hours, of Wasim Ruholla and Asem Kabir. Their murders seemed to cross another line, reaching beyond the mayhem earlier directed solely at native Algerians, and it also touched al-Salaam on a personal level. He had been in contact with both men, attempting to negotiate a cease-fire in Algeria, that futile exercise no doubt combined with some private fund-raising of his own. Now that the moneymen were dead, executed without regard to their fabled "neutrality," al-Salaam had perhaps seen his own name included in the writing on the wall.

Boudiaf, for his part, had been shaken by Kabir's execution. He wasn't the only diplomat in Tripoli, to be sure, but they had worked well together, Kabir either truly sympathetic to the GIA's cause, or else skilled enough at faking enthusiasm, so that the end result was the same. One way or another, he had arranged for the delivery of cash and arms from Libya, paved the way for the GIA training camp in Colonel Khaddafi's backyard.

And it was all gone, now, swept away in the space of two days, as if by a flash flood in the desert. Tripoli would send someone else in due time, Boudiaf had no doubt of that, but they would be starting afresh as strangers, uncertain of each other and cautiously feeling their way. Kabir's replacement might not share the dead man's affability, his gift for feigning camaraderie and rubber-stamping pleas for aid.

Boudiaf felt his mood beginning to sour, but caught himself before he slipped back into anger and depression. For the moment, he was still unscathed—although his army had been badly mauled—and luck was riding with him in regard to Malik al-Salaam. Instead of being forced to lure the American with lies and flattery, the man had come to him, a veritable gift from God. They would have an opportunity to talk, and if his first impression of the Yankee as a hypocrite and interloper was confirmed, Boudiaf would solve the problem swiftly, without fuss or muss.

Conversely, there was still a chance—however small—that he might find the American to be a true believer, someone dedicated to the cause of militant Islam, rather than crass self-promotion. Not that there was anything wrong with ambition, per se; Boudiaf was an ambitious man himself, albeit in a godly cause. If al-Salaam turned out to be a kindred spirit, in defiance of all odds and first impressions, why, so much the better.

In that case, Boudiaf and the Armed Islamic Group would have their first clear shot at America, the Great Satan. An alliance with the Islamic Brotherhood could expand the GIA's jihad into the Western Hemisphere, with unlimited potential for righteous destruction.

Vaguely conscious of his mood swings, Boudiaf reined in the brief surge of manic enthusiasm. If forced to quote odds, he would have said it was ninety percent certain that al-Salaam would prove to be a godless profiteer and hypocrite. In which case, he would be eliminated.

As for the struggle with his mortal enemies, however, there was still much do be done before Boudiaf could claim a victory. Co-opting or eliminating Malik al-Salaam was part of it, but that still left the killers of Arif Boumedienne at large, the murderers of Asem Kabir unpunished, and the raiders who had slain so many of his men presumably unhindered, if they chose to harvest more.

Al-Salaam might lead him to the American, yet, but Boudiaf couldn't believe that a single intruder— even a small band of outsiders—was acting alone in Algiers and environs, responsible for all the mayhem that had rocked the GIA of late. In his experience, that kind of concentrated violence required manpower, organization and mobility. It required, if not an army, then at least a dedicated, well-trained striking force.

And, once again, he thought of Nabi Ulmalhama, his old rival, the commander of the Islamic Salvation Front. Boudiaf's first reaction, after the raid on his base camp in Libya, had been to blame the FIS. He had instinctively unleashed the Anointed Ones against Nabi's forces when the first trouble came to Algiers, and he still wasn't convinced that his judgment had erred.

His dark suspicion, as it happened, had been lately reinforced by certain reports from the field, his lieutenants reporting anonymous contacts—even some calls from alleged FIS insiders, repulsed by the fratricidal mayhem among true believers—that confirmed the Islamic Salvation Front as the source of his recent troubles. Clearly, it wasn't the *only* source, with at least one American found in the mix...but, then again, why should he assume that the FIS was immune to infiltration by outsiders and heretics?

It began to make sense, the logic taking shape in Boudiaf's mind as a two-pronged plan of attack. He would welcome Malik al-Salaam, interrogate him subtly if possible—more forcefully, if it was called for—and determine whether the man was aware of any other Yanks presently at large in Algiers. On the second front, he would proceed toward the annihilation of the FIS, expunging one more blot on the reputation of militant Islam.

Good things came to those who waited, Boudiaf believed.

And he had waited long enough.

IT HAD BEEN a difficult choice for Malik al-Salaam, deciding which rebel leader to call, when the two leading factions in the city were at each other's throats. He had decided on the Armed Islamic Group because, all things being equal, it seemed to have the better chance of victory—or, more precisely, a better chance of keeping him alive and in one piece long enough for al-Salaam to escape from Algiers.

According to the word from sources in the know, Houari Boudiaf and the GIA had more men, more guns and more money than the rival Islamic Salvation Front, led by Nabi Ulmalhama with support from Tehran. If he was questioned about his choice later— by the Iranians, for instance—he could always fabricate some plausible excuse for choosing the GIA to protect him. Perhaps Asem Kabir had supplied him with a contact number, while Wasim Ruholla had not.

It then became a simple matter of convenience, entirely logical, with no offense intended.

Easy.

Malik al-Salaam left his packing to the nervous members of his private bodyguard. They were good at folding clothes, those brothers, and the urgency of finding cover had encouraged them to do it quickly. He made a silent promise to forgive them if his suits came out of it with any unaccustomed wrinkles.

Better creases, said the small voice in his head, than bullet holes and bloodstains.

Yes, indeed.

The car was waiting when they got downstairs, a proper limousine, with one of Boudiaf's men at the wheel. Al-Salaam hurried across the open stretch of sidewalk, huffing a sigh of relief as he settled into the limo's broad rear seat, surrounded by his men. Dawn would be breaking soon, and as he bolted from the hotel lobby, al-Salaam had been oppressed by the mental image of a well-placed sniper staring at him through a telescopic sight.

Forget about it, man!

He was alive and on his way to sanctuary. That was all that mattered, for the moment. He could fret about his public image later, put whatever kind of spin on it he wanted to. The main thing that he wanted to avoid was getting killed.

Houari Boudiaf had been accommodating and inviting on the telephone—all charm, in fact—but al-Salaam was a suspicious man by nature, having grown up in the low-rent projects, running with street gangs and dodging honky ''justice'' by his wits alone.

Okay, so maybe when it came to dodging in the old days, he was something less than a spectacular success. His rap sheet demonstrated that beyond a shadow of a doubt.

But that was then, and this was now. The simple fact that Boudiaf invited him to wander by and make himself at home wasn't enough to throw the new, improved Malik al-Salaam off his guard. If anything, in fact, the welcome had been just a bit too warm and fuzzy for his taste. And while suspicion wouldn't cause him to reject the one safe haven in Algiers, al-Salaam had warned his bodyguards to stay alert and keep their eyes wide open while they were guests of the Armed Islamic Group.

And speaking of armed, there would be no surrender of the weapons his security detachment carried. If Boudiaf suggested they disarm, al-Salaam was ready to forego the local hotshot's hospitality and head directly for the airport. He would commandeer the limo, if it came to that. Let Boudiaf come forward and accuse him of stealing the ride if he thought the cops would sympathize with one of the most wanted men in Algiers.

Fat fucking chance.

Al-Salaam was getting edgy, and he tried to turn down the paranoia a notch or two for his own peace of mind. There was a difference, he realized, between staying alert and running scared. If he was forced to flee Algeria, he meant to do it in as orderly a fashion as he could, ignore whatever criticism came his way for the moment and deal with the petty shit later.

Assuming he was still alive.

That was the deal-maker.

Al-Salaam stared out the limo's tinted windows, watching a rosy dawn break over Algiers. Just looking at it this way, you would never guess the country had been bogged down in a civil war the past ten years or so. It didn't show up in the city, much—not like Beirut, at least, where whole blocks had been bombed and rocketed into crumbling ruins; not like Baghdad, where the scars of American air strikes were still plain to see, people ruined and starving from the economic sanctions everywhere you turned.

Algiers still put on a brave face and polished the knickknacks, keeping up a front. You had to move among the common people, leaving the hotels and limousines behind to see and hear what it was like, living at ground zero. Even then, while Algiers and the other urban centers had their share of bombings and shootings—a damn sight less before the past few days—most of the killing had gone on in the countryside, in villages which the reporters rarely visited, and which the wealthy city-dwellers seldom heard of in the first place.

Al-Salaam had hoped to change all that, negotiate some kind of truce that would reduce the bloodshed, while at the same time casting himself in the role of a hero-statesman, rubbing his success in the faces of those who openly doubted his motives, who questioned his love of God. He had failed in that respect, no doubt about it, but that was no reason why his Middle Eastern trip should be a total washout.

Not at all.

He had made valuable contacts in Iran and Libya,

Iraq and Syria, in Jordan and Lebanon, before he ever set foot in Algeria. With any luck at all, he could still count on some of those contacts—maybe all of them, praise God—for substantial contributions once he got back home. He had a law firm standing by to deal with the arrangements, set up the offshore accounts and all that, in case the IRS had second thoughts about the Islamic Brotherhood's religious tax exemption, somewhere down the road. One of the partners in the law firm was a longtime friend; he had defended al-Salaam several times, back in the days when he was plain old Rodney Allen Tuggle, and the fact that he had never managed to win an acquittal on Tuggle's behalf wasn't really his fault.

After all, in each one of the cases, he had been guilty as sin.

"We there," one of the brothers told him, al-Salaam glancing up at a black wrought-iron gate as the limo rolled through it. There were men with AK-47s posted on the inside of the gate, and al-Salaam could only wonder at the way things happened in the Middle East. Houari Boudiaf was number one or two on the "most wanted" list for every cop in Algiers, denounced daily in the state-run papers as a terrorist and murderer, but no one seemed to care that he was living right there in Algiers, behind an eight-foot wall, with shooters posted on the gate.

What was up with *that?* al-Salaam wondered, but then who cared, as long as he could keep the other crazy bastards off his back.

Right on.

Al-Salaam was smiling by the time the limo found its parking place outside a stylish-looking house, and more armed men appeared to usher him inside.

NABI ULMALHAMA scowled at the sound of a telephone jangling in another room. Someone answered on the second ring, but it was still an irritation. All the more so, since the calls had started coming around midnight.

And nearly all of them the same.

His soldiers were reporting in, and none of them had any welcome news to share. No victories for the Islamic Salvation Front; not so much as a single, cunning ambush executed by his troops against the GIA. Only more losses, or the simple lack of news that had become almost as wearisome as learning of a new defeat.

More troubling yet, however, were the other calls.

They were all distinctly similar; indeed, for sheer monotony of recitation, the callers might have been reading from a common script. In each case, word had come from some more-or-less trusted source on the streets, hinting at a new offensive in the offing, ready to be launched against the FIS by soldiers of the Armed Islamic Group. The callers and their sources were inevitably vague on details, but it hardly mattered, after all.

Nabi Ulmalhama had no clear reason to doubt the reports. On the contrary, with recent events in mind, the losses he had suffered to the GIA's so-called Anointed Ones, he would have been surprised if there wasn't more violence being planned among his ene-

mies. He despised Houari Boudiaf with passion un-
surpassed, but he would have questioned his rival's
intelligence, much less his courage, if the strikes inflicted in the past two days hadn't been followed up.

The GIA was winning, after all.

No matter how he tried to sugarcoat the truth or
turn the facts around and stand them on their heads,
it still came out the same. Both sides had suffered
losses in the recent mayhem, but Ulmalhama's group
had been smaller to start with, his losses thus pro-
portionately greater. More to the point, he could claim
no significant credit for any damage suffered by the
GIA, since his soldiers had scarcely laid a glove on
their rivals. The glory, therefor, belonged to someone
he hadn't even been able to identify.

But there was still a chance, he thought, to turn the
tables on his foes and rescue victory from the slav-
ering jaws of apparent defeat. He was forewarned this
time, which meant that he could not only take steps
to defend himself, but also to stage a preemptive
strike against his enemies.

The notion made him smile, and the expression felt
so odd on his face after hours and days of scowling,
that the smile in turn made Ulmalhama frown again.

There would be time enough for smiles—and even
celebrations—once he had succeeded in striking back
at his foes. If he kept his wits about him, and God
was smiling, Nabi might just have a chance to smile
at Houari Boudiaf's funeral.

For starters, he knew where the GIA leader resided,
knew the number of his bodyguards, and he knew
each time Boudiaf budged outside his fortress. Per-

haps, after all, the trick would be not waiting for Boudiaf to show himself on the street. Perhaps Ulmalhama's soldiers should look for him at home, take every man and weapon left to overrun the palace guards and end the threat, once and for all.

He heard footsteps approaching, turned and saw his houseman standing in the open doorway, one hand raised as if to knock. Ulmalhama saved him the trouble, acknowledging him with a nod and a scowl.

"What now?" he asked.

"The call was from Akim Bourassa," said the houseman.

"Who?"

"One of your men, sir." The houseman looked embarrassed, thereby further irritating Ulmalhama. "He's assigned to watch Houari Boudiaf tonight."

"And so he leaves his post to use the telephone?"

"He has a portable, sir."

"Well, then? What did Akim Bourassa have to say?"

"Houari Boudiaf has houseguests, sir. The Americans."

Ulmalhama's mind went blank, his inability to follow the conversation further infuriating him. "Americans?" he echoed. "By the prophet's beard, *which* Americans?"

"Malik al-Salaam and his men, from the Islamic Brotherhood."

It felt as if someone had thrown a switch inside his skull, illuminating floodlights Ulmalhama never knew existed. Suddenly, as if by magic, he saw everything. He understood the full depth of Houari Boudiaf's duplicity, the real agenda of the black American who had pretended to negotiate a cease-fire in Algiers. And to think that Wasim Ruholla had been taken in by the American's performance, induced to carry messages for Malik al-Salaam as if he were a lapdog for the Americans, instead of a spokesman for the ayatollahs in Tehran.

No wonder he was dead, the scattered remnants of his body scraped with shovels from the street and sidewalk outside his hotel. A monumental fool deserved no better fate.

"Oh, *those* Americans. Yes, I see." And it was all that he could do to keep from smiling, now. His course of action was so clear a blind man could have seen it. "I need Mohammed Zeroual," he told the houseman. "Send for him at once."

He didn't wait for an acknowledgment of the command, assuming rightly that it would be carried out, and that Mohammed would respond immediately. A few more minutes, then—perhaps as much as half an hour—and Nabi Ulmalhama could issue marching orders to his troops.

He would have his revenge.

It would be all the more pleasant, he thought, to eliminate two rivals in a single stroke. Before that moment, he had viewed Malik al-Salaam as a simple opportunist, courting favor with the so-called Muslims at home through a pilgrimage to the Middle East. His followers were no doubt picking up the bill through tithes and contributions, while al-Salaam used their money to buy more publicity for himself.

But now, the FIS leader realized, he had to treat

the American as more than a minor, peripheral irritant. Malik al-Salaam had conspired with the GIA from his arrival in Algiers to help Houari Boudiaf destroy the FIS. And in order to crush the Islamic Salvation Front, they would have to kill Nabi Ulmalhama.

Unfortunately for his enemies, however, Nabi still had some tricks up his sleeve. He wasn't dead yet, and he renewed his pledge to God that their common enemies would suffer for breaking the faith and taking His great name in vain.

In fact, so committed was he to the plan so full-blown in his mind, that Ulmalhama had decided to lead the troops himself. Mohammed Zeroual would try to talk him out of it, but he wouldn't be moved by any concerns for his personal safety.

It would be a failure—worse, an act of cowardice—to remain safe in hiding when his troops took the field this time, against the very worst of his enemies. And, while Ulmalhama had been called many things in his time, no one had ever branded him a coward.

A great battle was coming, and it would be fought the only way such conflicts could be waged: without quarter asked or given.

To the death.

GHOLOMREZA KORDIYEH had decided to forsake his Z-84 submachine gun for the final act of the drama, switching instead to the more powerful AKSU assault rifle. With the metal stock folded, the compact Kalashnikov was no larger than his SMG—and smaller when the Z-84's sound suppressor was considered—

but it chambered a more powerful 5.45 mm Soviet cartridge, while boasting a higher cyclic rate of full-auto fire: 800 rounds per minute, versus the Z-84's 600.

Bolan had agreed to the change, remarking that it would be best for both of them to carry identical weapons, in case one ran out of ammunition and was forced to borrow a spare magazine from the other. Their side arms would remain the same, the CZ-75s, and they had finished double-checking all four weapons, topping off magazines, dividing the last of Kordiyeh's RGD-5 antipersonnel grenades between them.

"I could get more men to help us," Kordiyeh suggested, and at once regretted it. It made him sound as if he doubted their ability to do the job alone. More to the point, it made him look as if he were afraid.

In fact, both things were true. Kordiyeh did doubt their ability to carry out the raid Belasko had in mind, two men against two dozen or more, and he was afraid.

He simply hadn't wanted the American to know these things.

"How many people did you want to get involved in this?" Bolan asked him, graciously ignoring the Algerian's blush of embarrassment.

Kordiyeh considered it, seeing the escape hatch, then reached out himself to close and latch it. "None," he said in reply. "You're right about the numbers. Any more would be a needless risk. We might wind up shooting one another."

The American nodded, feeding a long, curved magazine into the receiver of his AKSU. Brown plastic magazines were the norm for such weapons. They wore out more quickly than the older metal ones, but it hardly mattered, since there was a seemingly endless supply on the market, available at cut-rate prices from various sources in the former Soviet Bloc. Ammunition, likewise, was more readily available than decent food to certain families in Algeria and other parts of the Third World.

This night's effort, Kordiyeh thought, might be a small step toward changing all that.

Or then again, it might simply be a blind leap to his death.

Either way, he felt he had accomplished something with Mike Belasko in the past two days. The achievement would be difficult to quantify for a casual observer: on the surface, it might appear that they had done nothing at all beyond compounding the violence and misery of Algeria's long civil war. Kordiyeh knew better, though. Since the first strike on Libyan soil, through the recent blitz that had included Asem Kabir and Wasim Ruholla among the dead, he and Belasko had effectively reversed the tide of violence. For the first time in years, armed combatants of the terrorist militias filled the casualty lists, while innocent civilians had been virtually left alone.

Two days.

It sounded even more insignificant in those terms, when compared to ten long years of bloodshed in the streets and rural hamlets, with women and children slaughtered by the score. And yet it was a start. For the first time in a decade, it was the terrorists who lived in fear, instead of innocent farmers and merchants condemned by faceless enemies for their religion or their politics.

A start, if nothing more.

And if they carried off their final mission, even if they died in the attempt, it would be more than a start. The Armed Islamic Group, deprived of leadership and several dozen of its fighting men, would be dramatically reduced in its ability to terrorize the hinterland. That much would be a shining victory to Gholomreza Kordiyeh.

He only hoped that he would be alive to celebrate it with his comrades after all was said and done.

And if he wasn't, well, at least his name would be remembered, both by those who fought for justice, and among the enemies of peace who would recall his deeds and cringe a little, knowing that if one man could achieve so much, there would inevitably be another, and another, and...

"We'd better get a move on," Bolan said, already on his feet and shouldering the duffel bag that held his weapons.

"Yes. I wish..."

"Wish what?"

"I was about to say, 'I wish that we could stop the FIS, as well.'"

"Don't count them out, just yet," Bolan replied. "I didn't have you making all those calls for nothing."

"But, if they were coming..."

"They'd be on their way by now," said the American, then smiled. "I guess we'll have to wait and see on that. Whoever shows up, though, the party won't be dull."

CHAPTER SIXTEEN

After a brief drive-by recon of Houari Boudiaf's hard-site, Bolan knew one thing beyond a shadow of a doubt: he wanted to be inside that eight-foot wall when the feces hit the fan. Scaling the wall under fire was a fool's errand—not impossible, granted, but the next best thing—and the soldier didn't plan to throw his life away on some grand, empty gesture. Getting inside would be infinitely easier before the watchdogs knew they were under attack.

But from that point on, all bets were off.

As Kordiyeh had indicated, there was no way to guess how many men and guns would be waiting for them at the hardsite. A dozen seemed pathetically conservative, but he couldn't read Boudiaf's mind. There might well be three or four times that number. He would simply have to take his chances, knowing that the strike was unavoidable.

And if an armed contingent from the FIS showed up to join the fray, as Bolan hoped they would, what then?

Same game, same stakes, same rules. The only

thing that changed would be the odds against his coming out the other side alive.

Sunrise was still at least an hour off, as Bolan chose a spot to lock and leave the vehicle. With Kordiyeh beside him, the Executioner moved through darkness, a long city block to the hardsite, patrolling the fence on his side, looking for the best way in.

There were no natural bridges, no convenient trees that Boudiaf's men had forgotten to trim or cut down. It hardly mattered, though, since an eight-foot wall was no real obstacle to a determined man in halfway decent shape. It would have been more difficult with razor wire on top, or even broken glass embedded in concrete, but Boudiaf—almost incredibly, considering the circumstances in Algiers—apparently put all his faith in bricks and mortar, men and guns.

The sentries worried Bolan, but there was nothing he could do about them in the final analysis. If they worried him too much, he would never get inside the wall, never come close enough to take Boudiaf.

Timing.

He paused and listened on the outside of the wall, the southeast corner, farthest from the house and street. Another man might have felt silly, standing in the darkness with his eyes closed, listening to the night, but Bolan knew what he was doing.

The one question in his mind was whether he could pull it off.

After three full minutes of near-silence, he scrambled to the top of the wall and froze there, stretched out on his belly, feet splayed. No guards were visible from where he lay, and none opened up on Bolan as he lay there, vulnerable, totally exposed. There could still be shooters hiding in the dark, waiting for him to fully commit himself, proceed beyond the point of no return...

He gave it another moment, weighing the odds, then flashed a quick thumbs-up to Kordiyeh, outside, and rolled off the top of the wall. Landing in a crouch, the AKSU ready in his hands, Bolan held the new position until his comrade dropped behind him, covering the Algerian's move.

They were in... and the easy part was behind them.

From that point onward, it came down to picking a fight with a combat force of unknown size, many of the opposition hardened veterans, and trying to come out alive at the end of it all. Somewhere along the way, before he could claim success, Bolan had to find and liquidate the leader of the Armed Islamic Group.

MOHAMMED ZEROUAL had rounded up as many soldiers as he could on such short notice. There would have been more a week earlier, before the latest whirlwind of slaughter hit town, but as it was they filled five cars, with six more riding double on three motorcycles.

They made a strange procession, rolling through the streets of Algiers in that last hour before sunrise, the motorcycles leading, zipping through sparse early-morning traffic. It reminded Zeroual of a funeral cortege, and he suppressed a shudder at the thought. Someone would die, this morning, but he hoped that he wouldn't be found among the dead.

Zeroual had protested Nabi Ulmalhama's plan to lead the troops himself, playing every card he had, but it was finally no use. He had no authority to overrule his superior's decision, and his other arguments rang hollow in the face of Ulmalhama's need to reassert himself as leader of the FIS, a leader who could march—well, make that *drive*—his men to victory, despite their recent losses.

At least they were well-armed, Zeroual thought, each man packing an automatic weapon, most with one or more side arms concealed on their person. In addition to the standard guns, Ulmalhama had insisted that they drag along the Eryx short-range antitank weapon, a French rocket launcher that weighed thirty-four pounds on its own without the twenty-five-pound missile. Eryx was a special sort of launcher, capable of being fired within closed spaces since it had no backflash, but the weapon was so bulky that they had to place it in the trunk, effectively beyond their reach until the car was stopped and someone went outside to fetch it.

Brilliant.

Zeroual had argued against bringing the Eryx, as well, noting that the half-dozen rockets stacked with their launcher in the trunk of the Peugeot sedan made the car a mobile powder keg, but Nabi hadn't budged. He wanted every ounce of firepower he had arrayed against the enemy this time.

And there was just a chance, Zeroual grudgingly admitted to himself, that it would work.

Not the Eryx; that was foolish, an extravagance unused since they had purchased it two years earlier from a black marketeer in Lyons. The basic plan, though, when he thought about it now—sitting with an AKM in his lap, surrounded by thirty more soldiers, all with murder on their minds—might just be successful, in spite of his early misgivings.

If they could take Houari Boudiaf by surprise, kill enough of his people before the GIA gunners could mount an effective resistance, then they had a chance. If they weren't spotted blocks in advance of their target or betrayed by an informer. If they could just breach the gate to Boudiaf's compound, make their way inside.

If.

Ulmalhama had to have had similar thoughts, for he ordered the caravan halted two blocks from their target. The motorcyclists wore tiny headphones under their helmets, and they were summoned back with a command from their leader, to stop them from alerting the GIA guards.

"We might have trouble with the gate," Ulmalhama said to no one in particular. Zeroual agreed, half hoping that Nabi was about to change his mind, call off the raid entirely, while another part of him was anxious to proceed.

"There will be soldiers on the gate, of course," he said, validating his superior's concern.

"I mean the gate itself, Mohammed. They will not just open it and welcome us inside."

"Perhaps—"

Zeroual was relieved of any need to blunder through a hasty, makeshift plan when Ulmalhama interrupted him. "The Eryx. Someone must take it, go ahead of us and be prepared to blow the gates when we arrive.''

Zeroual suppressed a groan. "It will be light soon," he replied. "Whoever takes the launcher will be seen."

"He will have to hurry, then. It is only five hundred meters, after all. One of the cyclists, perhaps."

That would mean leaving one of the motorcycle passengers on foot, or packing him into a car that was already crowded. It meant securing the Eryx launcher across the cycle's rear seat, somehow, since it was too large and awkward for the driver to carry. On arrival at the target, the unlucky one would then have to unstrap and shoulder the Eryx, find his mark and blow the heavy gate, all without being seen and gunned down in the process.

It sounded like a pipe dream, spawned by too much hashish.

"I will take it," Zeroual blurted out, uncertain who had spoken for a moment, until he realized it was himself.

What was he thinking? Had he lost his mind? The heavy rocket launcher was an albatross, the next best thing to a bullet in the head for whoever had to carry it in battle. Still...

"I will take it," he repeated, reaching for the inside handle of the Peugeot's left-rear door.

He had a plan, and if it all worked out, Zeroual would be a hero to the FIS, and in the eyes of God. If it failed, well, it was even money that he would be dead in that case, with Ulmalhama and the rest of the strike team for company.

Zeroual stepped out of the car, walked around to the rear end and opened the trunk. He lifted out the bulky Eryx launcher, already loaded, and hoisted it onto his shoulder. As a hedge against bad luck and sloppy aim, he reached into the trunk—nearly toppling forward in the process, his heavy weapon scraping the trunk lid—and retrieved a second rocket.

With the AKM slung on its shoulder strap, spare 30-round clips in his pockets and the pistol on his hip, Zeroual was carrying some eighty-plus pounds of hardware. It was nearly too much, a heartbeat of panic as he feared that he would stumble, drop his load, or simply be unable to proceed on foot, but somehow he started walking toward the target, picking up his pace until it was nearly a trot.

Behind him, closing in, the motorcade began to move once more.

BOLAN AND KORDIYEH were well inside the hardsite, moving cautiously toward Houari Boudiaf's fortified home when the shooting started. An explosion came first from the direction of the gate, striking Bolan's eardrums with the wham-bam of a heavy antiarmor round.

And that, he knew, could only mean one thing.

It was ridiculous to think that any member of the home team would be detonating HE rounds on the property—unless, perhaps, they were under attack. The blast and its direction, coming from the compound's one intended exit, meant one of two things: either someone was either trying to blast his way in, or else the sentries on the gate had unleashed heavy firepower against some unwelcome visitor.

In either case, it was the best diversion Bolan could have hoped for, delivered at the optimum time. The blast would alert any guards on the property, drawing them toward the gate, while those inside the house scrambled for clothing and weapons, racing to reinforce the perimeter contingent.

All were moving away from the point where Bolan and Kordiyeh were making their way toward the house and Houari Boudiaf.

No words were necessary. Bolan broke into a trot, with Kordiyeh matching his pace, both holding their AKSU assault rifles at high port, across their chests. The chunky H&K grenade launcher slapped against Bolan's hip as he ran, suspended from a makeshift shoulder sling, a 40 mm HE round already loaded in the breech. It wouldn't give the soldier as much bang for his buck as the unknown weapon that had blasted the gate, but it would do.

Another hundred yards remained before they reached the house. The trees were thinning already, and he had a glimpse of sentries running toward the gate, away from his position. Some of the retreating shooters sprinted, others jogged, clearly hoping for at least some vague idea of what had happened on the street before they blundered into a potential trap.

He didn't wish them luck. The more who were engaged with other enemies, the more who died without his help, the better it would be for Bolan and for Kordiyeh. From just the personnel that he could see, not counting those inside the house, it was apparent that they were outnumbered ten or twelve to one.

Grim numbers, but they weren't the worst that he had faced.

And he was still alive. So far.

Automatic weapons were firing down by the gate, now, the characteristic sound of Kalashnikov assault rifles. Smart tactics would have called for several shooters, at least, to remain near the house and guard their principals, but the sounds of combat so near at hand had seemingly thrown caution to the wind, every gunner in sight making a beeline for the perimeter. Bolan took advantage of their haste, closing the gap between himself and Boudiaf's villa, with Kordiyeh running a pace or two behind him.

And they were almost there, veering toward a side door, when the door swung open, disgorging more troops. Too late, it was apparent that the sentries of the second shift were taking up the slack, rushing to cordon off the house while their comrades dealt with the intruders at the gate.

It took perhaps three seconds for one of the guards to spot Bolan and Kordiyeh, pounding toward him across the green strip of lawn. Their black garb, plus Bolan's height and features, instantly distinguished them from any members of the home team. The point-man shouted an alarm as he swung his SMG around to bring them under fire.

Bolan was faster, nailing the Arab with a 5.45 mm burst that stopped the gunner's heart and whipped the weapon from his dying fingers, all at once. He saw the shooter lurch backward, jostling two of his comrades and spoiling their aim, then his AKSU was spitting out death once again, Kordiyeh joining the fight with his own Kalashnikov.

It was over in seconds, the shooters dead or dying as they fell, but it wasn't the end of Bolan's fight, by any means. His primary target was inside the house, and the soldier knew he wouldn't find Boudiaf alone, unguarded in his villa. Every step he took from this point was perilous, potentially the last move of his life.

He went in firing through the open doorway, his steel-jacketed rounds drilling pots and pans, knocking shiny divots in the broad doors of a double-wide refrigerator. There was no one in the kitchen to oppose him, but he caught the sound of angry voices coming through the arch that led to an adjacent dining room.

He glanced at Kordiyeh, made sure his friend had heard the voices, knew that enemies were waiting for them on the far side of the open arch. Bolan edged forward, hating the delay, yet determined that he wouldn't be propelled by haste into a lethal trap.

How many soldiers in the dining room? A cautionary hiss had stilled the voices, now, but he was sure there had been two or three, at least, all speaking in Arabic. He didn't care what they had said, what they were thinking in the sudden silence; all that mattered now was neutralizing them before Boudiaf was able to escape.

Bolan chose a frag grenade from the half-dozen clipped to his belt, pulled the pin and edged forward, keeping to the right of the archway. The interior walls of the house were lath-and-plaster construction, solid enough to support the roof overhead, but flimsy when it came to stopping military ammo. When the storm broke, he would have to hit the floor, and quickly, to avoid being dropped in his tracks.

The Executioner cleared the last eight feet in two long strides and whipped his arm around the corner of the arch, releasing the grenade to do its work, and hit the polished floor as several automatic weapons started chewing up the walls.

HOUARI BOUDIAF had poured himself a cup of mint tea, was just about to take his first sip when the echo of a powerful explosion somewhere near the gate rattled the windows of his home. He flinched involuntarily and dropped the cup, hearing it strike the carpeting between his feet and bounce. Boudiaf brushed past his visitor and hurried toward the window of his study, facing toward the driveway and the grounds beyond.

He couldn't see the gate or the perimeter from where he stood. There were trees in the way, the long blacktopped driveway curving in an S-shape that gave new arrivals an exaggerated sense of the property's size.

Even with the trees and darkness, though, he still made out a flickering illumination, as of firelight from a distance. Something was burning at the gate, he thought.

What could it be?

A car, perhaps. The blast had sounded very much like the explosion of a rocket or propelled grenade, the sort of weapon used by infantry on tanks and ar-

mored cars—or by guerrilla fighters on commercial
aircraft, given half a chance. The trouble with that
theory was that his defenders had no rocket launchers
or explosives at the villa, other than a few stray hand
grenades. That meant the rocket—if, in fact, it was a
rocket—had been fired by someone from outside, and
what would it have set on fire?

The gatehouse, he decided. It was made of wood,
and cheaply, meant to shelter sentries from pouring
rain and little else. If someone fired a rocket at or
through the gate, it might ignite the guard shack. No
great loss, Boudiaf thought, but if his home was under
siege by enemies who brought that kind of military
hardware with them, they would soon be past the gate
and past his watchmen, closing on the house itself.

A whiff of too-sweet cologne told Boudiaf that
Malik al-Salaam had joined him at the window. The
American had managed to dispose of his teacup without dropping it, but his hand was trembling as he
reached to pull the curtains farther back, giving himself a better view of the grounds.

"What is it?" he asked foolishly.

"An explosion," the GIA's leader replied. "It
would seem we are under attack."

Boudiaf was pleased with the sound of his own
voice, surprisingly firm, under the circumstances. It
didn't echo the nervousness he felt, unwilling even
then to call it fear.

"Under attack by whom?"

"If I knew that," Boudiaf told him, sneering, "I
would have killed the bastards days ago."

Al-Salaam was famous for his oratory back in the

United States, but few disciples would have recognized his whining voice, just now. "This was supposed to be a safehouse," he complained, childlike. "You promised me."

"There are no guarantees in life," Boudiaf replied. "Take heart, however. You might have a chance to prove yourself tonight. A hero in the making."

Al-Salaam half turned to face him, his dark eyes narrowed with suspicion. "What are you talking about?" he demanded.

"These traitors to God are doubtless the same ones who murdered Asem Kabir," Boudiaf told him, by no means convinced of the fact. Still, it was possible, perhaps even likely. "Imagine the prestige, the reward from Tehran, if you help destroy the infidels." His voice turned cold and sly as he went on. "Imagine the disgrace if you refuse to stand and fight in God's name."

"I'm not a soldier," al-Salaam reminded him, his voice dropping almost to a whisper.

"Asem was not a soldier," Boudiaf replied. "It did not stop his enemies from killing him, you might recall."

"I'm under your protection, dammit! That was understood."

"Of course." The GIA commander swished a hand, dismissing the objection. "You will agree, however, that I had no way of knowing you would lead the enemy directly to my door."

"I didn't lead them anywhere," al-Salaam retorted, flinching at the sound of automatic weapons firing on the grounds. "Your troubles didn't start with me."

"Myself, I have no doubt that your arrival in Algiers and the occurrence of the first raid almost simultaneously is a mere coincidence. Some others might not be so understanding when they learn that an American led those who killed a dozen of my soldiers and my second in command."

"Say what?" Al-Salaam seemed unaware that he had lapsed into the street patois of younger days. "What damn American?"

"Alas, I do not know his name. Of course, I do not suspect that one of your men was responsible."

"Damn right, they weren't! Why would I—"

"But it might look better, all the same, if you assisted me in punishing the men responsible. The ayatollahs are a nervous breed."

A scowl carved furrows into al-Salaam's face. "What are you asking me to do?" he asked.

"Defend yourself," Boudiaf replied. "No more, no less."

"I need to see my men."

"Of course. For any tools you may require, see Akhmet. He's the one—"

"I met him," al-Salaam cut in. "If we're done talking, here…?"

"Of course."

It was a minor victory, humbling the proud American, but it was something. Even as the door swung shut behind his visitor, however, Boudiaf heard gunfire moving closer to the house.

No, wait! Those shots had sounded from inside the house.

He crossed the room, opened a bookcase and found

the hidden switch that let him swing aside the bright facade of artificial books. The secret gun locker displayed its wares, all polished wood and gleaming, oily steel.

Boudiaf chose his weapon, swiftly loaded it and went to join his men.

MALIK AL-SALAAM WAS steaming as he left the study, his anger almost making him forget the fear that gripped him. Almost, but not quite. Back in the bad old days, when he was on the streets of Motown—even when he did his time—al-Salaam had never been much of a fighter. He could hold his own when it was one-on-one, but he had better luck with sucker punches, coming from an adversary's blind side preferably with a tire iron or a length of pipe. The one man he had ever shot was only wounded in the butt, and that from ambush, al-Salaam firing while his victim's back was turned.

In prison, he had fought to keep the bootie bandits off his back, but only for a little while, until he got connected with the Muslims. After that, if anybody tried to mess with Rodney Allen Tuggle, they were messing with the whole Islamic Brotherhood. That wasn't healthy, and the cell-block wolves had gone in search of other fish to fry.

Now, here he was, stuck in the middle of a turf war, ten or fifteen thousand miles from home, with his "protector" telling him he had to fight or else be lumped together with the enemy. Al-Salaam had no idea what Boudiaf had meant about Americans participating in the recent raids around Algiers. He had suggested something similar himself when he was talking to the moneymen from Tripoli and Tehran, but he had been talking about American influence, the kind of shit the CIA had pulled a thousand times in Third World countries, using local contract agents. It had never seriously crossed his mind that American agents—mercenaries or illegals—would do the dirty work themselves in a country like Algeria, where white faces stood out like the proverbial sore thumb.

It stood to reason, of course, that Langley and the Pentagon had all kinds of killers on their payroll, including some who could pass for Africans or Arabs in a pinch. It made no difference to al-Salaam *who* was responsible, in fact, as long as he got out of the present mess alive, with no undue damage to his personal reputation.

Which meant that he would have to fight, however briefly, at least for appearance's sake. Or, rather, that his men would have to fight, while he stood by to supervise.

His troops were waiting for him in the sitting room where he had left them when he went to have his private meeting with Houari Boudiaf. All four of them were packing AKs, folding stocks and long, curved magazines. A fourth identical rifle lay atop the nearby coffee table, waiting for him.

"Where'd all this come from?" al-Salaam demanded.

"From that Akhmet dude," Kareem replied. "One with the scar all down the left side of his face."

"Uh-huh." So, Boudiaf had arrogantly taken his assent for granted, arming al-Salaam's men before their leader had agreed to join the battle. Well, at least it never hurt to have more guns.

"Man says he needs us to participate in the defensive operation," he told his bodyguards. "Reckons his people need a look at how to do it right."

He saw no need to mention that Boudiaf had come within a gnat's ass of denouncing them as infidels, accusing al-Salaam of plotting with his enemies to kill all kinds of folks the American had never met. There seemed to be no point in pissing off his men, potentially distracting them with dark suspicions of their host right now, when he needed them to focus solely on the common enemy.

"We get to fight? That's cool." Kareem was smiling broadly, looking forward to it, but the others clearly had their doubts. Mfume and Uhuru glanced at each other, frowning, while Dwendi kept his head down, fiddling with his rifle, making sure that it was cocked and locked.

"What I've been thinking," al-Salaam replied, "is that the best thing we can do is haul ass out of here, ASAP." Before Kareem completely lost his smile, he continued, "But the trouble is, we have to get around these shooters who come looking for the fellow's got his name out on the mailbox."

"Maybe we can't get around them," Kareem said. "Maybe we have to go right up the middle."

"Then, we do it. Whatever's necessary for our own defense. But keep in mind that this is *not* our war, and this is *not* why we flew halfway around the world. If I wanted to get my ass shot off in some damn pissing contest, I could do it back home in Detroit."

"I heard that," Dwendi said, without raising his eyes.

"All right, then," al-Salaam told his soldiers. "What we need is wheels, and where we find them is out back. There may be keys in the ignition, maybe not. Uhuru! You still got your knack with automotive vehicles?"

"You pick the car, I'll get it started, Brother Minister."

Al-Salaam scooped up the AK-47 from the coffee table, hefting it to get the feel. "Okay, let's go," he said, "before this shit gets any deeper."

BOLAN WAS UP and moving as the echo of the frag grenade's explosion rocked the dining room. He went in low and fast, looking for mobile targets, but the two men he could see were down and out. One's face was torn by shrapnel, while the other had been pitched across the room, headfirst, into a china cabinet, with force enough to knock him out.

The Executioner kept moving past the bodies, through another open archway, this one leading to a spacious living room. The furnishings were mix-and-match, a low divan and a reclining chair, with big, soft pillows on the floor for those who liked pretending they were in a desert sultan's tent. No gunners were in attendance, though, and Bolan veered toward a doorway that appeared to open on a corridor leading to more rooms in the east wing of the house.

Passing a flight of stairs, he caught a twitch of movement from the corner of his eye, somebody on the second-story landing, and he swung in that direction, leading with the muzzle of his Kalashnikov.

The shooter could have taken Bolan's head off, but he jerked the trigger of his SMG, instead of lining up the shot and gently squeezing it. The first short burst was several inches high, unleashing a cascade of plaster dust, and the Executioner hammered his target with a spray of 5.45 mm rounds before a second burst could be unleashed. The GIA commando rocked back on his heels, a dazed expression on his face, before he lost the fight with gravity and toppled over on his back.

Suddenly, harsh voices seemed to be shouting from all sides at once—away to Bolan's left, along the corridor and from the second-floor landing above him. None of the soldiers was visible, yet, and while he couldn't understand a word they said, it was clearly a counteroffensive in the making, Boudiaf's palace guard closing ranks to rid the house of invaders.

Kordiyeh came up beside him, turning to cover the stairs, while Bolan shifted his attention to the west-wing corridor. Down at the far end, several shadow-shapes were stirring, and he chased them with a short burst from his automatic rifle, keeping their heads down. Kordiyeh, meanwhile, had primed an antipersonnel grenade and lobbed it toward the landing, where at least three men were calling back and forth, advancing cautiously toward the stairs.

One of them recognized the hand grenade and bellowed a warning cry, his meaning obvious to anyone within earshot, even if they spoke no Arabic. The blast came seconds later, instantly followed by sharp cries of pain, and Kordiyeh charged up the stairs, slowing only on the last few steps and ducking, to guard against defensive fire.

Bolan had no time to watch his comrade's progress, since the shooters at the far end of the corridor had found their nerve and their target, advancing by fits and starts behind a screen of covering fire. The soldier ducked to one side, partly shielded by the doorjamb, where he knelt and freed another RPG-5 hand grenade from his belt.

Downrange, his enemies were still advancing, but he had to guess the range, sight unseen. If the grenade flew overhead, they would be forced in his direction, shaken at the very least, and Bolan would be waiting for them with his folding-stock Kalashnikov. If it fell short, the gunners would be driven backward, their survivors briefly hidden by the smoke and dust from the explosion.

The trick, if he could pull it off, would be to drop the frag grenade directly in their midst, catch them out in the open and riddle them with shrapnel, then finish it off with the AKSU. There was no way to gauge the range precisely without risking a glance around the corner, where bullets were zipping through the air like angry hornets. Instead, Bolan wound up the pitch and let fly as best he could, ticking off the numbers in his mind until the RPG-5 detonated in a thunderous flash.

Screams beckoned him into the smoky charnel house, and he followed, leading with his rifle. There were voices to be silenced, faces to be checked against the photo of Houari Boudiaf that he had memorized.

And if the master of the house wasn't among these men, then the Executioner would have to seek him elsewhere in the killing grounds.

CHAPTER SEVENTEEN

The cars were waiting, right where Malik al-Salaam had known they would be. It was a mixed bag, including the limo that had brought them to Houari Boudiaf's estate, plus a Mercedes-Benz sedan, two BMWs, a vintage Lincoln Continental and a classic Jaguar XKE. From what he saw parked out behind the Arab's house, it seemed to al-Salaam that Boudiaf had turned a pretty penny on the Muslim revolution, up till now.

The XKE was out, first thing, since it would only seat two people. Back when he was living by his slave name in Detroit, al-Salaam had grooved on Lincolns, lusting after those the slick mack daddies drove around to check up on their whores, but at the moment, looking at the rides lined up that way, he passed the Continental by and picked the limousine.

Three reasons. First, it gave them ample room inside to move around with all their guns. Second, the heavy vehicle had armor plating on the sides, bullet-resistant glass and puncture-proof tires. He had learned to spot those kind of frills when he was boosting rides in Motown, and had kept his hand in now that he could purchase cars more costly than the ones he used to steal. Third reason was, if Boudiaf had sent the limo to impress him, when the driver picked them up at the hotel, it meant he liked this car the best, and boosting it would show him just what al-Salaam thought of a "brother" who would offer him protection, then expect him to get down and dirty in the trenches with the common folk.

Screw that.

The limo was unlocked, but there were no keys handy. No problem, there. Uhuru was underneath the dash in nothing flat, the dome light showing him which wires to sever, strip and cross. Less than a minute in the driver's seat, he had the limo rumbling like a lion in its cage at feeding time.

The rest of them piled in, acutely conscious of the combat noises—gunshots, screams, explosions—that were coming closer by the moment. Looking through the tinted windshield, Malik could see what looked like three or four cars rolling toward the house, their high beams on and muzzle-flashes winking from the windows. Some crazy bastard on a motorbike was pacing them, but he got hit and dumped the scooter while they were still some sixty yards from the house. There was no telling whether he was shot by someone on the home team, or the crazy suckers in the motorcade, but dead was dead, whether the Reaper found you in Detroit or in Algiers.

"Let's roll!" al-Salaam commanded, and Uhuru got the limo moving. Up front, in the shotgun seat, Kareem had found a gun port and was popping off a few caps from his AK at some shooters running on the grass. Al-Salaam suspected they were Boudiaf's, but didn't care enough just then to call off his henchman.

He kept his own Kalashnikov handy, sitting all the way in back, while Dwendi and Mfume took the forward jump seats, one of them adjacent to a gun port on each side. Some bastard in the third car of the hostile motorcade cut loose on them with automatic fire, al-Salaam recoiling from the impact of the first few rounds against the tinted window glass, before he noticed that they just left hazy-looking scratches without punching through. The rounds that hit the door and fenders sounded like someone was out there with a ball-peen hammer, but they likewise didn't penetrate.

"Well, shit!"

The curse came from Uhuru, driving, and al-Salaam craned forward, scoping the gate ahead of them. There were some bodies scattered on the grass, one of them stretched across the driveway like a fleshy speed bump, but the problem seemed to be another vehicle, slewed sideways just inside the gate and half blocking their retreat.

"We've got a tank," al-Salaam called out to his excited driver. "Don't forget it. Ram that son of a bitch out of the way, and see if you can find the airport, while you're at it."

They would have to ditch the limo and the hardware somewhere along the way, but that was nothing compared to coming through a goddamned war zone with your skin intact.

"Hang on back there!" Uhuru called out a beat

before they rammed the bullet-riddled hulk and
shoved it well left of the driveway, leaving paint behind, but suffering no damage that would keep them
off the road.

"All right!" Mfume cheered. "We rollin' now!"

And so they were, away from the "protection" of
Houari Boudiaf and the chaotic bloodshed in Algiers.
With any luck at all, another day or two would see
them safely home again, where al-Salaam would immediately touch base with the new friends he had
made throughout his journey—those of them still living, anyway—and set about fine-tuning his intentions
for the U.S.

BOLAN COULDN'T be sure exactly how or when the
house caught fire. It was most likely one of the grenades that he or Kordiyeh tossed, but there might
have been some other cause, including, he allowed, a
conscious and deliberate attempt to cover his primary
target's retreat.

In any case, the fire had blazed out of control while
Bolan was preoccupied with finishing his adversaries
in the hallway leading to the west wing of the house.
The second floor seemed more involved than the
ground floor where Bolan was, and that not only cut
him off from checking out the upstairs portion of the
house, it also threatened him with being trapped inside the villa, should the roof collapse.

Cursing bitterly, reluctant to the last, he called out
a warning to Kordiyeh and started to retreat along the
same path he had followed going in. Past bodies, bullet-riddled walls and furniture, the evidence of frag

grenade explosions, Bolan made his way back to the kitchen exit, followed all the way by drifting smoke and sound effects produced as hungry flames took hold, devouring the house.

He checked outside before emerging from the house, concerned about presenting his opponents with an easy target. As it happened, though, the gunners he could see were all collected at the north—or front—side of the house, where they appeared to be engaged in a do-or-die battle with some other foe.

The strike team from the gate, he guessed, most probably a spearhead from the FIS. Bolan ruled out police, because there were no flashing lights or sirens, no loud hailers calling for the hardmen to surrender. Likewise, he dismissed the military, since he saw no armored vehicles or uniforms. The home team was engaged with a civilian force that came prepared to hold its own, and from the bodies he saw crumpled on the ground, the issue still remained in doubt. Regardless of the winner, though, Houari Boudiaf had lost his stylish home.

And still, it wasn't good enough.

From where he stood, Bolan caught a flash of tail-lights, winking at him from the distant gate. A long, black car was turning eastward toward the city proper. It looked like a limo, and the soldier briefly wondered if he had already blown it, if his target had slipped past him.

If so, he instantly decided, there was nothing he could do about it, no way he could ever catch the limousine, not even if he disengaged and ran directly to his waiting vehicle. He had to be sure about Houari

Boudiaf, one way or the other, before he abandoned the battleground. And if the burning house presented him with major obstacles, as far as learning whether Boudiaf was still alive, it didn't absolve him from making the effort.

Kordiyeh emerged from the house with a hacking cough, stray tendrils of smoke clinging to his hair and clothes like cobwebs, blown to tatters and lost as he ran. Pulling up beside Bolan, he paused for a moment, bent double, trying to catch his breath.

"Whoever...is still inside..." he said, "they have not much time."

"Boudiaf?" Bolan asked his ally.

Kordiyeh shook his head, stifling another fit of coughing. "I saw no one who resembled him."

"We can't assume he's dead, then," Bolan said. "We need to stay awhile."

The smile looked out of place on Kordiyeh's face, considering the circumstances. "So, we stay," he told the Executioner. "As you Americans would say, the night is young. The joint is humping."

"Jumping," Bolan said, correcting him, and even as he spoke the word, a portion of the villa's west wing jumped straight into the air, shattered walls and roof lifted by a comet's tail of flame, before they crashed to earth again.

Some kind of ammunition or explosives going off, thought Bolan. It made sense that Boudiaf would have a stash laid by, with all these shooters on the property. He briefly wished his target dead in the explosion, realizing even as the thought took shape that it would leave the issue unresolved, should it be true.

He didn't need to think or hear that Boudiaf was dead. Bolan would have to see the body for himself. And first, before that happened, he would have to find the leader of the Armed Islamic Group, wherever he might be.

Someone had spotted them, a gunner at the northeast corner of the house, somehow distracted from participation in the main event. He recognized intruders in the glare of spotlights covering the yard, and fired off a quick burst in their direction, pivoting to make a better job of it the second time around.

Bolan was lining up his own sights on the distant figure, taking up the trigger slack and counting on an easy kill—when, suddenly, the lights went out.

HOUARI BOUDIAF WAS startled, even frightened, by the sudden darkness that surrounded him. He had almost become accustomed to the smoke, telling himself that he would soon be clear of it outside, but now he had a whole new danger to contend with.

He knew the layout of the house by heart and could navigate from room to room, or floor to floor, while blindfolded. Of course, it made a difference that the villa was on fire, smoke turning the familiar rooms and hallways into makeshift gas chambers. It also made a difference that his burning home was under siege by men who sought to kill him, locked in combat with his bodyguards outside.

Boudiaf clutched the mini-Uzi submachine gun in his right hand, guiding himself with his left held out in front of him, his fingertips in constant contact with the wall. A few more yards, and he would reach the formal dining room, where he had entertained important guests in better days. From there, it was a relatively straight shot through the kitchen, out the back door, into the fresh air.

Well versed in urban combat tactics, Boudiaf asked himself what he would do in his rival's place, if he were storming Nabi Ulmalhama's house, had managed to surround it and set it on fire. He would cover the visible exits, assign his best shooters to watch every door they could find and make sure that nobody escaped from the building before it collapsed.

If he had thought of that, Boudiaf reasoned, so had his enemies, waiting for him in the outer darkness. There were three doors to the house—the front door, the kitchen door and one to serve the shaded patio—all covered now, he guessed, if the attackers had sufficient manpower. Escape through any one of them could cost Boudiaf his life.

Still moving as he thought the problem through, he changed directions, backtracked to another hallway and proceeded eastward. That wing of the house included two guest rooms, his library and one of the villa's four bathrooms. He could wriggle through one of the windows, Boudiaf thought, and have a better chance of escape from the house than if he bolted from one of the doors.

And once he was outside, well, that would be another problem, separate and distinct from the one that dogged him now. He had to take the breakout one step at a time, keep his wits about him constantly, if he was going to survive.

Boudiaf came to the bathroom, first door on his

left, and slipped inside, closing the door behind him. The smoke didn't follow him in, at least not en masse, though rank tendrils were twisting like snakes, creeping under the door. He stepped into the bathtub, checked the window, knowing he would fit once he had punched out the screen, and opened it as far as it would go. The problem didn't lie in fitting through the window, but rather in the threat of snipers waiting for him out there, in the night.

He had to forget about them.

If the guns were waiting for him, there was nothing he could do about it. They would nail him halfway through the window; maybe wait until he dropped through, then blast him as he tried to stand. Whatever, if the guns were waiting for him, he was dead.

But if they weren't...

Boudiaf cranked the window wide open and drove his fist into the screen, no time for finesse with the latches that held it in place. A quick glance outside showed him nothing to fear, and he rose on tiptoe, shoved his head and one arm through the window. He reached down to brace himself against the outer wall, while his other hand clutched the windowsill, and started to haul himself through, an inch at a time.

The windowsill scraped his chest and stomach, caught on his belt and refused to let him pass until he sucked in his stomach, rocked his hips back and forth in a painful simulation of coitus, finally breaking the link. Another moment, and he spilled out through the window like a drunken acrobat, landing painfully on his head and one shoulder.

Something popped, flared pain along his left arm,

but Boudiaf was still able to rise, albeit grimacing, and retrieve his mini-Uzi from the grass. His clavicle and shoulder weren't broken—he couldn't have moved his arm, if that had been the case—nor did he think that anything was dislocated. Still, it hurt like hell. Some kind of sprain, he thought, which he could deal with after he escaped with life and limb intact to find another haven from his enemies.

Fleeing on foot was impossible, Boudiaf realized, as he moved toward the rear of the house, where the cars should be parked. He kept to the shadows, an easier task since the fire devouring his home had shorted out the electrical circuits, killing the flood-lights outside when the power went down. He spared a quick glance for his soldiers, fighting for their lives at the front of the house, but felt no great inclination to join them. They were doing their job, protecting their master, and those who died as a result were guaranteed a place in Paradise.

What more could any humble warrior ask?

Boudiaf didn't carry car keys—he rarely drove himself, in fact, considering the problems with security around Algiers—but he knew where the keys were concealed in each one of his cars. There had been no need to lock the vehicles before this night, since no thief had ever been foolish enough to violate Boudiaf's property, and no one passed his soldiers on the gate without approval from the master of the house.

He chose the Jaguar XKE for speed, and because it was his favorite among the several cars. Sometimes Boudiaf drove it up and down the driveway on a whim, though he hadn't been brave enough to drive it on the street in better than a year. This, though, was a special case.

He slipped inside and found the Jag's ignition key beneath the floor mat on the driver's side, dropped his mini-Uzi into the passenger's seat as he slammed the door behind him, fastened his seat belt and gunned the powerful engine to life.

He would get through the gate somehow, no matter who was guarding it.

Dropping the Jaguar into gear, he released the hand brake and stepped on the accelerator.

One narrow escape from the jaws of death, coming up.

KORDIYEH WASN'T SURE how he had lost track of Belasko, exactly. The lights had gone out, and his eyes were still dazzled from exposure to the outdoor floods when someone started shooting at him, bullets coming from the front of the house.

He returned fire, short bursts to unnerve his adversary, and instinctively moved toward the shooter, instead of backing away. There was no safe haven on Boudiaf's estate, as far as Kordiyeh could tell, and if pursuit was unavoidable, he wanted to be the one chasing his enemy, instead of making it the other way around.

The sudden darkness worked both ways, unnerving everyone, leaving all eyes momentarily blind. As Kordiyeh regained his eyesight, following muzzle-flashes that winked in front of him like fireflies, he knew that he was headed toward the front lines of the battle, where Boudiaf's defenders were locked in a duel to the death with members of a raiding party, probably commandos of the FIS. It would be simple just to turn around and leave them to it, but Kordiyeh found he didn't have it in him to run.

He hadn't come this far and dared so much simply to watch from the sidelines while two bands of terrorists slaughtered each other.

He was taking more fire as he moved toward the northeast corner of the house, ducking, firing back with short bursts from his AKSU. Perhaps three-quarters of a magazine was gone, and he would have to reload soon if he wanted to stay in the game. No time like the present, he thought, and sprayed his final six or seven rounds into the winking darkness, dropping to one knee as he ditched the empty magazine and snapped a fresh one into place.

Kordiyeh's eyes were almost fully adjusted to the night by that time, and he could make out the shapes of several cars pulled up in front of the house. Men were crouched behind them and firing toward the villa, one or two of them apparently inside the cars, but none of the vehicles were in any shape to be driven away from the scene. All were riddled with bullets, their windows shattered, steam rising from ventilated radiators, each car sporting at least one flat tire.

The assault force had come this far, and it would go no farther.

Tired of watching, Kordiyeh found a place against the nearest bullet-scarred wall of the villa, tucked his stubby rifle underneath one arm and freed two RPG-

5s from his belt, gripping one in each hand. He primed the grenade in his right hand and pitched it toward the cars, then switched hands with the other, quickly armed it and lobbed it after the first.

Number two was still airborne when the first grenade blew, detonating in the space between two bullet-punctured vehicles. Two or three of the invaders fell, one vaulting through a clumsy backward somersault before the second RPG went off on the hood of a once-stylish BMW. The blast cleared whatever window glass remained in the vehicle and its immediate neighbors, dropping more gunmen as the shrapnel ripped through them, shredding flesh and bone.

A cheer went up from the villa's front porch, where a pocket of defenders had been surrounded, slowly whittled down by incoming fire. Encouraged by the havoc spread among their enemies, several members of the home team sprang to their feet, picking off dazed or wounded adversaries with their automatic weapons. For a moment, it appeared that final victory was theirs...until disaster struck them from the flank.

An equal-opportunity killer, Kordiyeh turned his AKSU on the suddenly exultant defenders, spraying their ranks with 5.45 mm bullets as he came around the corner, firing underneath the ornate safety railing on the porch. He took them from their blind side, dropping three before the others realized where the deadly fire was coming from. Two more went down as they were turning to confront him, and the others scattered, cursing, a couple of them vaulting the rail into darkness, preferring the company of their FIS adversaries to that of the unknown sniper behind them.

Another magazine empty, and Kordiyeh replaced it in two seconds flat. He was on a roll, unstoppable, rising from his crouch to seek the ones who thought they had escaped his wrath.

NABI ULMALHAMA had lived to regret leading the raid himself, but at the moment, he wasn't sure if he would live much longer. Stunned by the grenade explosions that had rocked the vehicle he used for cover, Ulmalhama read his doom in the renewed spate of gunfire from the porch, dark shapes rising and advancing for the kill. He was fumbling with his weapon, trying to aim with the blood of a scalp wound in his eyes, when another dark form joined the battle, springing from the shadows at one end of the porch and hosing the defenders with full-auto fire.

Ulmalhama's heart leaped into his throat. Was this one of his soldiers, who had somehow flanked their enemies in time to save him? Was there hope, even now, for survival? Perhaps for victory?

That slim hope was dashed in an instant, as the faceless gunman made his way around the far end of the porch, reloading his assault rifle. Instead of pursuing the scattered defenders, however, he turned toward the vehicles of Ulmalhama's one-time motorcade, scanning the darkness there, as if in search of survivors.

First one, then another of his men emerged from hiding, taking the new arrival for one of their own, but he quickly proved them wrong, dropping both men with short, point-blank bursts to the chest. Ulmalhama gaped at him, clutching his SMG, a shriek of outrage swelling in his throat...but he caught himself before the sound betrayed him, understanding for the first time who this was, standing before him.

One of them. The bastards who had torn Algiers apart, these past few days, striking targets on both sides, pitting the GIA and FIS against each other in a fratricidal war of attrition. Oh, granted, he still blamed Houari Boudiaf for much of his loss in the two days of mayhem, but now Ulmalhama had a chance to strike directly at the source, his chief tormentor—one of them, at any rate—and pay back his own grief in kind.

The trouble was, exactly how to pull it off.

He had been kneeling on the ground, keeping his head down, since the first drive toward the house had stalled, his cars and men pinned by hostile fire. Now, when he tried to rise and face his enemy, his legs betrayed him. The left one wobbled, popping at the knee, while the right one felt totally numb. The FIS leader staggered, hip-checked the car to his left, and kept himself from falling with a painful elbow jab to the bullet-scarred fender.

It was too much for his trigger finger, and he accidentally unleased a short burst from his submachine gun, easily six feet off-target, wasted bullets slapping stucco on the porch. His enemy, still faceless in the night, recoiled from the staccato fire, unleashed a burst from his Kalashnikov in answer.

One of the bullets drilled Ulmalhama through the shoulder, jolting him, but the wound was a clean one, through-and-through, and his slumped-over posture prevented him from sprawling backward. Ironically, the sudden pain of the wound cleared his head, suffusing his body with the chill of impending shock, at the same time that his legs felt suddenly electrified.

It was a miracle, he thought. A gift from God to sustain him in his contest with the enemy. He would triumph, yet, and he would wear his scars with pride.

Ulmalhama forced himself erect, pushing off from the car, putting one foot in front of the other as he circled in front of the vehicle. His left arm hung useless, but that was all right. He could fire the SMG one-handed, thrusting it in front of him like an oversized pistol, advancing toward his target like a human juggernaut.

The stranger fired again—a miss, another miracle—and Ulmalhama held down the trigger of his submachine gun, unloading half the magazine in full-auto fire. He saw the bullets strike his target, ripping a diagonal between his right hip and left shoulder, solid hits that took the gunner down, collapsing to his knees.

Now, finish it!

The proud commander of the FIS moved closer to his enemy, locking his elbow to hold the SMG steady, framing the stranger's head in his sights. Another pound or two of pressure on the trigger, and—

He was so focused that he didn't see the muzzle of the wounded gunner's automatic rifle rising, stopping when it reached the mark of Ulmalhama's waist. He didn't see the smile upon his adversary's face, wouldn't have recognized it if he had.

The guns went off together, hammering in counterpoint, their muzzle-flashes blazing in a brutal mirror image, overlapping for a heartbeat as the man with the Kalashnikov fell backward, Ulmalhama sprawling forward, facedown on the grass.

As if their showdown was the culmination of the battle, morbid silence had begun to settle on the killing field, broken but fitfully by moaning of the wounded who could find no comfort in the dark.

IT WAS the Jaguar's dome light that betrayed Houari Boudiaf. Bolan wouldn't have seen him, otherwise, would probably have gone to look for Kordiyeh. A flash of light was all it took, one glimpse of the familiar face before the dim illumination was extinguished, and the Executioner had found his man.

Which wasn't the same thing as stopping him, by any means.

Bolan was moving toward the Jaguar when he heard the engine fire, take hold and snarl with unrestrained power. The XKE lurched forward, jerkily at first, until Boudiaf found his rhythm with the gears. A few more seconds, and he would be rolling at speed, with no stopping him before he hit the open gate and left the smoky battleground behind him.

Bolan broke to his left, putting himself in front of the Jaguar, as he sighted down the AKSU's barrel. Aiming for the driver was a way to go, but Bolan was afraid the angle of the Jaguar's windshield might deflect his rounds enough to spare his target's life. If Boudiaf could drive, he could escape, whether he had to drive through Bolan or around him.

He'd take the engine, then.

He pumped a dozen 5.45 mm rounds into the sports car's long, low hood, each impact ringing like a hammer stroke against sheet metal, ugly divots sprouting on the paint job. Boudiaf reacted with a sharp twist of the steering wheel and stamped on the accelerator, but the Jag didn't respond as he anticipated. It began to swerve, all right, but it was losing power, stalling out from damage to the carburetor, fuel pump, crucial wires and hoses.

Bolan watched the XKE drift to a halt some forty yards away. The dome light flared again, his target bailing out the other side to keep the vehicle between them.

All right, he thought. So far, so good.

The Executioner had no view of Boudiaf from where he stood, so he circled to his right, around the Jaguar's rear. It was a fifty-fifty deal, only two ways to go unless he charged directly toward the car, and that would leave his enemy with solid cover, while the Executioner was totally exposed. This way, at least, he had a shot—or would, if the commander of the Armed Islamic Group had nerve enough to show himself.

When he had closed the gap by half, a dark shape rose behind the car, then ducked back out of sight again. Bolan held his fire, secure in the knowledge that Boudiaf had no clear shot unless both of them did. The closer he could place himself to the car and his target, the better off he would be when it came time to fire for effect.

He heard a scuffling sound and logged it, as there

was nothing he could do to pin down Boudiaf, short of firing blindly into the Jaguar itself. That, in turn, would betray his position, resolve any doubt in Boudiaf's mind about which way he should direct his defensive fire, while offering no prospect of a solid hit.

Save it.

He kept circling, slower now, half crouching as he moved in level with the Jaguar's trunk. Another ten, twelve steps, and he should have the first glimpse of his target since Boudiaf had ditched and gone to ground.

Bolan lunged around the right-rear fender of the XKE, his finger tightening around the Kalashnikov's trigger, but he froze on the spot, weapon silent, as he beheld the empty stretch of lawn.

Where was Houari Boudiaf? The Jag was too low-slung for him to wriggle underneath, particularly after it had plowed those furrows in the lawn, nearly bottoming out. And that could only mean—

Boudiaf came erect at the front of the car, facing Bolan across the Jaguar's length. He had been emulating the Executioner's moves, perhaps unconsciously, and he had kept the vehicle between them, but his eagerness betrayed him at the final instant.

The terrorist shouted something in Arabic, raising his weapon, and Bolan took no chances, crouching slightly as he fired through the Jaguar's rear window. The steel-jacketed rounds punched through the glass as if it were plastic, erupting from the windshield on the other side.

Boudiaf staggered, twitching as the slugs ripped into him, his SMG spitting rounds that began a few

inches off target and swung toward the stars as he
fell, toppling back out of sight. Bolan rounded the Jag
in a rush and found his adversary sprawled on the
grass, the light of life already fading from his eyes.

It took five precious minutes longer for him to locate Kordiyeh, near the front of the house. The villa
was burning so brightly by that time that Bolan had
no difficulty picking out his comrade's body, even
with the ugly, close-range wounds. He made no effort
to identify the dead man who had killed him,
stretched out facedown on the deck.

A quick scan showed no hostiles stirring anywhere
within his range of vision. Bolan had a choice to
make: he could remove the body, try to clear the wall
with Kordiyeh draped across his shoulder and spirit
him away, driving with a corpse in the rental car, or
he could leave the warrior where he fell, let the authorities take care of him.

The sirens made his mind up for him, wailing in
the distance, closing in response to some excited
neighbor's call for help.

No family, the brave Algerian had told him when
they met. All gone. All slaughtered in his homeland's
never-ending civil war. Perhaps they would be re-
united somehow, somewhere, now that Kordiyeh had
made the final sacrifice.

The Executioner had no fixed views about the af-
terlife, but he believed that debts were paid and valor
was rewarded, whether in this world or at some other
level, by the Universe itself. A soldier would be
judged as much by those who were his enemies and

how he dealt with them, as by professions of a given faith.

Turning away, Bolan retraced his steps past the collapsing house, the cars, off through the darkened trees. His job was finished here...but only here.

Unless he missed his guess, there was a final task to be performed at home.

CHAPTER EIGHTEEN

Detroit was mostly black, these days, and that was fine with Malik al-Salaam. "White flight" had drained the honkies off to various suburbs since the catastrophic riots back in 1967, though they kept their jobs in industry, commuting from their enclaves where the crime rate was distinctly lower than Detroit's, the unemployment rate a flyspeck in comparison to Motown's solid nine percent.

Al-Salaam talked about the black unemployment rate, sometimes, although he didn't get the hoots and cheers from crunching numbers on the dais that he got for lighting into Jews and blue-eyed devils. If he had to tell the truth, he would grudgingly admit that having close to one in ten young brothers out of work was bad for the economy, but it was great for the Islamic Brotherhood's recruiting program. Hungry, jobless men were often angry men, as well, and he could play that tune all day and night without a breather. Yes, indeed.

"White flight" was also fine with al-Salaam, because it gave the real people of Detroit a chance to elect their own brothers and sisters to office. Later on, when it turned out that those at the top of the food chain were just as avaricious as the greedy whites they had replaced, al-Salaam turned that to his advantage, too. It was the fault of "so-called Negroes," he informed the faithful, and the blue-eyed devils who had molded weak-minded brothers in their own sinful image.

Now, if someone from the Brotherhood was elected to reform the city government, you could expect some fur to fly. That brother—maybe Malik al-Salaam himself—would start cleaning house and not put down his mop until the whole damn place was squeaky clean.

Of course, hinting around that you might run for office was one thing; getting anyone from the established parties to take you seriously was a whole other ball game, especially if you had a list of felony convictions as long as your arm, thinly disguised by a midlife change of names.

So, politics was out for al-Salaam, except where he could throw his weight, his people's votes, behind a candidate possessed of qualities like courage, nerve... and gratitude to those who swung the balance in his favor. Sadly, for the chief of the Islamic Brotherhood, most candidates in Motown still depended on established party networks for their daily bread and butter, meaning that they might shake hands with him in public, during Black History Week, but they frowned on him disclosing information like the Jewish roots of slavery or the prehistoric lab experiments by Zanotec the Mighty, which produced pale, inferior honkies from the grafted genes of the original black man.

Go figure.

And with traditional politics closed to al-Salaam, for all intents and purposes, was it any wonder that a man of his dynamic genius turned to other avenues of reforming society? If whitey wouldn't do the world a favor and relinquish power to the brothers who deserved it, well, someone would have to yank the reins away from him by force.

Some time had passed since al-Salaam's excursion to the Middle East. He had been right about the honky press and Congress sniping at his back, taking his name in vain, but that had passed within a week or so. New problems came along, new targets for the media to crucify, and al-Salaam had gone back to business as usual...with a twist.

He had, in fact, maintained some of the more important contacts he had made while touring the troubled Holy Land. It turned out, after all, that while the ayatollahs in Tehran were having second thoughts— a couple of them even sucking up to the United States for foreign aid, no less—the powers that be in Tripoli were still committed to supporting the Islamic Brotherhood's campaign of revolution from within the U.S. Funds had been transferred to a Cayman Islands bank, the first fat suitcase smuggled through Miami two days earlier. It was time, now, for al-Salaam to take the next bold step.

He had a nice fat shipment coming in that very evening from the guys at Guns 'n' Bombs R Us.

Discretion would have indicated that he send Kareem or someone else to make the pickup, but al-Salaam was strong these days, damn near invincible, in fact. It had been nothing short of magic how he slipped out of Algiers when all the bullets were flying, and got home smelling like—well, maybe "like a rose" was pushing it, but not like something that you stepped in when you weren't looking, either.

Meeting this first shipment in the flesh was simply common courtesy. Besides, he was anxious to make sure he got his money's worth. He had a mental list of everything the brothers from across the water were supposed to be delivering—not written down, of course; he was too smart for that, the way the pigs loved building cases out of paper scraps and such.

The shopping list was awesome, even if he didn't get to write it down. Fifty Kalashnikovs, to start, the AKMs, with a dozen magazines each and twelve cases of 7.62 mm ammunition to feed them. A dozen Model 12 Beretta submachine guns, once again with spare magazines for each. As for the real party favors, he was expecting one Russian AGS-17 automatic grenade launcher, the infamous 30 mm Plamya that came with its own tripod, belt-fed from special drum magazines that held twenty-nine rounds. Too bulky for everyday use, the AGS-17 worked best in fortified locations or when mounted on a vehicle—as with a flatbed truck, strafing a certain police station, for instance. And if that wasn't enough, al-Salaam was also expecting rocket launchers, a half dozen each of the Russian RPG-7 and the more compact RPG-18, each with enough ammunition to keep his troops well supplied for the race war ahead.

A person couldn't stash that kind of hardware in a suitcase, toss it in a Caddy's trunk and sell it to the brothers on the street. Their meeting had been scheduled for 9:00 p.m., at a warehouse on the river, a quarter mile from Tiger Stadium. Some syndicate honcho owned the warehouse, and al-Salaam had greased him enough for the hardware to sit there until he had suitable transport and hideouts arranged.

Kareem was driving the limo—pearl gray and polished to a spit-shine gloss, with blacked-out windows all around to give the Brother Minister some privacy—while Uhuru, Mfume and Dwendi rode with their boss in the back. After Algiers, they were his four musketeers, the faithful brothers who had watched his back from the smoky hell of Houari Boudiaf's "safehouse" all the way home, never dropping a stitch. The fact that two of them were packing sawed-off shotguns and the other two had Ingram MAC-10 machine pistols said nothing about their out-of-town visitors, necessarily.

It was simply good business.

And al-Salaam was looking forward to his meeting with the Libyans, almost twitchy with the sheer excitement of it. This time next week, maybe next month, the Islamic Brotherhood would begin to make itself heard in a whole new way.

And whitey would be listening, you bet your ass.

"I DO NOT LIKE THIS," Baghel Riyadh groused to no one in particular. "I do not like waiting here."

"We are safe," Rabi Saghir replied. "Malik al-Salaam has guaranteed it."

"And who is Malik al-Salaam?" Baghel asked his comrade in arms.

"You know as well as I do," Rabi said. "He is the chief of the Islamic Brotherhood. He is a man the colonel trusts."

Riyadh had no immediate response to that. It was unhealthy to criticize Colonel Khaddafi, even half a world away from Tripoli. The gibes of the American press were one thing, of course, but for a loyal subject to question the colonel's judgment—most particularly in a conversation with other Libyan natives as loyal as himself—could be tantamount to suicide. Saghir might not betray him deliberately, but the colonel seemed almost psychic, veritably mystical, when it came to sniffing out doubters. One word in the wrong ear at home, and Riyadh would be reduced to landfill at some desert construction site.

"I still do not like this place," he said, shifting gears. He could hardly be condemned for criticizing a warehouse, least of all when their meeting place had been the American's choice, with some Italian gangster lurking in the background.

"It is fine," said Wafi Marwan. He was the leader of their team, a former captain in the Libyan army and an expert in all manner of weapons. It was he who would explain the operation of their sundry cargo items to the pickup team. His word was final, and Riyadh knew better than to argue with him.

But he didn't have to like the meeting place, no matter what Marwan or anyone said. He simply had to keep his mouth shut and hold his private feelings locked inside, where they belonged.

The fourth member of their group, Sadiq Hashim, had nothing to say on this or any other subject. He wasn't a mute, but he preferred to watch and wait in silence, cradling the Uzi submachine gun in his arms as if it were his firstborn son, fresh from a feeding at his mother's breast.

It was Hashim who saw the limousine approaching. He announced it with a short, low-pitched whistle, fading back into shadow near the broad warehouse entrance. He had chosen the position moments after they arrived, a vantage point that would allow him to cover the Americans, take them from behind if they proved treacherous, and close their escape route behind them.

All wasted effort, Riyadh thought, if this Malik al-Salaam was truly a friend.

He wondered, not for the first time, whether Colonel Khaddafi had ever been wrong about anything. He was a wise man, granted, even visionary; some said he was no less than the prophet himself, born again. Riyadh put no stock in such notions, although he was technically pledged to believe, as a loyal Muslim, that all things were possible with God. At the moment, however, questions of divinity were irrelevant.

He simply hoped the colonel knew what he was doing.

There would be hell to pay, he realized, if the illegal arms shipment was discovered—much less if four Libyan nationals were found in possession of the weapons. Another U.S. President had sent war planes against Tripoli for less, avenging an act that hadn't even taken place on American soil.

Riyadh edged back toward the point where heavy wooden crates were stacked in the middle of the floor. He slipped open the button on his jacket, then hooked his right thumb in his belt, so that his hand was only inches from the automatic pistol tucked inside his waistband. He could draw the gun and fire within a second and a half.

A stretch limousine swung into the warehouse, maneuvering for space. It rolled toward them, the driver cutting his high beams after Marwan raised a hand to shield his eyes. Another moment, and the lights went off entirely, as the driver shut down the limo's engine. One of the back doors opened, and a tall black man emerged from the vehicle, standing aside to hold the door for those who followed him.

Riyadh knew gunmen when he saw them, and these were obvious—the first three out of the limousine, anyway, with bulges showing underneath the jackets of their high-priced suits. Likewise, the driver, when he left his place behind the wheel and stood upright behind the limo's open door, partly shielding himself.

It wouldn't save him from Sadiq Hashim, behind him, but if any of the black men had noticed the flanker, they gave no sign. All eyes were pointed forward, toward Wafi Marwan and his companions. Toward the prize.

The last man to step from the limousine was different. He was slightly older than the rest, for one thing, and apparently unarmed. Riyadh was no great judge of Western clothing, but he guessed that the fifth man's suit had cost him more, in American dollars, than some Libyans earned in a year.

The fifth man had to be Malik al-Salaam.

He smiled, moving forward, brushing past his bodyguards as if they didn't exist. No fear was evident in his expression or his body language, nor could Riyadh pick out any single thing that screamed to him of treachery. Perhaps there was no danger, after all.

He stood and watched as the black man and Marwan clasped hands. They could have passed for long-lost friends unless you knew, as Baghel did, that they had never laid eyes on each other before that moment. Still, they exchanged proper greetings and faced each other as if they were meeting in a five-star restaurant or at some embassy party, instead of in a run-down warehouse with the stench of garbage in their nostrils.

"I trust your journey was comfortable," al-Salaam said.

Marwan shrugged. "We had no difficulties," he replied. "It will be better going home."

"Of course. I understand. To business, then."

"To business," Marwan agreed.

"My people need a basic walk-through on a couple of the larger items," al-Salaam remarked.

Marwan half turned, examining the warehouse around them before he replied. "This is not the best place for test-firing."

Al-Salaam smiled at that, but stopped himself short of laughing aloud. "A dry run, my brother. No fireworks. Okay?"

"As you wish."

When Marwan snapped his fingers, Riyadh hurried

forward, moving to his side. He waited for instructions, his eyes never leaving al-Salaam's.

"Show them the AGS," Marwan said in Arabic, "and the launchers, one of each. Instruct them briefly, without firing."

It was Riyadh's turn to snap his fingers, beckoning Rabi Saghir to join him and bring the short pry bar he carried beneath his jacket, thrust through his belt like a pirate's dagger. Together, they moved to stand before the largest of the wooden crates, the one with nothing stacked on top of it. Riyadh couldn't read the English inscription stamped on the side of the crate, but he knew it offered a false description of the contents. Who would advertise a Soviet grenade launcher marked for delivery to a group of notorious militant blacks in America?

Saghir used the pry bar, bright nails screeching as they were drawn from their sockets and the front of the broad wooden crate fell away. Inside, the AGS-17 grenade launcher was swaddled in a plastic tarpaulin, straw shoved in around it to cushion any shocks it might receive in transit. The two men pulled out the straw, scattering it carelessly across the warehouse floor. If al-Salaam and his men wanted to clean up after they were finished, he would leave it to them.

It took both men to haul the launcher from its crate. Already mounted on the tripod, though unloaded, the AGS-17 weighed 114 pounds. It had the look of an old trench machine gun from World War I, as Riyadh recalled the photos in a history book, but its impact was many times more deadly.

"A magazine," he told Saghir, standing back to

wait as his companion opened yet another crate, rummaging inside, shedding more straw as he lifted out one of the drums, already loaded with twenty-nine high-explosive rounds.

Accepting the drum, Riyadh turned to the Americans and forced a smile. "If you will step this way," he said, "I will show you—"

The rest of it dried inside his throat, because Marwan's head exploded. It was the most amazing thing Riyadh had ever seen...at least, until he heard the echo of a gunshot that reverberated through the warehouse like the crack of doom.

BOLAN HAD OPTED for surprise, though he was long past tired of waiting for a finish to the mission that had carried him halfway around the world and back again. Through all the waiting, watching, he had finally begun to doubt that al-Salaam had actually struck a deal for weapons in the Middle East. Or if he had, perhaps the grim debacle in Algiers had scuttled the agreement, left him high and dry.

The phone taps had proved otherwise, ten days after al-Salaam's return from Africa. The rest of it was simply waiting for the shipment to arrive, Bolan and Hal Brognola in agreement that the tag couldn't be made in circumstances that would leave al-Salaam a martyr in the eyes of decent men and women who supported him in one cause or another, despite his flights of racist oratory often quoted in the media.

In short, the Executioner would have to catch him dirty, with the outlaw hardware in his hands, and preferably in the company of some illegal visitors from the Khaddafi terror network.

Like tonight.

Bolan had known about the warehouse for the past two days, resisting an impulse to sneak in by night and hot-wire it for obliteration. Something could always go wrong with remote-control traps, and besides, he wanted to make sure that no one slipped out of the net.

He came loaded for bear, an H&K MP-5 submachine gun slung across one shoulder, but he left it there as he approached the warehouse on foot, trailing al-Salaam's limousine down the alley. They had left the door wide open, as if unconcerned with spies, but there was plenty of security inside. He counted nine men altogether, with the nearest standing almost close enough to touch, his back toward Bolan, covering the Islamic Brotherhood contingent from behind with an Uzi.

Bolan listened to them talking for a moment, standing with the Beretta 93-R in his left hand, the big .44 magnum Desert Eagle in his right. Silence and thunder, side by side, enough rounds between them to drop the nine targets three times each, with two shots to spare.

Two Libyans had the AGS-17 out of its crate, preparing to demonstrate the arming procedure, when Bolan gave the lookout one behind the ear, a 9 mm Parabellum shocker delivered at skin-touch range. Before the dead man had a chance to hit the floor, Bolan's Desert Eagle was locked on to target acquisition, open sights framing the face that spoke for the Libyan contingent.

Two down, the Arab staggering beneath a halo of crimson mist, legs crumpling beneath him, and the Magnum's report galvanized Bolan's seven remaining targets. One of the Libyans shoved his partner backward toward the cover of the crates, using one hand for the shove, while the other ducked inside his jacket, searching for hardware. Bolan shot them both from thirty feet away, a one-two punch from the mighty magnum pistol that punched both men off their feet and down into an awkward, boneless tangle of limbs.

Malik al-Salaam's first instinct was to break for the limo, its armor plating the best hope he had of surviving a firefight at such close quarters. Unfortunately for the Brother Minister, one of his bodyguards unknowingly blocked the way, facing Bolan with his back toward al-Salaam, a stubby 12-gauge pump shotgun nosing out from under his charcoal-gray jacket.

The Beretta whispered twice in Bolan's left hand, closing the gap between shooter and target at something close to 1,300 feet per second. Bolan's double punch snapped the shooter's head back, sprawling him across his boss's path, so that the chief of the Islamic Brotherhood lost it in midstride, arms outflung to catch himself as he fell on his face.

That still left three men in immediate condition to react, and Bolan took the farthest of them next, head and shoulders visible behind the limo, where he stood next to the open driver's door. He couldn't see what kind of gun the wheelman carried, and he didn't care.

Another magnum thunderclap reverberated through the warehouse, and the driver's face imploded, as if an invisible sculptor had slammed through the bridge of his nose with a hammer and chisel.

Two shooters remained, and they both had their weapons in the open, another shotgun and a little SMG that could have been an Ingram or a mini-Uzi. Bolan hurled himself to the right, away from the backlit open doorway, unloading at his targets with both pistols while he was still airborne. Incoming fire rattled on the wall behind him, shotgun pellets and hot rounds from the little SMG combining to chew up the corrugated steel. The reports of his Desert Eagle joined the ear-numbing racket, while the sleek Beretta's contribution was registered only in recoil, through Bolan's palm and wrist.

Downrange, even before he struck the floor, the Executioner could see his adversaries taking hits, their bodies twitching from the impact, while the muzzles of their weapons swung off-target, their final shots wasted on ceiling and walls. They dropped almost shoulder to shoulder, dead fingers releasing the hardware they no longer needed.

Malik al-Salaam made a grab for one of the fallen SMGs, stretching for it, his fingers scrabbling at the grips when Bolan fired from his place on the floor. His last round from the Desert Eagle caught the man in his shoulder with the force of a dropkick, flipping him over and onto his back.

Bolan scrambled to his feet and crossed to stand above the last survivor of the carnage. Al-Salaam was likewise trying to struggle erect, despite the shock of

his wound. Teeth clenched against the pain, he
wedged himself against the limo's right-front tire, his
wounded shoulder sagging, leaking blood.

He blinked at Bolan and remarked, "A white dude.
Hell, I should've figured that. You FBI? Detroit PD?
I mean, what *is* this shit?"

"It's over," Bolan told him simply. "As of now."

"You dreamin'. It ain't over till I say it's over, dig
it? You think y'all can walk in here and pull this kind
of shit like it was 1955 or somethin', with J. Edgar
Hoover in the Lily-White House, man, you don't
know shit about my people."

"They were never yours," the Executioner replied.
"You used them for a while. That's over, too."

"Keep thinkin' that way, whitey. You're just dumb
enough to light the fuse that's gonna blow this town
apart. I tell you what, though. You can still get out
of this. I give you one more chance." Al-Salaam was
grinning like a madman now. "You let me go and
call an ambulance right now, we'll just forget about
the whole damn thing. I tell the papers that my brothers, there, got jumped by some of them Italian
dudes."

"No sale."

"No sale?" As understanding dawned in his eyes,
al-Salaam scrambled desperately toward a nearby pistol.

A silenced Parabellum round punched through his
forehead, slamming his skull against the tire behind
him. For a moment, Bolan half imagined that the dead
man might continue ranting, but then his eyes glazed
over and his head slumped forward, chin on his chest.

Finished.

There might be repercussions in the city, it was true, but Hal Brognola had a couple of reporters standing by to break the story of a link between Khaddafi, the Islamic Brotherhood and global terrorism. By the time the dust had settled in a day or two, Bolan suspected that Malik al-Salaam's rooting section would be reduced to a hard corps of fanatics, adrift and leaderless.

"No sale," he told the corpse, for emphasis, before he turned and walked away.

EPILOGUE

"No riots, after all," Brognola said, a note of cautious satisfaction in his voice.

"You weren't expecting any," Bolan reminded him.

"All the same, you never know."

As the big Fed had hoped, the story of the Libyan connection—once it broke, complete with pictures of the warehouse arsenal, an old file photo of Khaddafi grinning like a maniac and waving a Kalashnikov above his head—had rapidly deflated any latent sympathy for Malik al-Salaam. The vast majority of Muslims in America and elsewhere shunned the creed of terrorism, and a spokesman for al-Salaam's Islamic Brotherhood had gone on *Meet the Press,* suggesting that the late lamented Brother Minister had somehow been deluded by his radical connections in the Middle East. In future, al-Salaam's heir apparent had suggested, the Islamic Brotherhood would be primarily concerned with bettering the lives of its devoted members in America.

"So, what about Algiers?" Bolan asked.

"Hey, you know," Brognola said, a note of weariness creeping into his voice. "We made inroads, shook up the players, derailed their action for a while. You want to talk long-term, though, there's one country that's light-years away from stability."

Status quo, Bolan thought, and then caught himself. Maybe not.

He had to believe that Gholomreza Kordiyeh's sacrifice, the dedication of others like him, could and did make a difference, even in the chaotic atmosphere of a nation torn apart by seemingly endless civil war. Whatever force was used, the government would ultimately stand or fall according to its treatment of the people it was meant to serve. That lesson had been learned repeatedly in Germany, in Russia, in South Africa, in Chile, in Greece—anywhere, in fact, where human rights and freedoms had been crushed and smothered. It took years sometimes to effect a change, and sometimes it took blood. But the change always came, given time and the sacrifice of dedicated individuals.

"So, how's the R and R?" Brognola asked.

"Just getting started," Bolan said. "I thought I'd head out west and spend some time with Johnny."

Brother Johnny, that would be, the sole surviving member of the Bolan family. A warrior in his own right, strong and true.

"Sunshine," Brognola said. "Beach bunnies. *Baywatch.* I can see it now."

"I'll send a postcard," Bolan replied, as he prepared to disconnect.

"You do that," the big Fed told him, then sobered

in a heartbeat. "It was worth it, Mack," he said. "You know that, right?"

"I know that," Bolan said, and cradled the receiver, stepping from the open phone booth into Arizona sunshine. Far away on the horizon, he could see what looked like storm clouds coming his way, from the east.

It was always something.

But with any luck, Bolan thought, he could outrun them for a while.

The ultimate weapon of terror...

JAMES AXLER

DEATH LANDS®

Dark Reckoning

A secret community of scientists gains control of an orbiting transformer that could become the ultimate weapon of terror—and it's up to Ryan Cawdor to halt the evil mastermind before he can incinerate Front Royal.

Book 3 in the Baronies Trilogy, three books that chronicle the strange attempts to unify the East Coast baronies. Who (or what) is behind this coercive process?

Shadow THE EXECUTIONER®
as he battles evil for 352 pages of heart-stopping action!

SuperBolan®

#61452	DAY OF THE VULTURE	$5.50 U.S.	☐
		$6.50 CAN.	☐
#61453	FLAMES OF WRATH	$5.50 U.S.	☐
		$6.50 CAN.	☐
#61454	HIGH AGGRESSION	$5.50 U.S.	☐
		$6.50 CAN.	☐
#61455	CODE OF BUSHIDO	$5.50 U.S.	☐
		$6.50 CAN.	☐
#61456	TERROR SPIN	$5.50 U.S.	☐
		$6.50 CAN.	☐

(limited quantities available on certain titles)

TOTAL AMOUNT	$
POSTAGE & HANDLING	$
($1.00 for one book, 50¢ for each additional)	
APPLICABLE TAXES*	$ _____
TOTAL PAYABLE	$ _____
(check or money order—please do not send cash)	

To order, complete this form and send it, along with a check or money order for the total above, payable to Gold Eagle Books, to: **In the U.S.:** 3010 Walden Avenue, P.O. Box 9077, Buffalo, NY 14269-9077; **In Canada:** P.O. Box 636, Fort Erie, Ontario, L2A 5X3.

Name: _____

Address: _____ City: _____

State/Prov.: _____ Zip/Postal Code: _____

*New York residents remit applicable sales taxes.
Canadian residents remit applicable GST and provincial taxes.

GOLD EAGLE®

GSBBACK1